GRAND GESTURES

A PLANNERS AND DREAMERS NOVEL
BOOK ONE

LYNNE HANCOCK PEARSON

ACKNOWLEDGMENTS

This story takes place on the ancestral lands of the Coast Salish. I honor, with gratitude, the land, and its people.

Editing by: wordsmithalchemy.weebly.com

Proofreading by: joannemachin.com

Cover art by: Designwheelgraphics.com

Formatting by: TAFKAM

Visit the author at https://www.lynnehancockpearson.com

For Matt.

You are all that, and everything else.

CHAPTER 1

*H*olding an ice pack to the side of her face, Jane chanted into the phone, "Pick up, pick up, pick up."

"Hey, what's—" her sister answered.

Jane blew out a breath, interrupting, "Thank God! Beth, I need you to do something."

"Umm…sure. What is it?"

"You know the presentation for Duncan Properties today?"

"Yeah. Do you need a clean shirt? I told you to start carrying an extra. You are an accident waiting to happen."

Jane scrunched up her face, then stopped when it hurt. "Sort of. I need you to do the presentation for me."

Silence. She pulled the phone away from her ear to check the connection. "Hello? Beth, are you there?"

"I can't do that." Her sister's voice came out as a squeak. "We had a deal. I create the presentation; you make the pitch."

"I know. I know. But this is an emergency, and I'm not going to make it in time." Her cheek getting numb, she pulled the ice pack away, the red blood blending in with pink and blue paint on the soggy gauze wrapping.

"Call them. It's not for another ninety minutes. Just let them know you'll be late. We need this gig, and me making the pitch is a sure way we won't get it."

Beth did stink at making presentations, but she would have to suck it up this time.

Clutching the phone tighter, Jane whisper-shouted through clenched teeth, "We can't postpone. Finding a mutually agreeable date and time was a nightmare. You know the plan, and you helped me write the pitch. You can do this."

"Jane, I can't. You have to—"

"I'm in the ER." Technically, it was an urgent care clinic, but close enough.

"Are you okay? What happened?"

"I'll be fine. Nothing major, but there are a bunch of people ahead of me, and I'm not going to get out of here in time."

"I hate you right now." Beth's voice wobbled.

Waiting in silence, Jane crossed her fingers. Beth absolutely had to do this.

"Fine. But this is the one and only time I do this."

"I promise. Do you see the folder? It's sitting next to my laptop on the table."

"Yeah, I got it. Hang on. Okay, I found the folder and have the address. Will you be able to meet me there?" A desperate hopefulness echoed in Beth's voice.

Examining her blood-spattered clothes, Jane shook her head, forgetting her sister couldn't see her. "Nope, sorry," she spoke, disappointment choking her words.

Silence again, then the sound of Beth taking a deep breath. "Okay. You will owe me big time." Then she hung up.

Jane put the ice pack against her cheek. Leaning back against the wall, she sent up a quick prayer. She had faith in her sister, but a little help from on high would not go amiss.

wo well-dressed men stopped in front of the steamed-up windows of one of the many coffee shops in downtown Seattle. Liam Cross peered out from under the hood of his anorak, lips thinning in a sneer. "Seriously? Are we meeting in a coffee shop? Don't they have a storefront? What about a business license?"

"I knew this would piss you off." Chuck grinned up at him, raindrops bouncing off his smooth, clean-shaven cheeks. "They're renting a commercial kitchen while they're looking for the perfect location. You know what rent is like down here."

This time an eye roll accompanied the pressed lips. Liam Cross was the CFO of Duncan Properties and knew precisely the state of commercial properties in Seattle. "We have a conference room in our offices. Why didn't we meet there?"

"The office staff is far too nosy, and I want this to be a surprise."

If Chuck had taken Liam's suggestion and started planning the event six months ago, he would have been able to book the premier event planner in Seattle. But no, Chuck put it off, and now it was some small inexperienced company that would no doubt do a slipshod job for massive amounts of money.

"Fine." Liam yanked open the door. "Who are we looking for?" He scanned the coffee shop, eyes landing on, then dismissing the few students and businessmen sitting at the small café-style tables. His attention focused on a single woman occupying a large rectangular table in the back. She waved a tentative hand. "Is that her?"

"Huh." Chuck frowned. "Jane has dark hair. This must be her sister Beth." Shrugging slightly, he wove his way through the tables, Liam following in his wake, grumbling about the lack of professionalism.

The small blonde woman rose from the table and scurried into a hallway at the back of the coffee shop. Liam shook his head. This was getting better by the minute. Chuck stopped by the table where the woman had been sitting and looked down at the neatly arranged papers, then at the hallway. They waited, Chuck rocking back on his heels, hands stuffed into his trousers pockets, appearing to have all the time in the world. Liam shed his anorak and draped it over the back of a chair with a quiet huff of annoyance. Another tick against the company.

They waited some more.

"Do you think she's okay? Should we go check?" Chuck swiveled his head between the hallway and Liam.

"Her stuff is here. I think she's coming back."

"It's you!" Chuck gasped as the blonde emerged from the hallway, phone clutched tightly against her chest.

"I never got your name, and your suggestion worked a treat. See." He opened his jacket and yanked up the front of his sweater. He pointed at his shirt. "Completely gone." He swiveled between Liam and the blonde, beaming like a toddler showing off their belly. "A few weeks ago, my pen exploded. You know, the one Delia gave me that left blobs of ink all over the page." He twisted to address the woman. "Delia is my sister. Liam thinks she spends her money foolishly, but I—"

"Chuck." Liam sighed. "Get to the point. You had ink on your shirt."

"Right!" He kept on beaming. "I figured the shirt was a write-off. But she"—he tipped his head at the woman who was now smiling tentatively, bright spots of color riding high on her cheeks—"told me to use hairspray on it. And it worked like a charm. I wanted to thank you, but I didn't get your name."

The woman held out her hand to Chuck. "It's Beth. Beth Beckett of Grand Gestures Event Planning."

Liam watched a smiling Chuck take Beth's hand in both of his. Watching the pair stare at each other, he felt like the spinster aunt chaperone in a Regency romance movie. "And where did this fortuitous meeting occur?"

While Chuck seemed thrilled, Beth looked embarrassed, chewing on her lip and looking down at the table beside them. "The coffee shop on the corner. We were waiting for our orders, and Beth asked me if it was blueberries or cherry juice."

Seeing Liam's quizzical expression, the blonde—Beth—cleared her throat. "I, umm, had been working on a blueberry reduction, and the color of the ink looked similar."

"I see," said Liam, but he really didn't.

"And now to find out you're with Grand Gestures." Chuck looked delighted. "What a coincidence."

Liam didn't think so.

Chuck still held Beth's hand. "Are you all right? The way you raced off to…" He tipped his head to the hallway.

Beth withdrew her hand and fluttered it over her belly. "I'm fine. Just a little…nerves."

Liam groaned silently. If there was one thing his best friend and boss could not resist, it was coming to the aid of damsels in distress. The pretty, brown-eyed blonde in front of him fit the bill. Biting the corner of her bottom lip, she moved behind the table, ducking her head and rearranging the papers in front of her. Chuck continued to smile. Liam pulled out a chair opposite her and seated himself. He would make this fast and drag Chuck out of there before he offered to slay a dragon or pledge his devotion. "Shall we get started?"

Frowning, Beth darted a glance between Chuck and Liam. "I'm sorry, I wasn't expecting two of you. Are you Mr. Duncan?" she asked Liam.

"*I am*," Chuck said, tipping his head at Liam. He sat and pulled his chair closer to the table. "This is Liam Cross. He works for me." Liam kicked him in the shin, a bland look on his face. Chuck ignored him. "I was expecting your sister Jane."

Tucking her long curly hair behind her ears, Beth sank into her chair, continuing to fiddle with the papers. "She, umm, was detained at an, umm, event that went longer than expected. But I have all the information for your parents' party right here." Turning to the chair beside her, she pulled a tablet out of a bulging, worn tote bag and went through the process of turning it on. "Sorry, it's old and takes a minute to warm up."

"If your sister makes the client presentations and runs the events, what is your role in the company?" Liam asked without bothering to look up from the text to Chuck he was composing.

Not very professional, if you ask me.

Beside him, Chuck glanced at his own phone, then ground his heel into Liam's foot. Liam ignored him. He knew he was being abrupt. He glanced at Chuck's reply.

Don't be a douche.

Liam's official role at Duncan Properties was to make sure money was spent wisely. His self-appointed role was to protect Chuck from himself. If that meant he came off as a jerk, so be it.

Hands clutched around the tablet and sitting up straight like a novitiate in front of the Mother Superior, Beth said, "I design the invitations, create the decor and the menu, and oversee the food preparation."

Before Liam could continue the interrogation, Chuck intervened, smiling. "I can't wait to see what you've come up with."

Liam sat back and crossed his arms, foot jiggling under the table. It was worse than watching his cousin's painful piano recitals. Listening to Beth stutter and stammer, he realized that while she was awful, the presentation was excellent. For the fortieth anniversary of Chuck's parents, Chuck Sr. and Carol Lee, the surprise party would be on board a luxury sailboat in the Ballard Marina. The couple met working summer jobs while students at UW. Their first date was on a sailboat Chuck Sr. "borrowed" from the marina. After the party, the crewed sailboat would take them on a three-day cruise around the San Juan Islands. Corny, yes, but Chuck's parents would love it.

Stuttering to a stop, Beth presented a folder to Chuck. Flitting her eyes up at Liam, she whispered, "Here is the, umm, cost breakdown," then sat back, hands clenched tightly in her lap.

"Excellent." Chuck whipped out his checkbook and pen without bothering to open the folder. "Who should I make the check out to?"

Liam grabbed the folder, opening it to a page filled with neatly itemized costs. Working with commercial real estate in Seattle, he was used to large numbers, but the cost of the party nearly had his eyes popping out. Grabbing the pen and checkbook from Chuck, he said to Beth, "Please excuse us for a moment." He pulled Chuck out of his seat and propelled him to the front of the store.

"What is wrong with you?"

Chuck glared at Liam, glancing around his shoulder to give Beth a reassuring smile.

Stepping sideways to block his view, Liam said, "This party is going to cost a huge chunk of change."

"My parents aren't worth it?"

Liam shook his head. "That's not the point. I don't want to give money to a fly-by-night operation. You're so enchanted by that pretty face you're not thinking straight."

Chuck wrestled his arm out of Liam's grasp. "Grand Gestures has a great reputation. I did my work. After talking with Jane, I checked out the references. All glowing."

"That may be. But I have some questions that I seriously doubt Bambi over there will be able to answer. And why the hell is her sister not here? You'd think she'd make an effort for this kind of money."

Pulling out his phone, Chuck dialed while Liam continued to grumble.

"Hello?" came a throaty female voice.

"Hi Jane, it's Chuck. I'm going to put Liam Cross on the phone. I love the presentation, but he has some questions." Chuck thrust the phone at Liam, saying in a low voice, "Knock yourself out. I'm going to talk to Beth."

Caught unaware, Liam stood awkwardly, phone in hand, watching Chuck hurry back to Beth.

"Hey, Cross. Are you there? I can't see squat."

Looking at the phone, he saw a shadowy female face studying him. In the corner, his own scowling face looked back at him. He hated video calls.

"So you're the money guy. Chuck said to send the invoices to you." The background changed as Jane moved around, but her face remained shadowed. "Do you have something specific I can clarify for you?"

"I get that you specialize in *grand gestures*." The words came out of Liam's mouth as if he'd placed air quotes around them. "But that's a pretty expensive gesture."

"My, aren't you charming."

Liam sputtered. "I'm an accountant. I don't *need* to be charming."

A snort greeted his statement. Staring at the screen of the phone, Liam could only see himself. With his eyebrows caterpillared together, he did not look charming.

"I didn't know the two were mutually exclusive."

He bit back a comment that no one would consider charming and blew out a breath.

"Want me to explain the itemized expenses? I promise to go slow." Her voice dripped with sweetness. "Perhaps you'd like to take notes."

Practically strangling the phone in his hand, Liam said, "No, thank you. But you can explain why your price is so high. Please."

"I'm guessing you didn't read the itemized expenses completely, just glanced at the bottom line on the first page."

Reaching up, Jane pulled a hair tie from her dark mane, releasing it to fall to the top of her shoulders. The light shifted, and he could see her finger-combing the heavy mass. Who did that in a business meeting? While talking to the woman on a borrowed cell phone in a coffee shop was not a typical format for a business call, still…Liam's mind drifted further, wondering where she was to act so freely. Pulling the folder open once more, Liam quickly glanced over the information, his attention catching and clinging to the words *Fully refundable deposit.*

"When the deposit is returned, the out-of-pocket expense will be reduced by one-third."

"Oh," Liam said, slightly mollified but unhappy he hadn't caught that himself. He hadn't looked at the second page. "I'll review the contract and get back to you early next week."

"You do that, Skippy. Chuck has my contact info. Later."

"Huh." He stared at the blank screen. She hadn't hung up on him, so why did he feel insulted? She'd answered his question and accepted his response, but…didn't suck up. Used to people kissing his ass, he now expected it. Jane Beckett had all but dismissed him. And called him Skippy. He did not look like a Skippy. He looked like a—he shook his head. The woman had him off-balance.

And what was on her face? Before she disconnected, the light shifted, and he caught sight of one side of her face: dark straight brows, firm full lips, and a flash of white under her eye. Why did he care? This was business, not a swipe right/swipe left thing. He glared at the screen, wishing he could bring up her image and study it. Heaving an irritated sigh, he returned to the table to ensure party planning was the only thing being discussed.

❄

Staring into the bathroom mirror, Jane poked at the bandage under her left eye. The local anesthetic had worn off, her cheek throbbed, and when she squinted her eyes, the stitches pulled uncomfortably. Grimacing at her reflection, she popped a couple ibuprofen and headed to the kitchen.

At the last minute, Chuck had rescheduled the meeting for the same day as the tournament. The timing was tight, and she would have made it if she hadn't been hit. She moved about the cramped apartment, tidying up stacks of folders, rearranging her workspace at one end of the dining room table, and picking up Beth's empty coffee mug and rinsing it out in the sink. Anything to keep her mind off the meeting. They'd worked on the presentation together. Beth knew it well; she would be fine.

Hearing the front door unlock, she pulled two glasses from the cupboard and a bottle of wine from the fridge. She filled the wine glasses while she watched her sister trudge into the apartment.

Beth dropped her tote on the floor and collapsed on a stool at the counter separating the tiny galley kitchen from the living area. Burying her head in her hands, she groaned. "Don't make me do that ever again." Reaching one hand out, she grasped the wineglass in front of her like a lifeline.

Backing away from the counter, Jane waited for Beth to look up. When she did, Jane grinned, then immediately winced.

"Oh, honey, what did you do to yourself?" Eyes narrowed,

10

Beth crooned in sympathy before straightening up and cocking her head to the side. "Wait, did you do that at the paintball tournament?"

"Technically, I didn't do it. Some newbie with an itchy trigger finger nailed me."

Beth pointed at the bruise surrounding the bandage. "Weren't you wearing safety goggles?"

"Yep. I took a direct hit. The force pushed my glasses back into my cheek." Faking nonchalance, Jane sipped her wine. "We won the tournament, so it was worth it." At one point, she'd played paintball most weekends, but now, with all their time and money focused on Grand Gestures, it happened rarely. She'd worked out a deal with Bullseye Paintball so she could play for free in exchange for marketing advice, but time to play was a rare commodity.

Groaning again, Beth took a healthy slug of her wine.

Knowing a lecture was headed her way, Jane redirected the conversation. "So, other than the fact that you suck at presentations, Chuck was happy?"

Sighing, Beth tucked her hair behind her ears and nodded. "Yeah, he was happy. Not so sure about Liam Cross, though."

Jane scowled, then stopped herself. Scowling and stitches did not go together. "He seemed like a bit of a dick."

"I wouldn't say that. He seemed...cautious. Lots of questions, which...."

"Flustered you." As Beth nodded, Jane silently cursed Liam Cross for upsetting her sister. He might have been protective of the Duncan money, but Jane was protective of her painfully shy sister. "I didn't know he would be there. I'm so sorry." She reached out, taking Beth's other hand and prying apart the tightly clenched fist.

Raising her wine glass, Beth shot her a tight smile. "I'll survive." She took a sip and put the glass down on the counter. "There's more."

"Oh?"

"Remember a couple weeks ago when I spent the night working on the blueberry reduction?"

"Sure." Jane didn't remember *exactly*. To her credit, Beth often stayed up all night working on recipes.

Beth shifted in her seat. "I was scarfing chocolate-covered espresso beans the entire time and was a little jazzed."

"Right. I sent you for a walk to burn off the energy."

"I power-walked downtown and stopped in a coffee shop for a cup of tea. This guy was beside me and had a huge stain on his shirt, and I started talking to him."

Jane's eyes bugged out. "You started a conversation with a strange man? Why?"

"The stain was the same color as the blueberry reduction, and I thought the guy had been cooking as well and wanted to know what he'd been making. Turns out it was ink, and I told him about using hairspray." She sighed. "The guy was Chuck Duncan, and he remembered me."

"No way!"

"I just about died when he walked in today." She pushed a hank of hair out of her face.

"What's so bad about that?"

Beth groaned. "I needed to make the presentation, and the last time I saw him, I blathered away a mile a minute. I freaked out and ran to the bathroom."

"Oh, Beth. Did he recognize you?"

"Yeah. When I came out, he knew who I was right away."

"And?"

"He was very nice. He told Liam about it, but Liam looked…less than pleased. Me racing away from the table as they walked toward me certainly didn't help. Maybe that's why Liam gave me the third degree."

Jane squeezed her sister's hand. "Don't worry about it. Money guys are like that. So busy looking at the costs, they can be jerks. I'm sorry I had to put you through this. I should have canceled—"

"It's fine. We're in this together. You don't have to do everything yourself. So we're good."

"Thank you. Now give me the details while I get supper together."

In her tiny galley kitchen, Jane pulled out leftovers from a retirement party they'd done the other day. She peppered Beth with questions about the presentation. Did Chuck like the concept? Did he think the yacht would be suitable? Did he anticipate guests with special needs or food requirements? They were running on a tight schedule and didn't have time to mess around. Her back to Beth while reheating four mini quiches, she asked, "I'm thinking finger foods would be the best choice. What do you think?" Beth didn't answer. Turning slightly to see the toaster oven and look at Beth at the same time, Jane saw a blushing Beth focused on her phone, lips parted in a soft smile.

"What's that?"

With a guilty start, Beth dropped her phone on the counter. "Just playing *Words with Friends*."

"With who?"

Not meeting her eyes, Beth reached a hand up to worry the small silver locket hanging around her neck. "Umm, Chuck."

"Really?" Jane schooled her face to remain expressionless, not wanting Beth to see her excitement.

"When you were talking with Liam, Chuck and I talked a bit, and…umm…we both like *Scrabble* and *Words with Friends*. That's all." The words came out in a rush.

"That's nice." Jane shifted to give the food her complete attention. For the first time since her divorce three years ago, Beth was interested in a man. Not to make a big deal of it, but on the inside, Jane was dancing with happiness. It would probably lead to nothing, but Beth talking to a guy, even if it was just a game on a phone app, was a good thing. Maybe Beth should do more presentations, get her confidence back. Enough to consider dating again. Jane shook her head at that thought; neither of them had time to date.

Jane pulled plates from the cupboard and placed them on the peninsula. Running Grand Gestures out of their apartment meant tight quarters. Both their laptops were set up on the dining room table, with presentation binders stacked on the floor beside it. Beth's cookbook collection dominated the bookshelf, and a laundry basket filled with clean, folded uniforms sat on the couch. One of these days, they'd have their own kitchen to work out of and a storefront where they could meet with clients. If the anniversary party for the Duncans was a success, they would be closer to their goal.

Dishing up the quiche, Jane said, "We've got five weeks until the party. Tell me what you're thinking."

Beth pushed away her phone and pulled a pad of paper toward her. They settled into the best part of the job—envisioning the event.

CHAPTER 2

A file folder landed on Liam's desk, dragging his attention away from the spreadsheet on his computer screen.

"Here you go, boss." His assistant, Kevin, stood back, tablet at the ready, waiting for further instruction. He grinned cheekily at Liam's grimace of distaste. He couldn't break the younger man of his insistence on calling him boss. On testy days, Kevin was known to refer to him as Cross Boss. That annoying habit aside, Kevin was an excellent assistant, if a somewhat nosy one. Now, raised eyebrows on an otherwise impassive face indicated his curiosity was piqued.

Liam pointed his chin at the folder. "That's the company Chuck wants to hire for his parents' anniversary party."

Stepping forward, Kevin opened the folder and laid out the bright, colored images he'd downloaded of Grand Gestures. "They haven't been around long, but they have a sterling reputation. These are photos taken by clients, along with testimonials. Their financials are promising. Their fee structures place them above suburban backyard birthday parties, but not so high that they're unattractive to the upper-middle-class or, rather, people who have more money than brains."

They exchanged wry smiles. Despite his dapper wardrobe and penchant for expensive martinis, Kevin spent his money wisely and believed others should do the same, a reason why he and Liam got along so well.

Gathering up the pages, Liam stuffed them into the folder and set the folder on top of the one Beth had given him on Friday. He leaned back in his chair, pinching the bridge of his nose.

Kevin pulled up one of the two leather armchairs in front of Liam's desk and settled in. "What's bothering you about this? The contract is in order, and the reviews are glowing. Duncan Properties has certainly spent more money than that on events before."

Liam laced his fingers behind his head and stretched, causing his immaculate white dress shirt to tighten across his chest. "There's a girl."

"Isn't there always?" Kevin dragged his gaze from the tablet display to meet Liam's eyes. "Is Chuck smitten?"

"Yes." Liam rolled his eyes. "Beth Beckett came in place of her sister. Apparently, she's the creative side of Grand Gestures. Very pretty. Probably a nice person, but she sucked at making the presentation. And the more she stammered…."

"The more Chuck fell for her." Kevin matched Liam's eye roll. "He can't resist riding to the rescue."

"Beth couldn't answer my questions, so Chuck got Jane on the phone. Her answers were satisfactory, but she seemed to be hiding something." Liam shook his head. "The deposit is due by the end of the day, but I'm reluctant to sign this contract without meeting her face-to-face."

"Is the deposit refundable?"

"Yes, up to two weeks before the event date."

"Then what have you got to lose?" Kevin spread his hands

in front of him, pink palms contrasting with his smooth, dark brown complexion.

Liam shifted in his seat, bringing his hands down to tap on the folder. He had more important things to think about, so why were that disembodied voice and shadowy figure occupying his thoughts? He'd seen Jane's photo on the website. The two sisters seated at a table, with an elaborate tea set up before them. They appeared to be in their mid-thirties. Heads close together, they couldn't be more different, despite the obvious family resemblance. Both had wide generous mouths and dark brown eyes above narrow, straight noses. But whereas Beth had soft, curly blonde hair, Jane's was midnight-black, hung straight to her shoulders in jagged edges with thick bangs to her eyebrows. She looked like an edgy punk rocker—complete with a small tattoo on the side of her neck. Over the weekend, he'd gone back and studied the image. From the website, he'd learned that Beth had completed culinary school while Jane's background was marketing. The copy alluded to a long history of event planning, yet Grand Gestures itself was young.

He sighed. "Chuck met Beth before Friday without knowing who she was."

He went on to tell Kevin about the ink stain conversation. When Liam finished the story, the younger man held his hands out, palms up. "Coincidences do happen."

"Yeah." Liam drummed his fingers on the desktop. "It just seems too convenient. And Chuck..." The chance encounter followed by a lucrative contract dangling in front of the small company was too convenient. What lengths would the Beckett sisters go to? Chuck was just too damn trusting.

"So check them out in person. They have an event tonight down at the Market." Kevin pulled the sleeve of his caramel cashmere sweater back to look at his watch. "It's an engagement party for the daughter of one of our clients, Johnson Produce. I could get us on the guest list."

Considering the opportunity, Liam steepled his hands. "I would hate to disappoint a client. Should I bring a gift?"

Picking up his tablet, Kevin scrawled a note to himself. "I'll have one purchased and delivered this afternoon. I've added the time and address to your calendar."

"Excellent."

Kevin stood and shoved the chair back to its usual position. "Well aware of that, boss," he said before sailing out the door.

Liam smiled to himself and went back to his spreadsheet.

*P*ushing through the crowded restaurant, Liam nodded at business acquaintances who were surprised by his appearance. The presence of Liam Cross at a social function was practically unheard of. He made his way to the bar to find Kevin chatting with the handsome bartender. Liam's looming presence finally noticed, the bartender glanced between Kevin and Liam with raised eyebrows. Glancing over his shoulder at Liam, Kevin shook his head. "A coworker." He pulled a business card out of his wallet and handed it to the bartender before picking up the drinks in front of him. "Call me."

Following in Kevin's wake, Liam growled at the slim man, "Coworker?"

Kevin placed a martini glass on a small high-top table and handed Liam a glass of red wine. "This early in the chase, he doesn't need to know you're my boss." He turned back to the bar and sent the bartender a saucy wink.

Hiding his grin in his wineglass, Liam glanced around the room. Well-dressed people mingled in the restaurant while others braved the cool spring evening on the patio facing Seattle's harbor. Waitstaff carrying trays of canapes deftly wove their way through the throng. In addition to the open bar, a champagne fountain was manned by an attentive server handing out old-fashioned champagne glasses to a waiting crowd. Farther along, a step and repeat banner printed with "Congratulations Ahmed & Felicia" was set up and professionally lit. A photographer arranged an older woman in a brilliant blue sari next to a smiling young couple.

Liam drew Kevin's attention back to him by raising his wineglass in their direction. "The happy couple, I presume?"

"Yes. Felicia is the operations manager of Johnson Produce. Her intended is Ahmed Fazir of Fazir Financial Consultants." Kevin pointed with his own glass. "That's his mother, Zara Fazir."

"Fazir Financial? We're negotiating with them for two floors in the Castle building on Fourth Avenue. Zara Fazir drives a hard bargain. I should talk to her."

Kevin placed a staying hand on Liam's arm. "Easy tiger. Other than introducing yourself and congratulating her, you will not speak to her. She is hosting this event and will not be pleased if you bring up business."

Liam scowled down at him. Kevin was right, dammit.

The younger man went on. "Besides, you're here to stalk Jane Beckett."

"I'm not stalking her." This was *due diligence*. Their company would be forking out a pile of money for the anniversary party, and he was there to make sure Grand Gestures was worth it.

Kevin's eye roll met Liam's glare, so Liam continued to scan the room, focusing on the party itself. The restaurant had been emptied of its usual tables and chairs, which were replaced by high-tops around which people congregated. A conversation area of low sofas and chairs was arranged in one corner while a trio played soft jazz diagonally across from there. The volume was loud enough to provide ambiance but not so loud that guests needed to raise their voices to be heard. Canapes disappeared quickly as guests sighed appreciatively over the food. Liam watched the waitstaff quickly and efficiently enter one swinging door with empty trays and emerge out of another with full trays, all without appearing rushed or harried. Someone was doing a good job in the kitchen. Both the guests and the hostess looked happy and content.

"Carlos says that Grand Gestures contracts with the restaurant frequently."

"Carlos?" Liam turned to Kevin with a frown.

"The handsome bartender. Keep up." Kevin tapped him on the arm in a light reprimand. "Grand Gestures creates the menu specifically for the client so that the food is always original. The kitchen staff prepares the food under Beth's supervision. She also creates a beverage menu and chooses wines to pair with the food."

"Will dinner be served as well?"

Kevin shook his head. "Not at this event. However, plates are prepared for the older guests." He nodded toward the low couches where servers were placing plates and cutlery on the large coffee table before an appreciative group of older women in saris.

"Dolmades?"

Liam switched his attention to the server in front of him holding up a tray of stuffed grape leaves in one hand and a stack of gray napkins in the other. Both he and Kevin helped themselves and thanked the waiter. Taking a bite, his eyes widened in appreciation. Kevin, whose palate was far more sophisticated than his own, smiled. Reaching out to stall the waiter, Liam snagged another napkin and piled four more dolmades on it. The waiter grinned before moving on to another table.

At Kevin's raised eyebrow, Liam mumbled, "Lunch was a long time ago."

"Look at this." Kevin held out a gray napkin imprinted with "Ahmed & Felicia."

"So?"

Kevin flipped the napkin over. The back side was imprinted with two interlocking Gs in emerald green and a website address. "Brilliant. Subtle and effective advertising."

Before he could comment, a commotion near the entry drew Liam's attention.

Sipping his martini, Kevin turned to watch a drunken woman attempt to get past the bouncer at the door. Out of nowhere, a slim brunette in black slacks and a gray button-down shirt appeared to intercept. Kevin raised an eyebrow at Liam. "This will be interesting."

*P*arty crashers annoyed the hell out of Jane. *Drunken* party crashers pissed her off. Jane pasted a polite smile on her face as she hurried to the entrance, trying not to look like she was hurrying.

"Hello, miss, are you here for the engagement party?"

The stiletto-wearing blonde peered at Jane. "Yes. I'm a friend of Felishhaa." She spoke in that careful cadence employed by drunken people who did not want the world to know they were drunk, but the slur—and the stagger—gave her away.

Jane eyed the bouncer, who held up a clipboard with the list of invited guests and shook his head. She turned back to the blonde, attempting to change the woman's tottering course away from the other guests. "This is a private party, miss. Perhaps you can send Miss Johnson your best wishes tomorrow."

Sidestepping, the blonde attempted to get past Jane. She waved her phone. "No. Felishhaa wants me here. I need to post photos of the party. It's not an event unless I'm here." She spoke to Jane as if she were a backward child with no knowledge of social media.

Jane knew all about social media. It could kill a fledgling

business, yet if she did it well, social media posts would give more exposure to Grand Gestures, draw in more business. Speaking politely through gritted teeth when she really wanted to shove the drunken woman out the door, she continued, "That may be, miss, but this party is hosted by Mrs. Fazir, and she did not invite you."

The blonde changed tactics, shoving her phone into her clutch and pulling out a twenty-dollar bill. She thrust it at Jane. "How about you head back to the kitchen and pretend you didn't see me?"

"Delia, I think it's time to leave."

A man's hand reached around Jane and grabbed the hand holding the money. A smile appeared on the blonde's face. She straightened and thrust store-bought boobs at the newcomer. "Liam Cross," she purred. "Well, you've just made my night."

A big body slid past Jane, leaving the scent of cedar and starch in its wake. She watched the man turn the blonde and smoothly guide her through the door held open by the bouncer. Drawn like a magnet, Jane followed. What was it about busty blondes that they could scoop up hot men just by showing up? Reaching the curb, she saw the blonde tugging on the man's arm in an attempt to get him into the cab with her. He shook his head, stood back, closed the door, and sent the cab on its way with the pouting woman pressing her face up against the window.

"I was handling that," Jane grumbled to his back, standing with one hip cocked and her arms crossed. Nothing was more infuriating than a man assuming she couldn't take care of herself. Handling difficult customers was part of her business, and she didn't appreciate a man thinking she needed help.

He turned, and Jane was faced with the masculine glory that was Liam Cross. Dark hair with a slight wave, thick straight dark brows over deep dark eyes, cheek bones sharp enough to cut paper, and lips, even when pressed together in a tight line, hinting at a fullness begging to be bit. Jane shifted, feeling small next to his long, lean frame. Her gaze followed his hands as he deftly buttoned his well-cut suit, drawing her attention to his slim waist. She wondered if he had those arrowed cuts on either side of his flat belly, the ones that made women weak at the knees. She shifted again, knowing that she wasn't much to look at in her workday attire. At least her shirt was clean, and she'd put on gloss instead of lip balm at Beth's insistence. His gaze was fixed on her face, specifically on her left cheek. Belatedly, she remembered the cut on it. With Beth's help, she'd used concealer to cover the bruise. She resisted the urge to hide behind her hair and flipped it back over her shoulder. "Bar fight. You should see the other guy." *Where the hell did that come from?*

Head cocked, he blinked once, slowly. "Liam Cross." He held out a hand. "I take it you're Jane Beckett."

Surprisingly, rough calluses scraped against her skin. Jane jolted as her hand was engulfed in his. She frowned, quickly withdrawing her hand and crossing her arms again. "I don't recall your name on the guest list."

Liam gestured over her shoulder. "I came with him. Kevin Armstrong, my...coworker."

Jane turned to see a slim Black man give her a finger wave and a broad smile. "Ahh," she said, glancing between Kevin and Liam. "I see."

Eyes wide, Liam held up a hand. "No! We're not—that is, we work together. That's all."

"So is that your significant other?" Jane gestured at the retreating cab.

If possible, Liam's eyes went even wider. "God no!"

"That drunken diva is none other than Delia Duncan," Liam's coworker said as he joined Liam and Jane. He held out his hand to her. "Hi, I'm Kevin Armstrong."

To her surprise, instead of shaking her extended hand,

Kevin took it in both of his and squeezed it while searching her features. "Is it really from a bar fight?"

Slightly tongue-tied, Jane shook her head and mumbled, "Paintball."

A broad smile lit up Kevin's handsome features. "Even better." He looked up at Liam. "This woman is a badass."

Liam scowled, clearly unhappy about something.

"Delia Duncan. Why is that name familiar?" Jane looked at Liam, but it was Kevin who answered.

"Someday, when we have time to linger over an adult beverage, I'll give you the long story. The short story is she's Chuck Duncan's younger sister and party girl extraordinaire."

"Kevin. That's enough," Liam ground out.

"What?" Kevin smirked up at Liam. "Not a word I said was untrue." He winked at Jane, then squeezed her shoulder before turning to the restaurant. "I'm going back inside to have another of those divine martinis. Lovely party, Jane. Well done."

Jane watched Kevin saunter up to the brawny bouncer, say something that made the larger man blush, then continue on inside. Turning to Liam, she looked up to meet his eyes. "What do you think of the party? Did Grand Gestures measure up to your standards?"

He looked guilty but held her gaze. "You and your sister know what you're doing. I'm sure the anniversary party will be a success."

Smiling smugly, she headed back to the restaurant door until Liam's parting words halted her.

"However, I will be keeping a close eye on the invoices."

She glanced back over her shoulder and spoke through gritted teeth. "I wouldn't expect you to do anything else." She wanted to make a smart-ass remark, but the Duncan party was too important, so she settled for a finger wave. "Bye, Skippy."

Striding back into the restaurant, she forced herself to unclench her jaw and loosen her hands. The man was a dick, but there wasn't time to think about that. Or about his hands, or lips, or smell. Zara Fazir stood next to the champagne fountain and smiled broadly at Jane before returning to her conversation. Smiling internally, Jane strolled through the party and, seeing everything was running smoothly, followed a server into the kitchen. Organized chaos greeted her.

Beth was in her element. Barking out orders to the line cooks, plating desserts, and inspecting trays before they exited the kitchen, she was so focused on the food a chorus line of male strippers wouldn't have been able to distract her. Clearly not needed, Jane exited the kitchen and walked toward the bar. Seeing his raised hand, she joined Kevin at his table.

"Do we pass muster?" Jane leaned an elbow on the high-top, shifting her weight from one foot to another. She wasn't wearing heels, but anything other than sneakers or hiking boots was damned uncomfortable.

Kevin raised his glass in salute. "Most definitely. The food, the ambiance, the scenery"—he tilted his head toward Carlos, the bartender—"everything is perfect. Can I buy you a drink?"

"I wish. Things will start wrapping up soon. In about an hour, I should be able to partake. Do you want to stick around?" She surprised herself with the invitation, but Kevin appealed to her as the best friend she'd longed for her entire life.

He bumped her shoulder with his own. "Unfortunately, no. Boss Cross is a serious taskmaster. I need to be on my toes tomorrow, so I can't stay much longer."

"Boss Cross? I thought you were coworkers."

"We *are* coworkers. I'm his assistant."

"Come work for me! I need an assistant." Jane gave him big puppy dog eyes. "Please…"

Kevin laughed and sipped his martini. "Honey, I don't think you can afford me."

She heaved a dramatic sigh. "Probably not. But in a year or so, I'm going to ask you again."

"Event planning is going well for you and your sister?"

"It is. We've got—are you really interested?" Seeing she had his full attention, she continued, "We're doing really well. We could be booked every night of the week with successful parties like this. Tonight alone, I've had five people approach me."

Kevin tapped a finger on the lettering of a napkin. "And there's no telling how many of these will lead to a request for service."

Jane grinned. "You like that, huh? It was Beth's idea. I thought it would be cheesy, but she did a nice job."

"She did, indeed." Kevin picked up the napkin and tucked it into a pocket. "If business is booming, why are you frowning?" He held up a hand to stop her from protesting. "I've got until the bottom of this glass for you to tell me your troubles, so don't waste time."

Wondering why she felt able to unburden herself to him, she did just that. "We've got a great setup with Megan, the restaurant owner. This place is closed on Monday nights, so we can rent it for events like this. Plus, she allows us to rent her kitchen in the mornings for Beth to use. It's a win-win for everyone. But, in order to expand, we need our own commercial kitchen. In order to get a kitchen, we need a bank loan. So far, the banks don't want to lend to us because we don't have a commercial kitchen."

"Catch-22," he murmured.

"Yep."

Shoulder to shoulder, they leaned on the small table, watching guests bid their goodbyes to one another and make their way out the door. Kevin finished his drink and straightened up. "If I had a magic wand, I would make all that possible for you, but alas."

Jane smiled, then her eyes narrowed as she realized who she'd been speaking to. "You're not grilling me to report back to Liam Cross, are you?"

"Pfft." He waved a hand in dismissal. "He wouldn't be interested. He's satisfied by what he saw tonight; Grand Gestures does great work. I doubt you'll hear from him again."

"Oh. That's...good."

If Kevin noticed her slightly dejected tone, he didn't mention it. He leaned in for a cheek kiss, waved at the bartender, and joined the line headed out the door.

Not having to see Liam Cross again? Why did that not make her happy? With a shake of her head, Jane cleared tables, mentally counting down the minutes until the night was over.

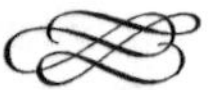

CHAPTER 3

A couple days later, Jane returned from her workout to find her sister still in her yoga clothes at the table, opened laptop, opened notebook, sharpened pencils, a stack of sticky notes, and cell phone arranged neatly around her. Scrutinizing the screen of her laptop, Beth didn't bother looking up. "I've made a fresh pot, and there's a yogurt parfait in the fridge for you."

"Thanks." Jane really wanted a bagel, but if her sister went to the trouble to make her a healthy breakfast, she'd eat it. She filled up a mug for herself, then held up the coffee pot. "Want some more?"

Beth held up her mug for a refill and smiled her thanks. Her nose wrinkled as she took in Jane's faded blue gi. "How was your class?"

"Hot and sweaty. Do you want a hug?" Arms wide, Jane made as if to round the counter.

"Oh God, no." Beth held up a staying hand.

Workouts were one of the ways the Beckett sisters differed. Kickboxing suited Jane's restless energy. Gone were the days when she belonged to an upscale gym. Now, in exchange for teaching once a week in a small studio, she had free membership. The class gave her the daily dose of social contact she needed. The quiet calm of yoga stretches and meditation was more Beth's style. She did them in private, in the front room of their apartment, different moves to energize her in the morning, and then to calm her in the evening. Her figure was fuller, softer, and curvier than Jane's, but she was as strong, agile, and fit as her slimmer sister. Beth pulled her hair out of its messy bun on the top of her head and let the riot of curls fall around her shoulders. "Go have your shower. When you come back, I'll have the invitations ready for you to look at."

Half an hour later, Jane emerged from her bedroom, wet hair brushing her shoulders. It was a work from home day, so she wore dark cargo pants, a raspberry-colored camisole with a built-in bra, and a raspberry hoodie. Beth had changed from her workout yoga clothes to her go-to work from home outfit: dark yoga pants and a soft sweater—this one in peach with a hood and pockets. Her hair was back up in its customary messy bun with a pencil buried in it. By the end of the day, three more pencils would probably be up there with it.

Jane poured herself another coffee and plopped down on the chair next to Beth. "I'm ready. Hit me with your brilliance."

Rolling her eyes, Beth angled the laptop for Jane's viewing. She clicked a key, and the invitation came into view. Sleek, understated, and elegant, in shades of blue, the details were spelled out with the shadow of the Seattle skyline in a lighter shade of blue as a background.

"Oh, wow!" Jane enlarged the image, studying the text. For what they were charging, they could not afford typos on the invitation. "Perfect. Send this to me, and I'll forward it to Chuck."

"Umm. No, I can do that." Beth didn't move her gaze from the screen, but a flush crept up her face.

"Okay..." Jane sipped her coffee, slightly confused. When they'd started Grand Gestures, Beth had firmly stated that she wanted few interactions with clients. Jane's paintball incident was the one and only time Beth had had to step in.

"Do you need his contact info?"

"I've got it." Beth's blush deepened as her eyes met Jane's. Then she waved at the laptop screen. "His email is listed on the contract. I've got it." Just then, her cell phone dinged with an incoming text. She snatched it up quickly, but not before Jane saw that it was from Chuck and turned away to hide her smile.

"Oh my God!" Beth's phone fell to the table with a clatter as she turned big eyes toward Jane. "He wants me to print out the invitation and deliver it to him in person. Why? Why would he need that when I can send it as an attachment?"

"Honey..." Jane's eyebrows rose. She waited patiently for the penny to drop. When it did, when Beth's open mouth indicated that she'd figured out what the text from Chuck meant, Jane leaned in and squeezed her sister's hand, speaking softly. "Yeah. He wants to see you. The invitation is an excuse."

Beth rose from her stool and began to pace, wringing her hands and chanting, "Ohmygod, ohmygod" over and over. If it wasn't Beth, it would be funny. But it *was* Beth—Beth who had barely spoken to a man other than employees and their father in over two years since catching her husband, Tony the Asswipe, boffing a bridesmaid at a wedding where he'd been the photographer and Beth had been the wedding planner. Jane had picked Beth up and dusted her off, but to say the cheating had left her shattered was an understatement.

Sipping her coffee, Jane wondered how best to encourage her sister. Chuck Duncan seemed like a nice guy. Meeting him to deliver the invitation was a great way for Beth to kick-start her social life. She picked up Beth's phone and scanned the text. "He wants you to meet him in the coffee shop on the first floor of his building. That seems doable. It's the place that makes those key lime tarts. You know, the ones Ava raved about and suggested we start serving." She saw the moment when Beth stopped thinking about Chuck and focused on the tarts. "We could pick up a couple, bring them back here, and deconstruct them."

"We?" Beth's brow furrowed.

"Sure. I'll come with. I'll sit in the back of the coffee shop and do some work."

Beth sighed with relief, then looked down at herself. "I should…"

"You look great. Maybe take the pencil out of your hair, though."

Sitting at one end of a long table in the coffee shop, Jane threw a wadded-up napkin at Beth.

"Hey!"

"Stop picking at your cuticles. It's unprofessional to greet a client with bloody nail beds."

Beth scowled and threw the napkin back at her.

"What did you think of the tart?" Jane nodded at the empty plate on the table. They'd both sampled it, concentrating on the flavors. She dipped a finger into the crumbs and icing sugar dusting the plate, then licked it off. "Can you recreate it?"

"Of course I can," Beth spoke as if insulted. "Although I think a shortbread crust would be better than graham wafers." She dug through her purse for a pen and notepad. "I'd better write that down now while I'm thinking about it."

"Thinking about what?"

Both sisters looked up to see Chuck smiling broadly in front of them.

Beth dropped her pen and blushed. Jane returned his

smile but said nothing. Under the table, she nudged Beth's knee with her own.

"The key lime tart would be better with a different crust," Beth answered, barely above a whisper.

"Really?" Chuck pulled out a chair and seated himself across from her. "Why's that?"

Beth leaned forward and began to go into detail about crust composition, Chuck hanging on her every word. Neither noticed when Jane got up and headed to the counter. Waiting for her coffee, she watched Beth and Chuck. They looked good together, Beth smiling and gesturing, Chuck nodding and laughing. It might not go anywhere, but seeing her sister so engaged made Jane smile. This was the boost of confidence Beth needed. As extroverted as Jane was, and with as many people as she talked to, she couldn't remember the last time her heart went pitter-pat, if ever. She shook her head. Over the years, she'd met a lot of nice men and dated some. But they were just that. Nice and maybe a little bland. None of them had challenged her or lingered in her thoughts long enough to want to spend more than a few evenings with them. Perhaps someone was out there; meanwhile, she had a business to run. With that thought, she accepted her drink and stepped outside the coffee shop.

For the fifth time in the hour since Kevin had sent him the video clip, Liam watched as Jane received a paintball to the goggles, then charged forward, gun raised, screaming, "Right back atcha, sucker!" The clip ended with an image of Jane, goggles removed, blood streaming down her face, holding a trophy and grinning like a maniac. Kevin was right. The woman was a badass.

The elevator dinged, and Liam exited, emerging in the lobby of the Duncan Properties building. He had a meeting a half-mile away and planned to stretch his legs. His step faltered when he spotted Jane leaning against the wall next to the doors, scrolling through her phone. Dressed casually in sneakers, cargo pants, and a raspberry-colored hoodie, she stood out from the people in business suits passing by her. Liam stepped behind a large potted plant to study her unnoticed. She scowled at her phone, then winced, a finger coming up to rub against the small white bandage under her left eye. Her hair was pulled back and up in a high ponytail, revealing the tattoo under her ear. She wore no makeup. She was unlike any woman he'd ever known. He wanted to soothe her injury and explore her tattoo with his lips. He shook his head. *Where the hell had that come from?*

He must have made a noise, because her head came up and her gaze locked on him. Warm brown eyes crinkled at the corners when she grinned at him.

She shoved her phone in a pocket as he approached. "Hey, Skippy, what were you hiding from? Bears?"

"I wasn't hiding. I was…." *What* was *he doing?*

"What then?" She cocked her head to the side and smirked. "You were spying on me!"

Her peal of laughter drew the attention of others. Scowling at her, Liam grabbed her by the arm and marched her out of the building and away from the doorway. "Would you keep it down?" He let her go when they were up against the windows of the coffee shop. He looked around to see if anyone was paying attention. Propriety meant everything.

Hands in her pockets, Jane stood with one hip cocked and grinned up at him. "I'll keep it down," she mock-whispered, "if you tell me why you were spying. Afraid I was casing the joint?"

"What?" Where did this woman come from, and why was she so—he couldn't find the words to describe her.

"Just messing with you." She peeked around him into the coffee shop, her grin softening to a smile.

He turned and searched through the window, wondering what had made her look so content. His gaze settled on Chuck and Beth looking way too cozy over coffee and baked goods. "Oh. That's not good."

"What's not good?"

Shit. He'd said it out loud. There was no taking it back. Jane was staring at him, clearly expecting an explanation. "Your sister, Beth, is…lovely."

"Yes. Yes, she is. So what's the problem?"

Liam shifted on his feet, avoiding her gaze. "Chuck is—" *Easily led astray. Weak when it comes to women.* Nope. While they were both true, he could say neither out loud. God, he'd be happy when this party was over and he could get Chuck back onto the straight and narrow. "Your client. Chuck is your client."

Speaking slowly as if to a person with limited English, Jane nodded. "Yes, Skippy, Chuck is our client. A client who asked to meet to go over the invitation for an event."

"Chuck asked for the meeting? With both of you? And stop calling me Skippy."

Jane peered through the window at Chuck and Beth, then turned back to Liam, lashing him with her ponytail. "Beth did the design. She's the one who can address any changes. What does it matter? Our client, Chuck, asked for the meeting, and here we are, *Liam*."

"Yes. Here *you* are." Grand Gestures was operating on a shoestring; they needed this event. They needed Duncan Properties. Perhaps they were thinking beyond their business. Perhaps they thought Beth snaring Chuck was the answer to their problems. As if she were able to read minds, Jane interrupted his thoughts.

"He came to us, wanting a lavish affair in a short time span. We are bending over backward and will do a kick-ass job. When—not if—we do well with this event, Duncan Properties may throw more work our way or provide a glowing reference. That kind of goodwill, we can't buy. So if Chuck Duncan asks for an in-person meeting to go over the invitations, *we* will accommodate him." Her wide eyes fairly dared him to contradict her.

Liam glared down at her, undecided if she was speaking the truth or had deliberately left Chuck and Beth alone to encourage more than a business relationship. But damn, the woman was confident. And determined. For now, he'd let it go, but he would be watching closely and have a word with Chuck after the party. Before he could say anything else, Jane yanked open the coffee shop door and sauntered over to join Beth and Chuck. Whatever she said made the two look around at him, Chuck grinning broadly, Beth smiling politely, and Jane smirking at him. He raised a hand in a wave, then turned to make his way to his meeting. Why did he feel like he'd missed something?

*E*xiting the elevator, Liam glanced around the busy floor on his way to his office. Spotting Chuck at his desk, Liam nodded at Kevin, then changed direction, stopping to lean against the open door of Chuck's office. The blond man was engrossed in his phone and didn't notice Liam until he cleared his throat.

"How'd your meeting go?" Chuck asked.

"Not bad. How was yours? I saw you in the coffee shop with that woman from Grand Gestures."

"Beth." Chuck's ears pinked as he said her name. "She was showing me the invitation."

"Not giving you more laundry tips?"

"What?"

Liam shook his head. "Nothing. I'm glad they're doing a good job."

Chuck's phone beeped, drawing their attention to it. Chuck glanced at the screen, then turned it face down on the desk. Liam wasn't sure, but it looked like a video game. "After work, do you want to get something to eat, then head to the batting cages?"

His glance shifting between Liam and his phone, Chuck shook his head. "Thanks, but there's umm, some things I've got to work on at home."

He studied his friend's innocent expression. "'Kay. I'll see you tomorrow then."

Liam headed to his office, nerves twisting his gut. Was it happening again? Was he going to have to clean up after another woman broke Chuck's heart? The next five weeks were going to be a trial.

CHAPTER 4

$\mathcal{J}$ane stood in the lobby of the Duncan Properties building, waiting for Kevin. Since the bonding experience at the engagement party, the two had become friends, texting frequently. She'd shared that Grand Gestures had eight, *not five*, potential events due to the party. They wouldn't be able to accommodate them all, unfortunately, but it was a nice problem to have. In the area for a meeting, she'd invited Kevin for lunch, looking forward to his company at a time when she wasn't working.

The elevator dinged, drawing her attention. Spotting Kevin, she waved and smiled. Her smile dimmed when the large frame of Liam Cross emerged behind him in a suit and tie. Jane was dressed for business as well, in the meet-the-client outfit Beth put together for her: a gray pantsuit, emerald green tank underneath, and zebra-striped Rothy's. She looked fine but felt Liam's scrutiny. "Put on your big girl panties," she muttered and strode forward.

Kevin pulled her in for a cheek kiss and stepped back, flapping a hand at Liam. "You okay with the boss man joining us?"

No! "How nice." Jane extended her hand; cheek-kissing Liam would be awkward.

He appeared to be of a like mind. When their palms connected, he frowned and quickly let go. "Ms. Beckett."

"Mr. Cross." Her hand tingled from the contact, and she surreptitiously flexed her fingers behind her back.

"Excellent. Niceties have been observed, so let's go." Kevin tucked Jane's hand into his arm and guided her out the door. "I thought we'd head to Nonna's. I think you're going to love their seafood salad."

Exiting the building, they turned left toward Pike Place Market. Lunchtime crowds mixed with tourists meant full sidewalks. Unable to walk three abreast, Liam led the way. While Kevin chattered in her ear, Jane observed Liam's broad shoulders in the perfectly tailored suit. With each long stride, she caught a glimpse of his rounded ass cheeks. *Stop that!* She dragged her attention back to Kevin. Nothing good would come from ogling Liam Cross.

At the restaurant, Liam held the door for her, and she smiled her thanks, oddly flustered by the intense look in his eyes. The foyer was crowded, but, recognizing Kevin, the hostess led them to a booth, leaving them with a smile and menus. Kevin sat next to Jane while Liam occupied the bench opposite them.

"Who are you meeting with today?" Kevin asked while perusing the menu.

Jane flicked a glance at Liam, who was scrolling through his phone as if no one else was present. Was he doing that deliberately, or was he raised without manners? She decided ignoring his presence would be the best way to proceed.

"Imani Singh of Singh Communications wants us to plan an event for a product launch for them."

That got his attention. Out of the corner of her eye, she saw him put away the phone and glance between her and Kevin.

"Singh Communications would be a big feather in your cap. Have you done this kind of thing before?" Kevin quirked an eyebrow at her.

She shook her head. "Not exactly. Beth and I have been brainstorming, and I think we have a solid plan for them. It can't be worse than coordinating a wedding proposal in a scavenger hunt." She smiled inwardly when the flip remark earned her a scowl from Liam.

"Where will you be doing the cooking? Still at that restaurant in Pike's Place?" Kevin unfolded his napkin and placed it on his lap before turning and doing the same for Jane.

"Thanks, *Mom*." She grinned and pointed at Liam. "What about him?"

Kevin waved dismissively. "He's on his own."

She laughed, then answered his question, "We're looking into a sports venue, and we've worked out an agreement with a food truck company. Jorge used to cook for us before going into business with his cousins. They have four trucks and a commercial kitchen in SoDo. It's huge, and our schedules mesh. Beth is thrilled to not be constantly working against the clock."

"She's very talented. Can you convince her to share some recipes? Or maybe let me sit and watch her work?"

Jane nudged his shoulder with hers. "Her recipes are carefully guarded secrets, and I don't know how she would feel about cooking in front of an audience."

Turning to her fully, Kevin tapped a finger on the table. "A video of her at work would do wonders for your Instagram feed."

Jane scrunched her nose. "I believe you. But Beth would die before cooking in front of a camera."

"Why don't you have your own kitchen?" Liam's deep, rich, velvet voice sounded from across the table.

The question caught her by surprise. She didn't think he was paying attention. She rubbed her fingers together in the international sign for money. "We're working on it. A couple larger events like Singh and we should be able to satisfy the bankers."

At his furrowed brow, she continued, "The banks are leery about lending to us. They can't pigeonhole us. We're not a restaurant or catering company but prepare food. We need to prove to them that we have a good track record before they will open up the checkbooks."

"What about investors?"

"Nope. Investors are going to want to tell us how to do things."

"There are angel investment groups. You could—"

Jane held up her hand. "Thanks, but this is our company, and we will do it ourselves."

The waiter's approach put a stop to further discussion. They placed their orders: the seafood salad for Kevin and Jane, beef dip for Liam.

Her phone rang, and Jane glanced at the screen. "I have to take this. Would you mind?"

Kevin rose from the bench, and she scooted out, making her way to the relative quiet of the sidewalk.

"Jorge, what's up?" She plugged one ear to better hear the owner of the food trucks.

"It's more like what's down. A pipe broke on the floor above us. Water has run down through the walls, and our kitchen is flooded." Jorge continued to share more bad news. "The power went out, shutting down the fridges and freezers. I'm afraid everything in yours will have to be tossed."

Knees weakening, Jane leaned against the building. "Everything?" They had a retirement party scheduled for tomorrow night. All the supplies had been in those fridges. Beth was supposed to be prepping today. *Oh shit.* "Is Beth there? Does she know?"

Jorge cleared his throat and lowered his voice. "Yeah. I got here fifteen minutes ago, and she was right behind me. She's kind of a mess, which is why I'm calling you."

"Right." Shoving a hand through her hair, Jane stared blindly through the restaurant window. "I'm at the Market. I'll get there as soon as I can."

"'Kay. Drive safe. I'll look after Beth until you get here."

She disconnected and went back into the restaurant for her bag. She carefully schooled her expression not to reveal her panic. Everything lost, a flooded kitchen, four events in the next two weeks. What the hell were they going to do? Speaking tonelessly, she avoided the eyes of both men. "Something's come up, and I have to leave." She cleared her throat, swallowing back tears. "Kevin, can you hand me my bag, please?"

Grabbing her messenger bag, Kevin stood from the table, a worried expression on his face. "What's up? Can I help?"

Darting a glance at Liam, she shook her head. "No, but thanks." She settled the bag over her shoulder with shaking hands and turned to leave. Kevin's hand stopped her.

"Hey." He squeezed her arm. "Call me tonight. You hear?"

Unable to answer, she nodded, turned, and wove through the tables to the door, anxious to get to Beth.

When Jane arrived at the warehouse where Jorge operated his business, her sister was standing over a compost bin overflowing with what should have been canapes for thirty people. Beth didn't acknowledge her. The food wasn't spoiled, but the laws covering food handling were strict, and Grand Gestures was not about to risk their license. Her thrifty sister had set aside some for them to take home to eat, but still, a lot was thrown out. Silently, they stared at the waste, each lost in their own thoughts. Beth's face was blank, but her eyes were rimmed with red, and her shoulders slumped. Jane searched her mind for something reassuring to say, but she came up empty. Tomorrow's party was in an office in Bellevue. The food could be replaced, but where would they be able to prepare it? There wasn't a kitchen on site they could use. Her brain was tired from churning like a hamster on a wheel. How much money was in their account? Did they have time to shop and prep? Where would they do it? Tomorrow was Friday. A big night in the restaurant business, no one would be willing to give up their kitchen. If they canceled the party now, with such short notice, they could kiss Grand Gestures goodbye. No one would hire them again. *Think!* She forced her tired mind to go through the Rolodex in her brain. There had to be someone she could call.

"Truck twelve will be back by six. Tito and Naomi will clean it up, and then it's yours for the next few days."

Both women looked up, uncomprehending expressions on their faces as Jorge joined them.

"What?"

The barrel-chested man placed a beefy hand on Jane's shoulder. "You've got one of my trucks from six tonight on."

The women stared at him.

He shrugged. "It's gonna be cramped, but it will work. We can crank up a generator, plug in a fridge, and store your food until tomorrow night."

Jane looked to Beth. She'd be the one bearing the brunt of the work. "What do you think?"

Beth glanced from Jane to Jorge to the compost pile and back to Jane. She bit her lip. "I'll have to change the menu. Will the client care?"

"They don't even know what the menu is. They requested vegetarian canapes and left the rest up to us."

"Are you sure about this, Jorge?" Beth looked up at the big man. "You'd be cutting your income down by twenty-five percent."

Jorge waved dismissively. "You helped me get my start. It's my turn to help you. Don't cancel anything. The truck will work for your thing tomorrow, and I'll ask around. We'll figure shit out, find a kitchen you can use until—"

Beth jumped him, wrapping her arms around the much larger man.

Jane joined in. "Thank you, thank you, thank you."

Looking both uncomfortable and pleased at the same time, Jorge disentangled himself. "Enough. Don't you have things to do?"

Jane and Beth grinned, Jane wiping her nose on her sleeve while Beth used her apron.

"Right," Beth said. "I've got to make my shopping list, and you have that meeting."

"Right," Jane said. "Let me return some messages, then I'll join you." Turning away, she pulled out her phone to see three texts and two calls from Kevin. Smiling, she called him back as she settled into her car.

"A food truck. You're going to be working out of a food truck?" he asked in a disbelieving tone.

She tried to downplay the gravity of the situation, not wanting her new friend to worry about her. "Until we get stuff sorted. It'll be fine. Just a little water damage."

"Sweetheart, I saw your face. I don't believe you. Now spill."

She gave him the details. Beth's tears, her fears. Even with Jorge's generous offer and reassurance, Grand Gestures would be scrambling until they could secure a proper kitchen.

"Jorge is right," Kevin muttered. "Don't cancel anything. I know you have that meeting today. I need to sort some things out, but I want you to call me when you're done."

"Umm…sure."

"I mean it. Promise?"

"Yeah. Gotta go." Jane disconnected, wondering what he was up to. But she had no more time to spare. She had a soggy kitchen to clean and a client to pitch to.

Three hours later, she was driving back to SoDo to wait for the arrival of truck twelve when her phone rang. She engaged through Bluetooth. "Sorry, Kevin. I should have called you sooner. The meeting went well. I'll tell you all about it later. I'm on my way to meet Beth." She'd made the presentation on autopilot while she went through her mental Rolodex again, trying to sort out the kitchen situation. Had she jinxed herself boasting to Kevin and Liam at lunch? Kevin's voice interrupted her thoughts.

"Then you and Beth will meet me at the AME church on Fourteenth Avenue."

"What? Why?"

"First African Methodist Episcopal Church is my mother's church. It has a commercial kitchen because they run a soup kitchen out of it. I've arranged with them for you to rent it for the next six weeks with a possible extension. You and Beth can chat with them about scheduling."

Jane blinked at the brake lights of the car in front of her. "You did what?"

"You heard me. I called the church. They're happy about the additional income. This is me waving my magic wand. I'm sending you the address, pictures of the kitchen, and the city license. Text me when you're on your way." As if sensing she was about to balk, he said, "Don't be stubborn. It's not weak to accept help once in a while." He disconnected before she could say anything else.

She pulled into a warehouse parking lot and brought up Kevin's text. The kitchen was large and clean, with good-quality commercial appliances. She enlarged the photo of the license, noting the dates and signature. Blinking back tears, her shoulders slumped in relief. This just might work. If nothing else, they'd make it through tomorrow's event, buying some time until the SoDo place could be cleaned up. She drove out of the parking lot with a much lighter heart, thanking her stars for the generous hearts of the people in her life.

❄

"I'm taking a personal day tomorrow."

Kevin's voice distracted Liam from the spreadsheet he was studying on his screen. "Hmm?"

"Personal day. Me. Tomorrow." Kevin stood in the doorway of Liam's office, unrolling his shirtsleeves and buttoning his cuffs. He looked up to catch Liam's eyes and rolled his own. "You have three meetings tomorrow. They're on your computer's calendar with alarms set. The files that you will need are in your inbox. Incoming phone calls will be routed to Chuck's assistant. You'll be fine."

Liam blinked. Kevin took his vacations, at times arrived late, or left early for medical appointments, but never, in the three years he'd worked for Liam, had he taken a personal day. And he rarely left before six o'clock. "Are you…well?" He scrolled through his memory, trying to recall if the day was significant. It wasn't his birthday. Kevin had programmed that into his calendar the first month he started working for Liam. Kevin's father had died years ago, but he thought his mother was alive and in good health. "Is your mother…?"

"She's fine."

But Kevin obviously was not. After Jane Beckett's abrupt departure at lunch, he'd been pensive. He was clearly distracted, although his work, as always, was impeccable. "Did you hear back from Jane? Is something wrong with her sister?"

Kevin shook his head. "Beth is fine. They had a situation, but they've handled it."

Liam leaned back in his chair, fingers linked behind his head. "A situation? Lost the Singh Communications account? I'm not surprised. Grand Gestures is a scrappy company, but

45

they're small. And Jane Beckett is hardly professional. That scar and tattoo. I doubt they'll—"

"Stop disparaging them," Kevin interrupted him, his eyes narrowed, his lips thinned. "Scars and tattoos don't make people poor business risks. If it takes Grand Gestures a while to succeed, it's because misanthropic misogynists like you are holding them back." Kevin's glare continued, burning a hole in Liam's face.

Liam blinked.

"So"—Kevin jerked his chin at the door—"I'll be in on Monday. Goodnight."

"Goodnight," Liam murmured, staring at the now vacant doorway. Misanthropic misogynist. Was that what he was? Cynical? Perhaps. Skeptical? Definitely. But misogynistic? He had to think about that. He shifted in his seat. He and Kevin never had words. He felt like he'd been scolded and that, possibly, he'd deserved it.

That afternoon, he'd followed Kevin into the elevator, blathering on about cost projections, assuming they'd be eating lunch together like they'd done multiple times. Jane's presence in the lobby caught him by surprise. But Kevin being Kevin, he included Liam. And he'd been…civil. All right, he'd been *barely* civil—and petulant, to boot. The woman annoyed him. Kevin clearly thought she was something else. What was it about the Beckett women that his two closest friends were smitten? During lunch, he'd stared at Jane while she spoke. She was animated, attractive, and confident, clearly uncaring about the thin scar on her cheek. She didn't attempt to hide it or the small sunburst tattoo below her left ear. When she'd returned from her phone call looking like death warmed over, he'd been confused by his emotional reaction. He'd wanted to push Kevin aside, be the one to reassure Jane. Instead, he'd sat like a bump on a log, mute. After that, the afternoon dragged on. Now he was alone, feeling like he should apologize. For what and to whom, he didn't know.

❄

Catching sight of Kevin waving from the sidewalk in front of the church, Jane pulled over to the curb and lowered the passenger window.

"You made it!" Kevin leaned into the car. "Turn right into that alley and there's parking next to the big red doors. That's the entrance to the kitchen. Where's Beth?"

"She should be here any minute. She's driving a silver delivery van with GG on the side of it. Will you stay here and flag her down?"

Kevin backed up and nodded. "Yep. The doors are unlocked. Go ahead and start unloading. When Beth gets here, I'll give you the grand tour."

Jane gave him a thumbs-up, checked her mirrors, then followed his instructions, parking near the large red doors. Grabbing two bags of groceries, she let herself into the kitchen.

"Are you Jane or Beth?" A tall, slim Black woman with a regal crown of braids greeted her.

Automatically, Jane straightened her posture. "I'm Jane Beckett, ma'am. Kevin told me to let myself in."

The woman approached with a hand extended. "That would be my son. I'm Eleanor Armstrong. Here. Let me help you with that." She took a bag of groceries and hefted it onto the large island in the middle of the kitchen.

"Thanks." Putting the other bag beside the first, Jane stepped back and extended her hand. "Nice to meet you. Your son is a godsend."

Eleanor's lips quirked. "When he's not a trial and a tribulation, he is that. I'm glad he called. Like everyone else, the church could use more income. It never occurred to us to rent out the kitchen. This is a win-win for both of us. I printed out a quick contract. Do you want to look it over now or wait until your sister gets here?"

"Thanks, I'll look at it later. Kevin didn't say you worked here."

"I do." Turning to the island, Eleanor pushed a file folder toward Jane before unpacking the groceries. "I'm the office manager here."

"She does everything but deliver the sermon. Check that. She's delivered a few sermons here and there." Kevin entered the kitchen, smiling big, arms laden with grocery bags. He put them down, rounded the island, and kissed his mother on both cheeks. "When she dies, she'll sit at God's right hand."

"Flatterer." Eleanor pushed him away, moving toward Beth, who had arrived moments ago and now stood next to Jane. Introductions were made again, and Eleanor took them on a tour of the kitchen, pointing out the industrial stand mixer, dishwasher, eight-burner stove, commercial refrigerator, and walk-in freezer. "I know you have a time crunch, so for now, put your goods wherever you need to. Monday morning, we can delineate space for you and space for us. Will that work?"

Beth and Jane nodded like bobbleheads. The kitchen was scrupulously clean, the equipment well-used but also well-maintained.

"Questions?"

They shook their heads.

"Then here are the keys, and I'll get out of your way."

Eleanor left, and the two sisters started unpacking food items. Kevin removed his jacket, hung it on a hook on the back of the door, and asked, "Where would you like me to start?"

"Thank you, but we've got this." Jane threw a grateful smile his way.

"No, no," he said, rolling up his shirt sleeves. "I don't get a chance to work with food, and I am happy to be your minion."

"Are you sure?" Jane looked between him and Beth. "I'm sure we can use another pair of hands. Beth?"

She nodded. "Yep. You know this kitchen better than us. Can you dig out as many baking sheets as you can find and then fill the sink with hot soapy water? There will be a lot of dishwashing ahead of you tonight."

"Not a problem. Let me fire up the coffee maker."

Beth smiled her gratitude while Jane hugged him.

They worked steadily through the evening, recreating the food they could in the short span of time they had, substituting some items for others. Beth was organized and focused, Jane and Kevin following orders. At midnight, they called it quits.

"Kevin, you are a lifesaver. I can't tell you how much it means for you to be here." Jane leaned back against the counter and bumped shoulders with him.

He smiled. "This was fun. What time should I be here in the morning?"

Jane shook her head. "No. You've done enough. We can't ask you to do that."

"Yes." Kevin crossed his arms and leveled a glare at her. "You didn't ask. I like you, and I like this work." He glanced around the kitchen. "This is different from my regular day. It's creative, productive, and if you've done it right, you've made people happy."

Beth and Jane exchanged glances.

"Are you thinking of quitting your day job?" Jane asked.

Kevin snorted. "I wish. I'm far too practical to do so. Perhaps in the future. It's..." He shifted his feet, and the look he gave Jane was full of admiration. "I'm impressed by your drive and determination. I've seen businesses start up and fail so damn often. You two deserve to succeed. And if I can help—why not?"

For the second time in one day, Beth hugged a man. "Thank you. Can you meet us back here at eight?"

Kevin pulled away from her, then squeezed both her hands. He blinked away a tear. "I'll be here."

CHAPTER 5

Needing a file retrieved, Liam reached for the intercom. It went unanswered, and he swore, finally remembering that Kevin wasn't at work. Deciding to check in with Chuck, he left his office and strode past Kevin's empty desk toward Chuck's office, where Chuck's assistant, Kami, sat guard in front of it. She pasted on a smile as he approached.

"Hi, Mr. Cross. How can I help you?"

"Would you please find the Axis file? They're one of our oldest clients, and some of the records aren't digitized yet."

Kami scribbled on a notepad. "Certainly. I'll have it for you shortly."

Liam shoved his hands in his pockets and frowned at the closed door of Chuck's office. "Is he on a call?"

She shook her head, dark curls dancing. "He took a personal day."

The frown took over Liam's face. "Hmm," he grunted and turned back to his office. Chuck was taking a personal day. Kevin was taking a personal day. What the hell? Then he forgot all about it, sat at his desk, and buried himself in spreadsheets.

An hour later, he rose to stretch his legs. Walking through the office, he spotted Kami and two other women clustered together, heads bent over a cell phone and giggling. He headed in their direction. Kami looked up and smiled.

"Have you seen Kevin's latest Instagram post? He's having a great time today."

At Liam's headshake, she extended her phone toward him. On the screen was a smiling Beth. Kevin stood on one side of her, Chuck on the other, both kissing her cheek and mugging for the camera. All three looked sweaty and had flour on their faces. Scowling, Liam scrolled through the caption. *Grand Gestures brought in the B team. Good thing Chef Beth knows how to hold people accountable.* Liam thrust the phone back at Kami and stomped back to his office, slamming the door as he passed through it. Growling, he stormed around his office, slamming his fist against the back of his chair each time he passed it. Chuck and Kevin were kitchen help for Jane and Beth. That pretty blonde was dragging his best friend further into her net. Grabbing up his cell phone, he opened Instagram.

Liam was a social media snob. Kevin set up an Instagram profile for him, but Liam never posted. He lurked. He looked at the profiles of people with whom they did business. Now he looked for Grand Gestures. Whoever did their posts knew what they were doing. Gorgeous shots of food, interspersed with larger photos of event settings, some tagged with clients' names, with the odd photo of Beth and/or Jane. They looked approachable and professional, like the kind of people you would want to help you plan an important life event. He went to Kevin's page and found the post of him with Beth and Chuck. The joy on their faces was a knife to his gut.

They were off having a great time and hadn't bothered to include him, hadn't even bothered to tell him. Chuck was his best friend, dammit. Truth be told, Chuck was his only friend besides Kevin. Liam sighed, feeling empty. He was in his late thirties, and his only friends were the men he worked with. And whose fault was that? His life revolved around Duncan Properties. He couldn't even remember the last time he'd gone on a date.

He looked at the photo again. This time, he noticed Chuck's arm wrapped around Beth. Chuck should not be anywhere near that woman. Could he not see that it would only end badly? You'd think he'd realized by now that women were nothing but trouble. No doubt he was whipping out his checkbook to sort out whatever crisis the Beckett sisters had landed in. And Kevin…he was rumpled and sweaty and covered with flour. Liam had never seen his assistant look so relaxed and happy. The knife in his gut twisted.

Right before his eyes, a new post popped up, this one with Jane. Gone was the boring pantsuit she'd worn to lunch. In its place was a high-necked tank top that showed off her toned arms to perfection. The shirt had been white at one point, but the woman must have wiped her hands on it because it was liberally coated with food stains. A smile lit up her eyes as she pressed her cheek against Kevin's for the selfie. Neither Jane nor Beth had personal pages, which disappointed Liam. He wanted more photos of Jane. He wanted to peek inside her world and learn what she was passionate about. He knew she played paintball, but what else? Was she seeing anyone? Did she turn that megawatt smile in the direction of anyone in particular? He hoped not. Going back to Kevin's profile, he enlarged the post to see the front of Jane's shirt. It was an image of a bullseye with paint splotches around it. The script superimposed over the image read BULLSEYE PAINTBALL. Liam typed the name into the search field and struck pay dirt. Within the many photos of paint-spattered patrons was an image of Jane holding a trophy aloft while blood oozed down her cheek. Not hesitating, Liam took a screenshot of the image and saved it to his photos.

Shoving the phone into his pocket, he drifted over to the windows. From his corner office, he could watch the ferries moving across the bay, taking people to the islands, possibly getting away early for the weekend. It was two o'clock on a Friday afternoon. He had no more calls or meetings for the day. Nothing was stopping *him* from getting away for the weekend. He had no plans. Sundays, he often had brunch with Chuck and his parents, but they were off in Leavenworth.

His phone dinged with an incoming text. Not leaving his spot by the window, he pulled out his phone. Chuck.

Can't make it tonight. See you Monday.

Liam gazed sightlessly out the window. He didn't have firm plans with Chuck, just an unspoken agreement to meet for a drink on Friday nights. In fact, it wasn't unusual for Chuck to cancel on him. But this time, Liam had a feeling Beth was the reason Chuck had begged off. And there was nothing he could do about it.

❄

Jane slurped down the last of the latte Chuck had brought her. They'd been drinking the coffee in the church's kitchen, which was fine, but Beth received a text from Chuck asking her to meet for coffee. When she told the others, Kevin commandeered her phone, called Chuck, and told him to bring them all lattes. When he arrived, Kevin went on to convince him to take over vegetable peeling and chopping for the carrot tarts and broccoli toasts they were making.

Two hours later, they were almost done. Seven different appetizers were packed up and ready to be delivered. The party was small, so Beth would be handling food service while Jane performed bartending duties, beer and wine only, which made it easier. The glassware and dinnerware would be delivered by their usual supplier, and the alcohol and soft drink order would be held in a cooler, ready to be picked up. She and Beth had plenty of time to shower and change before trekking across the lake to Bellevue.

The back door opened as Beth sprayed down the prep area with sanitizer while Jane returned from stuffing the dirty kitchen towels and washcloths into the church's washing machine. Eleanor Armstrong entered, carrying a box of fruit.

"Perfect timing," she said. "Our delivery from the gleaners has arrived. Kevin, will you please help them bring in the rest?"

Kevin saluted smartly and went to do his mother's bidding.

Eleanor placed the box on a counter and surveyed the kitchen. Beth and Jane stood motionless, awaiting her verdict. The church was being generous, and they wanted to make a good impression.

"The place looks great! How did things go?" Smiling, Eleanor ambled over to where the foil-covered trays of appetizers waited to be loaded in the van.

Beth hurried over to the fridge and pulled out a plastic container. "I love your kitchen. It's set up so well, it was a dream to cook in. Here are a few of the appetizers. I thought you'd like one." Her face turned red. "Of course, you don't have to eat them. I…"

Eleanor popped a pastry filled with goat cheese and sundried tomatoes into her mouth, eyes widening. "Oh my. That is tasty. I'm keeping these for myself."

Lips pursed, Jane watched Beth's sigh of relief. It frustrated her that her sister didn't believe in her own talent, no matter how many people praised her.

Chuck had been observing but now sidled up to Jane as

Kevin and two others came in the back door, carrying boxes of produce and baked goods. "I hate to sound ignorant, but what is gleaning?"

Eleanor heard him and explained, "Gleaning is a term from the Bible. After the fields were harvested, farmers were instructed to leave some grain to be picked up by the less fortunate. Local grocery stores and bakeries contact us when they have food they need to get rid of, food that's close to expiring but not rotten. The church hosts a free meal on Sunday mornings. We use the gleaned food to make the meal, and what we don't use, we make available for our guests to take home." She studied Chuck with a quizzical expression. "I'm sorry, I don't believe we've met."

Kevin put his box down and came over to make the introductions. "Mom, this is my friend, Chuck. Chuck, this is my mother, Eleanor Armstrong."

Holding Chuck's extended hand, Eleanor spoke to Kevin, "Friends, huh? Kevin doesn't often introduce his friends to me."

"Mom!" Kevin rolled his eyes. "We're not dating. We play for different teams, so don't get excited."

"A mother can dream." She patted Chuck's hand and let it go before turning to Beth. "We have a rotation of professional cooks who come in to oversee the meals. We rely on church and community volunteers to serve and clean up, and we have a team who go out to the stores to pick up the food —those are the gleaners. Some of our guests are our best volunteers."

"Mom's program is a model for others in the city."

Eleanor frowned at her son. "It's not *my* program."

Holding up a hand, Kevin started ticking off his fingers. "You got permission from the city. You found the gleaners. You reached out to the restaurants. You organize the volunteers and oversee the meal service. It's *your* program."

Blushing, Eleanor began unpacking a box of vegetables. "Someone had to do it," she muttered.

"Mrs. Armstrong, if you'd like, you can add my name to your list of cooks. I can't commit to specific dates at the moment, but you can call me—"

Eleanor beamed at Beth. "Thank you, I will give you a call."

Jane had a feeling she'd been volunteered as well. She narrowed her eyes at Kevin accusingly. He, in turn, widened his eyes innocently. She picked up her jacket and messenger bag. "We'll get out of your way. Kevin and Chuck, thank you so much for your help. It meant the world to us."

Waving at Kevin and his mother, she followed Chuck and Beth out to the parking lot. He said something to Beth, then got in his car and drove off. Pulling out her keys, Jane strolled over to where her sister watched the departing vehicle, a blush high on her cheeks. "That turned out well. Are you looking to add him to the payroll? Because we can always use a big, strong man in the kitchen."

Beth blushed further and dug through her own purse, avoiding Jane's eyes. "That was...very nice of him. A kind gesture."

"Yes, it was." Jane leaned against the van, deciding that teasing her sister wasn't a good idea.

"Because that's all it was—a kind gesture. He's not—we're not—"

Jane held both hands up. "Not saying anything. I'll meet you at home." She waited for Beth to get in the van and take off before walking toward her car. She was both exhausted and energized.

The past twenty-four hours had been a roller coaster ride. Kevin had truly waved his magic wand, because working out of the church kitchen was perfect. She'd worried that it was too perfect. It had all but dropped in their lap, and she wanted to pay the church for the use of the kitchen while looking for something else. Do a cost/benefits analysis, figure out if GG could be hurt in any way by working in the church's kitchen. She'd voiced her hesitation to Beth, who'd given her the stink eye. Her sister then enumerated the benefits. The location gave them easy access to downtown Seattle; depending on traffic, they were about ten minutes away from their apartment. There was massive space to prepare food for events, and they wouldn't be racing against the clock when others wanted to use the kitchen. The pricing was more than fair, the equipment was in great shape—and *why* did Jane have to find fault with *everything*? Seeing the exhaustion on Beth's face and realizing her only misgiving was because she hadn't found the facility herself, Jane acquiesced. She, Eleanor, and Beth discussed terms and decided on hours of use. They looked over the contract. The sisters signed it and received a key. Jane glanced up at the church and smiled. Who said there wasn't a God?

Visualizing her to-do list, she reached into her bag for her planner. *Crap.* It must still be on a counter inside. Grabbing her bag and keys, she retraced her steps and let herself back into the kitchen.

"Is this yours?" Eleanor held up Jane's most prized possession. Held together by stout elastic bands, the leather planner was bright yellow. It bulged with notes, business cards, menus, and a pencil case.

"Thank you! I'd be lost without that."

"I know what you mean. Hang on for a sec." Eleanor hustled back to her office and returned, holding up her own bulging notebook. "I'm a Happy Planner gal. How about you?" She placed the book on the island and opened it up to display her spread for the week. It was a veritable rainbow. Tasks for the day were neatly printed in different colored ink. "I used to have a personal and a business calendar, but now, they're so intertwined, I track everything in one place." She tapped a bright pink sticker worded with a reminder to meditate placed next to a box about sorting recycling.

"I am in awe. It's so neat."

Eleanor laughed. "That's next week's spread." She flipped a page backward. "This is what it looks like at the end of the week." It was still neat, but there were additions in black ink, some things lined out, and notes in the margins.

Jane nodded. She started the week off with neat notes and to-do lists but, by Saturdays, was madly scribbling all over the place. "What's your system? What do the different colored inks mean?" She herself simply noted a W for a work note and a P for a personal note. Sadly, the only thing personal these days was exercise and paintball.

Eleanor flipped to the front of the book and pointed to a box with names in different colored ink. "The colors tell me who is responsible for each task. I'm purple. The pastor is green. The custodian is gray. The admin is light blue. I got that idea from one of my planner pals."

Jane raised a questioning eyebrow.

"I belong to a Facebook group dedicated to paper planners. On Thursday nights, we have a Zoom meet-up. We geek out over pens, stickers, washi tape, that kind of thing. I pour myself a glass of wine and make my spread for the upcoming week. One of the women has five children, and she assigns a different color to each kid. I thought the idea was brilliant and have incorporated it here at the church. It took the staff a while to get on board, but we now use the same colors on the wall calendar in the office." She leaned against the island and tapped Jane's planner. "How do you delineate who does what for Grand Gestures?"

Jane blew a raspberry. "This is just me. Beth is free form. See?" She pulled out a piece of paper covered with doodles of recipe ingredients, invitation ideas, and freehand circles and rectangles indicating the table set-up for an event. "I'm too much of a control freak to work like that."

"But you mesh?"

"Oh yeah." Jane laced her fingers together. "She's the creative, and I'm the business. We work well together."

Eleanor moved over to the coffeemaker and poured herself a mug. She held one up for Jane in silent inquiry.

"No, thanks. Any more and I'll be jittery."

The older woman smiled. "I know what you mean. I pace myself throughout the day." She stepped back to Jane's side. "When Kevin called me yesterday, I looked you up online. Grand Gestures is doing well, it seems."

"Yes. However, we're still tap-dancing pretty damn hard. Being able to use your kitchen is a godsend."

"We're not a business, but I know what it's like getting something off the ground. We've found corporate partners who assist us with funding and volunteers. Have you considered looking for investors to give you some breathing room?"

She'd worded it differently, but Eleanor was echoing Liam Cross's question.

"I may consider that in the future. Right now, I don't want to have to rely on someone else. I want to keep things close." She wasn't about to go into the ugly tale about the last time she'd relied on someone other than family.

"What about Beth?"

"Beth wants what I want."

Eleanor wrapped both hands around her mug and nodded at their planners. "I won't keep you. You've got a party to get to."

Scooping up her notebook, Jane murmured a goodbye and headed back to her car, wondering if her last answer was the right one.

CHAPTER 6

What the hell was he thinking? With whiskey warming his belly and muddling his mind, signing up for a paintball session seemed like a great idea. In the light of day and with a headache pounding in his brain, not so much. He intended to argue his way out of the non-refundable fee he'd paid in his drunken state. Settling his sunglasses more firmly over his eyes, Liam hauled his sorry ass out of the car. His back hurt, his head hurt, and his hands hurt.

Fingering a fresh blister on the palm of his hand, he cursed himself for not wearing gloves at the batting cage the night before. He'd left the office wearing his work clothes and drove directly to the sports field in Magnuson Park. For two hours, he'd slugged away at balls. Personal day. Liam had never taken a personal day. Other than dental and medical checkups, he never took a day off. He couldn't remember the last time he'd done anything fun without Chuck. He'd whacked the ball time and time again, thinking about his best friend potentially getting his heart stomped on. Again. Worn out from swinging the bat, he'd stopped off for booze and takeout, then headed home to stalk Jane Beckett online.

Bullseye Paintball was located in an old salvage yard off Aurora. The parking lot was half full of minivans and SUVs, out of which kids erupted, whooping with glee. Wincing at the noise, Liam made his way around parents and kids alike to the office and pulled open the heavy door.

"What are you doing here?"

Shit!

Wearing black cargo pants tucked into combat boots and a black hooded sweatshirt, Jane Beckett lounged against the registration desk. She flicked her bangs out of her eyes with a toss of her head and smirked at him. "You're not playing, are you?"

Her dismissive tone rubbed against his raw nerves. "Yes. Why wouldn't I?"

Sipping from a travel mug, Jane's gaze roamed up and down his body, taking in his khaki shorts, fresh white collared shirt, and sneakers. Her lips twitched. "Oh, no reason at all."

The door opened, and the small office filled with kids, backing Liam into a corner and saving him from having to reply. Jane shifted her attention to the kids and raised her arms in the air.

"Who's ready to have fun?" she yelled.

"Yay!" the kids replied at the top of their lungs.

"Who's ready to get dirty?"

They yelled louder.

"Who's ready to plant a garden?"

The kids looked confused.

"I'm just messing with you!" Jane grinned and opened the door to the playing field. "Head out and find Jason. He's going to fit you with safety equipment and guns."

The kids stampeded out, leaving two dads dressed in camo-chic, looking both excited and nervous. One of whom wore an air cast on one leg. "Oh dear," Jane said, "you're not going to be able to play with that."

The man in the cast replied, "Stan and I discussed strategy. I figured I'd prop myself up in a corner and shoot from behind cover."

"Yeah," Stan said. "You and I can run and juke, draw their fire, and Carl can pick them off. He can as well." He looked toward Liam. "Sorry, I didn't catch your name. Whose dad are you?"

Three pairs of inquisitive eyes turned toward him. "Nobody's. I'm not part of the party." He felt like a fool. How the hell to get out of this while saving face?

"Liam's never played before. He's here to scout the place for a team-building event for his company."

Carl and Stan nodded at Jane's remarks. Liam shot her a quick smile of thanks.

Then she cocked one hip, crossed her arms, and threw him under the bus. "We've got tactical gear you can borrow for firsthand experience, Mr. Cross. How about it?"

"Yeah," Carl said. "You'll be able to see how much fun it is. And help us out. There's twelve of them, and with my bum leg, they'll make mincemeat out of us."

Stan nudged Carl's shoulder. "Don't scare him." He turned to Liam. "It won't be that bad. The girls are experienced. We'll tell Jessica, that's our daughter, to tell them to go easy on you."

Out of the corner of his eye, Liam caught the grin Jane was attempting to hide behind her hand. Great. She was laughing at him. There was no way he could get out of this and still keep his man card. "I'm in." He extended his hand to Carl but glared at Jane.

Thirty minutes later, he found himself cowering behind a stack of wooden pallets with a barrage of paintballs coming at him. *What the holy hell?!* This was *not* fun. This was terrifying. He looked back and spotted Carl wedged between empty oil drums, cackling maniacally as paintballs pinged off the metal. What was *wrong* with these people?

Carl waved at him, yelling, "Three bogies on your left!"

Liam poked his semiautomatic paint gun around the pallets and fired off a half dozen rounds. A thwack followed by "Darn!" resulted. He resisted the temptation to look, instead shouting to Carl, "How'd I do?"

"One down. Good job."

Yes! A satisfied grin settled on his face. He was beginning to understand the appeal. "Shit!" He looked down to see a bright pink paintball had missed his calf by a hair's breadth and thwacked against the pallet. He'd exchanged his shorts and shirt for a thick coverall. It provided some protection, but that would have hurt like a mother. Sweating under the hot sun, the girls' squeals, and the popping of the paintball guns combined with the smell of the old tires drove Liam's headache to another level of pain. He did his best to ignore it, reasoning the game couldn't last too much longer.

The girls were good. They'd divided up into four groups of three, each one focused on taking out one of the adults. They'd gotten Stan almost immediately. Three determined dynamos penned him behind a junked car, then blasted him with pellets. Liam didn't know where Jane was, but he could hear jubilant whoops from her every now and then. Unlike Carl, Liam didn't have an excuse for hunkering down and staying in one place, but he wasn't going to move from behind the pallets until he absolutely had to. That time looked to be now.

"Carl, can you see them?"

"I think there are six left. Watch that pile of tires to your —crap!" Carl rose from his hidey hole, paint splattered on the top of his helmet. "Sorry, dude. I'm out."

Liam visualized the layout of the field. On the other side of his pallet stack was open ground beyond which was a three-story structure with window openings all around. On his left were three upended large wooden spools. He'd been fired at from the stack of tires to his right. Was that a blonde ponytail? He fired off a burst. A blast of paintballs pinged off the pallets above his head. He was trapped. A blur of motion to his left had him bringing his gun around. Finger on the trigger, he pointed the barrel off to the side at the last moment. Jane popped up from a somersault. "Easy, Rambo." She raised her pistol—because, *of course* Jane would have her own personal paintball gun—and fired over his shoulder.

A disgruntled voice cried out, "Crap on a stick!"

Jane leaned back against the pallets and grinned. "Two down. That leaves four. They've taken cover in the tower. You head to the spools. I'm going to the tires. I'll cover you."

Exposing himself to four amped-up girls armed with weapons sounded like a bad idea. "How about if I stay here and cover you?"

"Seriously? You can't take them out from here." She nudged him with an elbow. "Come on, Cross. Grow a pair. It's their party. Let's show them a good time." She got up on her knees, turning to face the pallet.

Grumbling, Liam crouched, ready to make a run.

"Go! Go! Go!" she yelled.

Under a volley of heavy fire, Liam dashed across the dirt, diving behind the giant spools as paintballs exploded against the wood. A banshee scream drew his attention. He peered around one spool to see Jane, wearing a shit-eating grin, race behind the stack of tires, drawing fire away from him.

Catching his eye, Jane held up three fingers, counted down, pointed forward, and took off like a juggernaut. Not thinking, Liam followed. Screaming at the top of his lungs, his finger pulled the trigger of the semiautomatic, aiming at the tall paint-spattered structure. He pulled again. Nothing happened. He checked the hopper. Pink paint blossomed on his chest at the same time he realized he was out of ammo. He waved, acknowledging the hit but remained rooted to the spot, eyes frozen on Jane.

Crouched low, she approached the tower at lightning

speed. Had she used him to draw fire? Regardless, she was at the tower, back to the wall, gun raised, peeking into the first-floor window. Satisfied the room was empty, she vaulted through the window, landing silent as a cat. Popping up, she grinned at Liam before disappearing from view.

Walking backward, Liam joined Carl and Stan on the raised observation platform. Both men high-fived him, then turned their attention back to the action. The rules of the game did not allow inactive players to call out directions, which was killing the girls beside them, who jumped up and down, squealing with anticipation. They could hear the other girls in the tower calling to each other, a round of fire, then two paint-spattered mini warriors emerged to join them. From the top window, the heads of the two remaining girls showed, guns at the ready, searching the playing field. Liam fully expected Jane to give up, allowing the birthday girl to claim victory. Jane didn't. She crept around from behind the tower, stood silently against the wall, and waited. The girls inside chattered nervously, while the girls on the observation platform covered their mouths to keep from shouting out. Jane waited some more. Then she moved, expertly nailing the girls in the middle of their chests. A whoop went up from the platform. Liam let out a breath he didn't know he was holding. The girls came down from the tower and shook hands with Jane. The three walked back together, speaking animatedly, thoroughly stoked from the experience.

"Your daughter's not upset," Liam said to Stan.

"Are you kidding? She went toe-to-toe with Jane Beckett. That's a badge of honor she'll crow about for weeks."

"But she didn't win."

Stan didn't hear him. He'd joined Carl and the swarm of girls excitedly discussing the game. Their daughter, Jessica, wore the biggest grin, gazing up at Jane like she was a warrior princess. Liam didn't understand it; as the event planner, he'd expected Jane to bend over backward for the client. Yet no one at the party looked upset.

Liam turned away from the group to find his clothes and change. A tug on his sleeve drew his attention.

"Mr. Cross, thank you for joining us. You were a worthy opponent." A smiling Jessica looked up at him, Carl at her back.

Catching Carl's smile, Liam snorted. "More like scared poop-less. You and your friends terrified me."

Jessica grinned. "Dad says there's plenty of food. Do you want to stay for the party?"

What he wanted was a hot shower and a cold drink in the quiet of his apartment. However, what he said was, "Sure. Thanks for letting me join you."

Jessica skipped off to join her friends. Looking around at the paint-spattered salvage yard, Liam couldn't imagine it as a venue for a girl's birthday party. He asked Carl, "Where will the food be set up?"

"There's a conference room off the office. You can see it right there." Carl pointed to three large windows next to the entrance to the field. "It's a pretty good setup. I'll show you after we change."

"You've been here before?"

"Just to see the place and arrange payment," Stan answered. Moving slowly to accommodate Carl's cast, the three men headed to the changing room. Inside, Liam got out of the hot, sweaty coverall and tossed it into the laundry bin. There wasn't a shower, but fresh towels and a bottle of body wash stood by the sink. Gratefully, he washed up and put on his shorts and shirt. He contemplated his shoes, now dusty and dotted with pink paint. They wouldn't be seen in public again. Too much explaining to do.

"Did you enjoy yourself? Will your company hold their event here?" Stan was folding up his and Carl's gear and tucking it into a duffel. He wore a white T-shirt with "Jessica's Dad" on the back, and Carl's matching shirt said, "Jessica's Pop."

"I didn't know Grand Gestures did team building. We had our wedding out at their farm. Actually, their parents' farm. The company was named Beckett Bridal Consultants. That was such a beautiful day." Carl smiled up at Stan. "BBC took care of everything—the officiant, the venue, the food, the photographer, our tuxes. I wore white, which was a big mistake."

"He attracts stains."

Carl tsked and resumed his story. "It's a shame BBC went under. I thought they did a great job."

"They went under?" Liam's ears perked up. He hadn't heard about this.

"Barbara and Steve retired. They're Jane's parents," Stan explained. "They'd been doing weddings for years and were done. They didn't go under."

Carl sat on a bench, stretching out the leg in the air cast. He shook his head. "I heard there was a lawsuit."

"Now you're just spreading rumors. Anyway, that was a long time ago." Stan turned to Liam. "Whatever you hire GG for, you'll be happy. Jane's a professional."

Squealing laughter came from the changing room next door.

"Sounds like the girls are ready. Let's go party." Carl grinned at his husband and followed him out the door.

A lawsuit involving the Beckett family. Liam filed that nugget of information away, determined to do more digging.

"*A* food truck?"
The man could not sound more disdainful. Jane rolled her eyes and stood back from the doorway to allow the girls to enter, each carrying a plate of food. It was Jorge's

truck, with a limited menu designed specifically for the party. Jessica wanted paintball. Carl and Stan wanted Jessica to be happy. Jane made it happen. The group of girls was enjoying themselves immensely. So why did she care what Liam Cross thought?

Seeing him enter Bullseye's office had knocked her over. Clearly fighting a hangover, he still looked like a GQ model. She had no idea why he was there, but she hadn't wanted him to leave. She wanted to know what he was like without his pressed shirt and polished loafers and if it was possible for him to enjoy himself outside the boardroom. So she'd opened her big mouth and thrown down the gauntlet. Had she shown off? Absolutely. She'd thought he might leave with his tail between his legs; instead, he was sticking around for the party. And she wasn't sure how she felt about that. He was not the client today. The plans for the Duncans' anniversary were too far along to be derailed, so she turned her back on him and joined the girls.

An hour later, she was laughing so hard she nearly peed herself. Not taking no for an answer, Jessica had drawn Liam into the fray. They taught the men the latest dance moves and recorded them on TikTok. Carl's cast excused his clumsiness. Stan was plain awkward, and Liam? Liam had no skills but was gamely following directions, looking like a man in serious need of a drink. He looked up and, catching her eye, mouthed, "Help me" over the heads of the whirling pre-teens. She laughed harder.

She passed a red Solo cup to him as he sank down on a chair beside her. "Here. You look like you need it."

He sniffed suspiciously. "What is it?"

"A cure for what ails you." She raised her own cup and drank deeply.

His eyebrows went up after taking a cautious sip. "Ginger ale?" He drank more deeply. "Thanks."

Jane nodded in acceptance, her fingers flying over her

cell phone. She snorted, then held the phone up for Liam to see. It was a video of him running toward the tower before being shot multiple times. Then the view shifted to the girls in the stands screaming and high-fiving. "Do you mind if I post it?"

"I suppose. But what's the point? Who's going to see it?"

"What are you, a dinosaur?" Jane took back the phone and stared at him incredulously. "Videos from events like this get shared over and over, putting Grand Gestures' name in front of thousands of people."

It was Liam's turn to stare. "But how many of those turn into clients?"

"Let me show you." Standing, Jane grabbed Liam by the arm and hauled him over to where Jessica and two of her friends sat eating birthday cake. "Do you mind if we join you?" Jessica shook her head and motioned for them to sit. Liam took the chair between Jane and a shy-looking girl with big eyes. Proving he wasn't a complete idiot, Liam shifted his chair away from the girl and angled his big body toward Jane. His cedar-scented cologne made her think of the outdoors—cool nights and moonlight and snuggling by a campfire with a dark-eyed man. Shaking off the image, Jane focused on the conversation and addressed Jessica. "What made you decide to contact me for your party?"

Jessica's eyes narrowed. "There were these boys at school talking about paintball. I said it sounded like fun. They said it wasn't for girls. Boys are stupid." Her friends nodded in agreement. "No offense, Mr. Cross."

"None taken," Liam muttered, biting his lip as if holding back a smile.

"I told Pop and Dad I wanted to play paintball. They weren't real happy about it. I'm an only child, and they can be a little too cautious." She looked over at her friends, who both nodded again. "So I did some research."

"She created a PowerPoint," Jane whispered to Liam.

"I explained why I should be able to play paintball. Showed the safety features and detailed the costs."

"She sent the PowerPoint to our parents," one friend said.

"It included video links," the other added.

"But how did you choose Grand Gestures to organize the party?"

Jessica wiggled in her seat and pointed at Jane. "I was specifically looking up girls who play paintball. There's a great video of Jane doing a 360 and taking out four guys. The hashtags led to here, Bullseye Paintball and Grand Gestures. Then I looked up Grand Gestures and showed my dads. They recognized Jane, and that was it."

"You looked up the Grand Gestures website?"

"No. Their Instagram profile. Their website is nice, but it's static. No offense, Jane."

"None taken." Jane grinned.

Liam held up a hand. "What do you mean by static?"

"It doesn't change very much." Jessica cocked her head to the side. "Are you on Instagram?"

He shifted in his seat. "I have an account. But I don't have time to post pictures."

"But you understand how it works, right?"

"Yes. People put up selfies and pictures of their vacations. It's for sharing photos."

Jessica shook her head, her friends following suit. "Oh, Mr. Cross. It's so much more."

Sitting back, Jane crossed her arms and listened while a CFO learned about social media marketing from a trio of twelve-year-olds. When they were finished, Jane thanked the girls and led Liam outside. He looked shell-shocked.

He waved at her cell phone. "So, you posting that video…."

"Um-hmm. With the right hashtags, I've promoted the venue, the food truck, and GG." Jane leaned back against the wall. "Duncan Properties doesn't need social media. But small companies like mine, we need to be in front of our audience constantly. But it works both ways. A few negative posts can put a company out of business."

"It's target marketing," Liam said with a nod. "Do you rely solely on social media to find customers?"

"No, but these days, that's where people are hanging out. It's well worth the time and effort."

Liam raised his cup and tapped it against hers. "ROI. Return on investment. Now you're speaking my language."

Grinning, she bumped his shoulder, liking the moment of quiet camaraderie. "How's the head?"

"Much better, thanks. How did you know I had a headache?"

"You flinched every time someone spoke to you."

He rolled his eyes. "I'm not around children very often. I'd forgotten how loud they could be."

"They are that." A burst of laughter drew her attention. "I need to get back inside. Can I get you anything?"

"No. I'm good, thanks. I'm going to hang out here for a bit."

She glanced into the party room and then looked back at Liam. "Are you taking off soon?"

"No. I'll wait to say my goodbyes to Jessica and the guys."

Nodding, she turned to go back inside.

A squeal drew his attention, and he peeked into the party room. Jessica ripped the paper off a gift and held it up triumphantly. Through the bobbing heads, Liam couldn't tell what it was, but it certainly excited the girls. He fished his keys out of his pocket and stood to find the men. This wasn't how he'd intended to spend his Saturday, and while his headache had subsided, his ass was dragging. That shower was going to feel so good.

A noise rose up behind him, and he twisted around to see the girls gathered around Jane, clapping and chanting her name. "Jane! Jane! Jane!"

She patted the air and spoke loudly, "Fine! I'll do it."

A cheer went up, and all the girls but Jessica settled into chairs. Jessica fiddled with the controls on a square device sitting on a table, then handed a wireless microphone to Jane with a thumbs-up. Karaoke. Liam shuddered. Was there anything worse? He watched Jane grin at the girls and run a hand up and down her pant leg. She looked...nervous. Liam leaned against the doorframe. His movement must have caught her eye, because Jane looked over and scowled, making a shooing gesture at him. He shook his head and grinned back at her. This was going to be good.

The opening strains of "I Will Survive" filled the room. Clutching the microphone and staring at the screen before her, Jane warbled along in a truly awful voice. The girls bounced in their seats, a dozen cell phone cameras pointed at the woman in front of them. Jane was white-faced, her hands shaking. Liam's smile faded. Petrified didn't begin to describe her. He glanced around. Carl and Stan were over by the food truck, talking with Jorge. He looked back at Jane. Wasn't the party supposed to be winding down? Was karaoke part of the activities? He didn't think so. Jane's jaw was set, and she recited the words rather than sang them. She smiled weakly at the girls in front of her holding cameras up—cameras! Liam groaned. How soon before this would be bouncing around social media? Shoving his keys into his pocket, he strode up to the makeshift stage, positioned himself behind and beside Jane, and began to move.

❋

*I*n third grade, Jane auditioned for a role in the school's Christmas concert with her best friend, Carolyn. The two girls rehearsed their piece together and were prepared and confident. They learned at the audition they would be singing alone and unaccompanied. Carolyn went first, singing in a clear and angelic voice. Jane stepped up to the microphone…and did not. When she finished, the music teacher suggested that Jane take a non-singing role as a dancing tin soldier.

The last time Jane did karaoke, they'd turned off the microphone. The only place she sang these days was in the car, with the music cranked very loud. Squinting against the lights of the cameras, Jane found Jessica and nodded. She started to sing. Badly. She would get through this but would pad the bill to compensate for the mortification.

From the corner of her eye, Jane tracked Liam's movements. She turned away from the girls and held the microphone away. "What are you doing?" she hissed.

"I'm your backup dancer." He twirled awkwardly and clomped a few steps to the left and back again, arms held out while shaking his hips. A cheer went up behind her. Glancing over her shoulder, she saw the cameras were now pointed at Liam. He stomped in time to the music, and the girls clapped along with him. "Just go with it." He jerked his chin at the microphone and rolled his eyes toward the cameras. "Trust me."

Jane blinked. Why? What was in it for him? As far as she could tell, he would gain nothing from humiliating himself in front of a bunch of pre-teens. There was no time to think about this now. Gritting her teeth, she said, "Fine," and turned back to the girls. She raised her arms. "Who's gonna sing it with me?" Three girls dropped their cameras and came forward. Jane handed them the microphone, stepped back beside Liam, and began to move in time to the music. They found an awkward rhythm, bumping into each other now and then, laughing when Liam's elbow connected with her shoulder. She hip-checked him in retaliation, and he stumbled before catching himself and grinned back at her.

Mercifully, the song ended. While others clamored for their turn with the microphone, Jane slipped away from the makeshift stage, closely followed by Liam. She slumped against the wall outside the party room, fanning her face.

"Well?"

Jane looked up at the man beside her. "Well, what?"

"Aren't you going to thank me for saving your ass?"

"Is that what that was? I thought that was you doing Zumba." She blew out her bangs. "Seriously, though, that was…."

"Painful? Excruciating? A fate worse than death?"

"It wasn't the worst experience I ever had."

Liam shook his head. "I'm talking about having to listen to you. I think I'm scarred for life."

"Hey!" Jane swatted his arm. "It wasn't *that* bad."

He shuddered, then twisted to prop one shoulder against the wall. "Seriously, you were clearly uncomfortable, and singing is not your forte, so why would you do that? Especially in front of cameras."

Jane folded her arms across her chest and gripped her elbows. Yeah, that could have gone all kinds of sideways. Videos of her tone-deaf self being played over and over, turned into a meme. "I didn't want my mom to take the training wheels off my bike because I was afraid to fall. But she did anyway. It took me a bit, but I got comfortable and stopped being afraid of falling."

She raised her hand as Liam opened his mouth. "Yeah, I know. I can't carry a tune in a bucket, and no matter how much I practice, singing will never be my thing. But if I don't get out in front of people, do things I'm not good at, what message am I sending? What am I telling these girls?" She studied his thoughtful expression. "Dancing is clearly not your forte. Why did you step up?"

Liam frowned and cleared his throat. "Well…same thing. I was modeling how to support someone who's struggling." He nodded emphatically.

"All righty, then." Jane bumped against his arm as she headed back into the party room.

The party wound down, and Jane was waving off Jorge's truck when a throat cleared behind her. She turned to see a tired-looking Liam run a hand over his jaw. Other than his paint-spattered shoes, he looked perfect. The greenish tinge from his hangover had disappeared. The tousled hair and stubbled chin looked good on him. Glancing down was a mistake. Her eyes got stuck on his hard chest and firm belly beneath his tight polo shirt. Her earlier impression still held true; he was model perfect. For the first time all day, she wondered what *she* looked like to *him*. And for the first time in forever, she actually cared.

He stopped next to her. "I don't know what I was expecting, but clearly, you delivered exactly what the client wanted."

She wasn't going to let him off that easy. "And what did you expect? Pretty princess dresses and pedicures?"

"Maybe? I assumed that if an event planner was hired for a kid's birthday party, it would be more elaborate. But this was really relaxed and—"

"Tailored to the client. We rarely do kid parties. But Stan and Carl are friends, the venue was a no-brainer, and the food truck—"

"Was perfect. I shouldn't have disparaged it."

"It was Beth's idea."

"It was a great one." The corners of Liam's mouth tipped up slightly.

Jane nodded, toeing the graveled parking lot and looking up at him from under her bangs, feeling like a teenager at the end of a date. She didn't know what to say, didn't want to leave, and didn't know why. *This* Liam Cross surprised her. While playing paintball, he'd gone along with every instruction, not drawing attention to himself, as if he were an added feature for Jessica's party, willing to be hit by paintballs and made fun of in TikToks. And then there was the karaoke save. Weekend Liam was a hell of a lot nicer than Corporate Liam, and she wouldn't mind seeing more of him.

Ding!

An incoming text broke the moment. Scanning the message, Jane scrunched her nose and sighed.

"Everything okay?"

"Yeah. Just Beth reminding me we're going to an art opening this evening. Somewhere over on Mercer Island."

Chuck had invited them yesterday. GG had a rare Saturday night off, and Jane was looking forward to doing nothing. But the light in Beth's eyes made her agree. When Kevin said he'd be there and they could stand in the corner and make catty remarks about people, she definitely agreed. Kevin was swiftly becoming one of her favorite people.

His posture went rigid as an impassive expression overtook Liam's face. "Really. Well then, I won't detain you. Take care."

Turning his back to her, he strode to his car, folded in, and took off.

Jane gaped at his taillights. What the hell happened there?

CHAPTER 8

*J*ane scanned the crowd, looking for Liam, telling herself she wasn't looking for Liam. There was no reason to think he'd be there. But the invitation had come from Chuck, and she associated Liam with Chuck, so…

"Quit fidgeting." Beth frowned at her. "And stop pulling on your shirt. You'll ruin the collar."

"It's too damn low." Jane had workout clothes and work clothes, nothing for going out, so Beth dressed her in one of her many soft sweaters, this one a V-neck in ivory. Balking at wearing a skirt, Jane instead wore close-fitting black slacks and red Rothy's. Beth wore a dress that set off her figure without clinging to it in a shade of peach that made her glow. Or perhaps it was anticipation. Beth hadn't smiled this much in ages, so Jane resolved not to ruin Beth's evening. The small gallery was packed with well-heeled patrons sipping champagne and gesturing at the artwork, marble statues of nude male and female figures. The sculptor was a family member of Chuck's. When he'd invited them, he'd downplayed it. Jane had half-expected an exhibit of barely decipherable lumps of clay, so she was impressed by the skill and detail of the pieces. Also, the price tags. She took two steps back. She could not afford to knock one over.

"You look fabulous."

Both sisters smiled as Kevin approached, arms wide to embrace them. Standing back, he appraised Beth, declaring, "That color was made for you. I insist you wear nothing else."

"That would mean buying new uniforms, and that's not in the budget."

Kevin rolled his eyes at Jane's comment, assessing her as well. "Would it kill you to wear a dress? And maybe heels?"

Jane shoved her hands into the pockets of her trousers and rolled up on her toes. "Our parents made us wear dresses to school. I haven't worn one since I graduated from high school, and I'm not about to anytime soon." She laughed at Kevin's exasperated sigh.

Beside her, Beth made a noise, and Jane turned to see what had caught her attention. Heading toward them from the gallery's entrance was Chuck, with a goofy grin directed at Beth, who blushed prettily. Announcing the need for a drink, Kevin pulled Jane with him and headed for the bar at the back of the gallery, where they stood and observed Chuck and Beth.

"This is good for her. Chuck is so sweet. Perfect to ease her back into dating." At Kevin's raised eyebrow, she continued, "Her ex-husband screwed around on her. She hasn't dated anyone since the divorce. This will help boost her confidence."

"You don't think it's true love? They both look smitten."

Jane tilted her head to the side and considered his statement. Jane knew Chuck and her sister spent a lot of time texting and seemed very comfortable together. "I suppose it could happen. Is Chuck a Don Juan? Should I worry he's going to break her heart?"

"No. He falls fast, and he falls often. If anything, he's the one whose heart could be broken."

The couple under observation stood in a corner, ignoring everyone and everything. Smiles illuminated both their faces. "Beth would never hurt anyone. Besides, it's early days, and this is the most they've ever been alone together."

"Their alone time is about to end."

Jane followed the direction of Kevin's raised glass. Liam had entered the gallery and was headed toward the couple. Her heart skipped a beat, and she bit the inside of her cheek to keep from smiling. Had he spent the past two hours looking at the karaoke video? Jessica and her friends had obviously put their heads together, because instead of Jane's mortifying singing, the video showed her and Liam dancing behind the three girls singing.

Steps away from Beth and Chuck, a leggy blonde intercepted Liam. Curling a hand familiarly around his arm, she leaned into him. Something like disappointment coursed through Jane. Shaking it off, she nudged Kevin's shoulder. "Who is that with him? She looks familiar."

"That's Chuck's sister, Delia. I'm surprised she's here. An art opening on a Saturday night is rather tame for her. Her parents have financed a series of businesses for her—all of which failed—and now she's an influencer. That and she lives off her trust fund."

"Must be nice," Jane muttered.

Delia's golden curls contrasted beautifully with Liam's dark hair. In a short, tight dress barely covering her assets, Delia chattered animatedly to him. Jane studied them over the rim of her wineglass, unconsciously standing straighter and flipping her bangs out of her eyes. Her movement must have caught his attention because Liam looked up, meeting her gaze directly. He said something to Delia, who pouted but followed as he wove his way through the throng toward Kevin and Jane.

Up close and sober this time around, Delia Duncan was perfection. Perfectly coifed, perfectly made-up, perfectly dressed, perfectly everything Jane wasn't. Mentally, she kicked herself. Putting on lip gloss and brushing her hair was the total amount of effort she'd put into dressing. The woman gave her a once-over, obviously found her lacking, and squealed in delight at Kevin. "Darling!" She air-kissed him. "It's been ages! Where have you been?"

"Some of us do work for a living, Delia," Kevin spoke through a tight smile.

"I insist you free Kevin for the evening. There's a party in Bellevue I'm going to, and I want Kevin to go with me." Delia batted her eyes up at Liam and shimmied her shoulders.

Words popped out of Jane's mouth without her permission. "Does Kevin get a say in the matter?"

Delia blinked.

Kevin snorted.

Liam's lips twitched. Stuffing one hand in his pocket, he gestured between the two women. "Delia Duncan, this is Jane Beckett. Jane, meet Delia."

Jane waved and shot her a perky smile. "Hi!"

Her smooth forehead remaining oddly wrinkle-free, Delia squinted at Jane. "Have we met?"

Jane wanted to say, *If you call me throwing your drunken ass out of a party meeting, then yes.* What she did say was, "Not officially. We were at the same function."

"Right." Again, she gave Jane the once-over, as if wondering what function they would both be present at.

"Jane's company is planning your parents' anniversary party." Liam tilted his head in Jane's direction, then away toward Beth. "That's her sister talking with Chuck. She's an excellent chef. I'm looking forward to the menu she's planned."

"Thank you, Liam. Beth will be pleased to hear that." Jane wasn't sure she'd heard correctly. Liam Cross endorsing Grand Gestures?

Towering above Jane on her four-inch stilettos, Delia said

in a haughty voice, "Since you're catering this event, I'll have a Grey Goose martini. After that, Kevin, we'll go to that party."

Weirdly, Liam moved closer to Jane at the same time Kevin placed his hand on her arm. Being taken for the waitstaff didn't surprise her; having two men at her back did. Before she could speak, Liam got there first.

"Jane is an invited guest, and Kevin is not your plaything, and he's not on company time. You do not tell either of them what to do." His big hand landed on Jane's back, settling slightly above the swell of her ass. He may not have intended to startle her into silence, but that was the effect.

Being reprimanded appeared to be new to Delia. She gaped in surprise, eyes darting back and forth between the men. "But she looks like a server."

"Liam, I didn't know you'd be here." Chuck's open expression and pleased smile brought down the tension. He drew Beth forward, saying, "Beth, this is my sister, Delia."

The two women smiled politely at each other. Beth's eyes went round as she caught Jane's, and they conversed silently, Beth wanting to know what was going on and Jane indicating she'd tell her later. Meanwhile, Chuck nattered to the others, his presence dispelling the previous awkward moment.

Kevin removed his hand and stepped to the side. "How did the paintball party go today? Need any stitches?"

Liam's hand pressed into Jane, and she leaned back into it. "All good. There was one trigger-happy newbie, but I think he enjoyed himself." Liam's hand drifted over to squeeze her waist as if thanking her for keeping him out of it. "In fact, I think your company would enjoy it as a team-building exercise." The comment earned her another squeeze. A thrill shot through her. Jane was far from inexperienced, but flirting wasn't one of her strong suits. Was this even flirting? She'd think about that later. Right now, the unexpected presence of

Liam's hand was making her giddy. "What do you think, Liam?" Twisting to look up at him, she lost her train of thought in his amused gaze and the twitch of his lips.

"I'll think about it."

His deep voice sent shivers through her, and she looked away, burying her nose in her wineglass. Looking up, she saw Delia's calculating gaze taking in the closeness of Chuck and Beth and her and Liam.

Delia pursed her lips and shook back her hair. "Well. This was fun. Kevin, would you like to go to a party with me?"

Kevin lifted his glass in salute. "Thank you for the invitation, Delia. That sounds lovely. Let me finish my drink, and we'll be on our way."

"Oh! Great." Delia bit her lip and nodded. "I have to say hello to a couple people, and I'll meet you by the door." She waved at the others and wandered off.

"You don't have to do that." Liam inclined his head at Delia while speaking to Kevin.

He shrugged. "She can be fun to be with. And *I* might meet someone." He finished his drink, set the empty glass on the bar, and waved as he walked off. "See you later, kids. Oh, and Jane, call me when you decide to re-think your fashion choices."

"I guess I'm going shopping." Jane glared at Kevin's retreating back.

Chuck said something about looking at the artwork and moved off with his hand on Beth's elbow, leaving Liam and Jane alone together. His hand moved from her back as he shifted to stand in front of her. "What was Kevin talking about?"

She waved a hand up and down in front of her. "He was giving me crap about my clothes. Then Delia confirmed that, so…"

Liam's gaze traveled over her from top to toe and back up, skittering over her breasts before returning to her face.

"Don't listen to them. You look great." His dark eyes met hers, his full lips turned up slightly.

Warmth suffused her, starting at her core and moving up until she felt her face flame. She brought up her wineglass only to find it empty. Feeling unsettled was not something she was used to. But Liam Cross did that to her.

Looking for safer ground, she asked, "Have you watched the video yet?"

He frowned, looking confused.

"Your epic dance moves." She gave her glass to a passing server and pulled her phone from her back pocket. Opening the app, she held the phone up for Liam. He stepped closer and bent down to see the screen. She twisted and grinned up at him when he groaned. "You know, if that whole CFO thing doesn't work out, you could try being a backup dancer. Look at those moves." She replayed the video, this time watching real Liam shake his head instead of watching video Liam stomp and shimmy. "You didn't put your back out, did you?"

Liam nudged her shoulder with his own. "For God's sake, put that away."

She chuckled, tempted to tease him more, but stuffed her phone in her pocket and turned to face him. He was watching her with amusement and something else. Interest perhaps? She wanted to hide behind her hair, pull her shirt up to reveal less skin, go help the bartender. Anything to avoid that penetrating gaze.

"Tell me about the tattoo." His gaze focused below her ear.

"What?"

He reached out with one finger and, not touching her, traced the outline of the sunburst on her neck, causing the flames in her face, neck, and chest to burn higher. He smirked at her reaction.

She should pull back. She should move away. She

should…She wanted to get closer. She wanted to…She shook her head, dislodging the thoughts of his hands on her body.

She'd had the ink so long she needed to think about the answer. "It's a reminder to choose light."

His head tilted, he studied her tattoo, then her face, as if memorizing each feature. "Instead of darkness. Yeah. It's a choice." He looked directly into her eyes.

She looked down, sure her pounding heart was visible through her sweater. Her glance took in his long legs encased in jeans, then traveled up. He'd paired a black button-down shirt with a black wool blazer that no doubt cost more than Jane's entire outfit. He looked solid and confident and hot, and why was he talking to her? She searched for something to say, to steer the conversation to safety. "Do you think that piece is to scale?" She indicated a marble foot, beautifully detailed to the point of appearing life-like. Unfortunately, Liam had looked past the foot to a marble sculpture of a man's trunk, a full-frontal nude with a half-erect penis. His smirk at her round-eyed realization turned into a smile, and then his head went back, his eyes closed, and he released a full belly laugh.

Jane wanted to die. She wanted the floor to open up and swallow her. She turned away, hoping to escape without him noticing, but his long arm reached out, took her hand, and pulled her back. Squinting up through her bangs, she mumbled, "I need another drink."

Grinning broadly, he tilted his head toward the door. "Would you like to get out of here?"

Flustered, she had no clue how to answer. She'd hoped to see him tonight, to annoy him and joust with words. But to be alone with him? To have him ask her out? Because that's what he was doing, right?

"Are you guys hungry? I can get us a table at Johnny's."

Chuck's interruption came at the perfect time, although it

didn't appear as if Liam was in complete agreement. His forehead creased briefly, but he nodded. "I could eat. Jane?"

Jane looked to where Chuck had his hand laced with Beth's. Her sister's smile and one-shouldered shrug were the answer she needed. "Umm, yeah. We Ubered over. Can we catch a ride with you?" She was addressing Chuck, but Liam answered.

"I've got my car. Why don't you ride with me? Beth and Chuck can go together."

Blushing furiously, Jane shook back her bangs and glanced at the expectant faces. "Sure. That works."

"Good." Liam's hand went to the small of her back, and he ushered her out of the gallery.

*L*iam smirked. Out of the corner of his eye, he could see Jane fidgeting beside him in the passenger seat of his Volvo S60, clearly out of her comfort zone, unlike earlier today, when she was relaxed, confident, and in control. Out of her paintball gear and in the soft sweater, she was a different Jane. Less intimidating but no less interesting. Seeing her in action with her quick wit, quick mind, and quicksilver smile, he'd decided he wanted to know more about her. Not Jane, whose sister had charmed his best friend, but Jane, the woman who teased and taunted him and smelled so good. No cloying perfume, no fruity shampoo, just Jane. Standing near her at the gallery, touching her, was a mistake. It was all he could do not to pull her against him and bury his face in her hair. Now she was in his car. Johnny's was on Lake Union, about twenty minutes away. Twenty minutes with Jane at his side, quietly freaking out—if the foot tapping was an indication. He snagged one of her hands and held it loosely on the middle console between them.

"If I can survive playing paintball with a bunch of tweens, you can survive a car ride with me."

She huffed out a laugh.

Following a much-needed shower after getting home from paintball, he'd wandered his apartment with nothing to do. The place was immaculate, thanks to a cleaning service and his tendency toward neatness. The work he'd brought home could wait. The book he was reading didn't interest him. A certain brunette did. A certain brunette who would willingly expose herself to ridicule.

Why would she do that? The client was certainly pleased; however, Jane said she'd done it to model fearlessness—not her words, but that's what it was. Being unafraid to do something she wasn't good at—in public. Would he have done the same? Nope. So why did he leap to assist her? Chuck must have rubbed off on him. Chuck, not Liam, rescued damsels in distress.

Jane hadn't needed rescuing. In fact, Liam stepping forward turned that excruciating performance from an embarrassment to a publicity coup for Grand Gestures. Liam snorted. There was no way she had set that up. But had she set up that meeting between Chuck and Beth? Beth's shy, winsome personality had certainly attracted the attention of his best friend, and they'd been spending a lot of time together.

Liam had an invitation to the art opening himself and decided it was a great opportunity to keep his eye on the pretty blonde. And now he had her striking sister beside him.

"You love it, don't you?"

"What?" she stammered, turning to him with wide eyes.

"The energy of putting on an event."

She blinked at him before smoothing her hands down her thighs. Her answer was slow but considered. "It can be a rush. We're making people happy. Well, with the exception of the funeral reception we did. Not doing that again. So yeah, I do enjoy the energy."

"Aside from playing paintball, what's your favorite part of an event?"

"This probably sounds weird, but it's the before part. Sometimes, clients are very clear about what they want, and that's easy and kind of boring. But when they are less particular and trust us, it's a lot of fun. We did a retirement party for a man. His wife gave us a small budget, a small guest list, and told us her husband liked chess and collected watches. That was it. Watching Beth work with that little bit of personal information was wonderful. Seeing her energy and enthusiasm, and making ideas come to life, that's the best part."

Liam looked over to see her gazing out at the water of Lake Washington, smiling at a memory. "Your sister is very talented."

"She is that."

"Did you two take over the family business?" As much as it was possible to do so while driving, Liam studied her response. Would she mention the lawsuit?

Tilting her head to one side, she flattened her lips. "Not exactly."

He remained silent, disappointment filling him at her lack of an answer.

"Beckett Bridal Consultants was the name of the family business. Mom and Dad started off doing wedding photography, back before hiring a wedding planner was a thing. But the business changed, and they had too as well. People were always asking Mom her opinion about flowers and food and stuff, so becoming a wedding planner was a natural for her." Jane laughed. "Beth and I spent most evenings and Saturdays decorating venues and making keepsakes. After college, I started working in accounting here in Seattle. Beth went to culinary school and worked with my parents. By then, they had fixed up my grandparents' farm out in Snohomish and turned it into a venue. They did quite well."

"Carl said they had their wedding there and BBC did a great job. He said your parents retired?"

"Yes and no." She grimaced and stared out the window for a few moments.

Liam wondered if she would change the subject. Instead, she shifted in her seat to face him completely. "The business grew, and Dad hired a photographer while he handled other stuff. Tony was good-looking and smooth and swept Beth off her feet. They married, and things were good for a while. They were working on this elaborate wedding, and the mother of the bride was a major pain. Didn't like anything Beth suggested for the food. Beth was a wreck. Then she caught Tony boffing a bridesmaid. The girl was seventeen, the younger sister of the bride. The shit hit the fan. The father of the bride threatened to cut his dick off. Tony was yelling that the girl said she was nineteen. The mother of the bride threatened to sue. Beth fell apart. By the time I got there, she was curled up in a ball and wouldn't speak to anyone. I took her back with me."

She lapsed into silence while Liam pulled into a parking space in front of the restaurant. Hearing the pain in Jane's voice, he thought about how much pain Beth had been in. How hard it must have been on the whole family. With his father long since passed away and his mother God knows where—and good riddance to her—Liam did not have any close family other than the Duncans, yet he understood Jane's protective nature. He'd picked Chuck up after a broken heart multiple times and didn't ever want to do it again. Turning off the car, he asked, "Then what happened?"

Jane shrugged. "Beth stayed with me for three weeks while my parents and I mopped up the mess. The girl wasn't completely innocent, but she was still seventeen. In exchange for not pressing charges against BBC, my parents refunded the costs of the wedding. Beth and Tony got the fastest divorce in the history of the state of Washington. And BBC dissolved. Mom and Dad were worn out, and Beth never wanted to make another wedding cake again."

"What made you decide to open up Grand Gestures?" he asked, his curiosity piqued along with his awareness of the woman drawing him in.

Jane settled back, her head against the window, her smile impish. "I was bored. I had a good job at Amazon. Great pay, excellent benefits. But I was bored out of my skull. Chained to a desk every day, staring at a computer screen. Every day, I'd come home from work and talk to Beth. Let her know about the people I worked with. One woman, her name was Bryn, was planning a baby shower for a friend. Practically pulling her hair out over the details. I told Beth about it, just shooting the shit, you know. It was the first thing that she expressed interest in. So I asked Bryn if she wanted some help. She practically kissed me." Jane nudged Liam's arm. "Beth and I had so much fun doing it. It brought her back to life. She took a job at a bakery—one that didn't do wedding cakes. Gradually, she came out of her shell. But I could see she was restless. Amazon had a company newsletter, so I put in a little blurb about event planning. I was inundated. Requests for bat mitzvahs, retirement parties, Christmas parties. We got to the point where we had enough requests that we could quit the day jobs. That was scary as shit. Giving up the security."

Liam watched the shadows play across her face. Give up the security of corporate life? He didn't think he could do it. Jane really was a badass. Fearless, brave, brilliant. He was happy to sit in the car and listen to her. Her passion was infectious, and soon he was smiling along with her. She gestured while she spoke, and he took the opportunity to study her hands: blunt unpolished nails, no rings, a few tiny scars—evidence that she was a scrapper. And a part of him didn't want to see her with any more scars. She talked about her business plan, liability insurance, income projections. He was impressed and surprised, but then embarrassed for underestimating her. About to ask her about product sourcing, a tap on the window drew their attention.

Chuck waved and motioned to the restaurant. Liam acknowledged him and turned back to Jane. She was facing forward, looking out the window, wearing a small smile.

"What?"

She gestured. "Chuck and Beth. They're so cute. He's the first guy she's shown any interest in since her divorce. He's good for her." Chuck had taken Beth's hand and held on to it as he guided her around a mud puddle and into the restaurant.

"Yeah?"

"Chuck doesn't seem like the kind of guy who would break someone's heart, and I think he's gonna treat her well." Frowning, she tugged her shirt higher on her shoulder.

"What's wrong?"

She did it again, drawing his attention to the smooth skin of her throat and the little divot between her collar bones. "This is Beth's sweater, and it's a little big. She's more into clothes than I am. Other than stuff for work, working out, and playing paintball, I don't have much of a wardrobe. Don't really need one."

Liam trailed his gaze over her form, wondering if the sweater was as soft as it looked. She looked great. Hell, she'd looked great in combat boots. "You don't get dressed up for dates?"

She shook her head. "No time. This is my first free night in forever, and I'm spending it with—that didn't come out right."

"That depends. How was it supposed to come out?" He twisted in his seat, bringing one hand up to the back of Jane's seat. Her hair brushed against him, and he was tempted to run his hand through it.

She flipped a hand at him. "It's some weird limbo, a place in between." She blew out a breath at his raised eyebrow. "This isn't a work thing, yet you're kind of sort of the client."

"It's well after business hours, and the money for the party is not coming out of my pocket, nor Duncan Properties'. So yes to the first and no to the second."

She cast him a fleeting glance before looking down at her intertwined fingers. Was she…nervous? If so, why? She was brash, bold, and beautiful. Surely, men threw themselves at her wherever she went. Propped against the side window, Jane was mostly in the shadows. The headlights of a passing car shined on her, highlighting her wide mouth, one corner tipped up.

"So what is this then?"

He tugged on a strand of her hair, letting his hand graze the back of her neck. "You tell me. What do you want this to be?" She watched him move toward her, the tip of her tongue emerging, then disappearing. He wanted to chase it. Taste it. She moved closer.

Her phone pinged, and she blinked and sat back. "We should…we should go in."

Liam almost growled when Jane opened her car door and got out.

CHAPTER 9

Jane joined Beth and Chuck in the foyer of the restaurant, Liam's presence a warm feeling at her back. She peeked at him over her shoulder to find his gaze fixed on hers. She shivered and was saved from having to say anything when Beth drew her attention.

On a Saturday night, Johnny's was packed. An old bar on Lake Union, it had been taken over by two women who turned it into an oyster bar featuring the best fish in Seattle. Jane looked to the service area, where the waitstaff picked up plates from the busy cooks. Peering through the slot, she made out a friend's face and waved. The hostess seated them at a booth, and Jane leaned over to speak to Beth. "Miguel is working." Then to Liam and Chuck, she explained, "He was Beth's right-hand man until he got the job here."

"The man makes the best crab cakes. It took me forever to duplicate them after he left us." Beth grinned.

Seeing her sister's relaxed posture made Jane relax; Beth was regaining confidence every day. The success of the business was responsible, but Chuck's attention was helping as well. He was thoughtful, kind, and treated her with respect.

She could almost kiss the man. Although he had a menu of his own, he leaned close to Beth and looked at hers.

The booths were narrow, and Liam's presence surrounded her. When he moved, his shoulder brushed against hers. He shifted, and his thigh pressed against the length of hers. Neither moved. Heat rose up her neck to her cheeks, and she ducked her head to avoid scrutiny. Beside her, Liam acted like everything was perfectly normal. Like he hadn't tried to kiss her. Had he though? She replayed the scene in her mind. His unwavering attention, him touching the back of her neck, leaning toward her. If Beth hadn't texted her—but she had, so there was no point chasing that thought. All Jane knew was that the handsome man sitting next to her made her heart go pitter-pat, and she wanted to chase that feeling.

She glanced over to see him alternately looking at his menu and the couple across from them. His expression was neutral, so she had no clue what he was thinking. She thought back to their earlier conversation in the car. Had she said too much? Did he think less of Beth because of her breakdown? Jane hoped not. As if sensing her studying him, Liam looked over and smiled.

"Beth, when you go to a restaurant, how do you choose what to eat?"

Beth gazed off to the side as if considering Liam's question. "It depends. Sometimes, I want to eat a dish that I don't make myself and just enjoy it. Other times, I will order a dish and compare it with my own. If theirs is better than mine, I try to figure out what's different, an herb or seasoning or the preparation itself."

"And if yours is better?"

She shrugged. "I give myself a mental high-five."

"I bet your dishes are always better," Chuck said with an earnest expression.

"I wish."

A loud commotion drew their attention.

"Jane!" Three men strode toward their table, the flustered hostess following in their wake.

"Boomer! Hey." Jane was pulled out of her seat, engulfed in a hug by the first man, then passed over to the others, who hugged her as well. Laughing, she slapped the first one on the arm. "What are you guys doing here?"

"My divorce is final, and we're celebrating!" Over the protests of the hostess, he dragged an empty table next to the booth and motioned his friends to get the chairs.

The manager hurried over, wearing a pained smile, and patted the hostess on the arm. "It looks like a party. Will we be expecting any more guests?"

"Nope!" Boomer smiled happily at the manager, apparently oblivious to the havoc he had created. "But a round of shots would be good. Fireball!" He shot his arm in the air, and Jane grabbed it, pulling it down and clutching it with both hands. Boomer leaned in and kissed the side of her head with a loud smack.

Gusting out a sigh, Jane glared at the other two men before smiling at the manager. "Some water would be great, and menus, if you don't mind."

The manager walked off, and Jane did her best at playing hostess. Looking at Liam and Chuck, she indicated the three men with a jerk of her head. "I play paintball with these guys. Boomer, Steve, and Roland, this is Liam and Chuck. You know my sister Beth."

The men exchanged up nods while a drunken Boomer slumped against Jane. Absorbing his weight, she in turn leaned against a stiff and resistant Liam. Feeling his withdrawal, her heart plummeted. Out of the corner of her eye, she saw him frowning down at his phone. For a moment, she felt like an airplane passenger in the middle seat, trapped between two strangers oblivious to her discomfort. "Screw this," she muttered, pushing Boomer to an upright position.

"Hey!"

He blinked blearily at her, then smiled in recognition. "Hey, Jane. What are you doing here? My divorce is final. Wanna celebrate with me?"

"All right, big guy. It's time to go." She rose from the booth and snapped her fingers. "Roland. Steve. Let's get him out of here."

The two silent men pushed their chairs back, obediently hauled Boomer out of his chair, and dragged him to the door.

Jane smiled apologetically, her gaze bouncing between a wide-eyed Chuck, Beth's sympathetic frown, and the top of Liam's dark head. "I'm going to pour them into an Uber. I'll be right back."

Jane's belly did a little flip, and she sighed. Her friends safely packed off, she was ready to spend an evening with the hot man watching her from the top of the stairs. She wished she had time to add lip gloss, but, what the hell, he'd seen her in her paintball clothes. With a bounce in her step, she walked toward him. "Sorry. That took longer than I thought it would."

"I'd thought perhaps you'd gone off to celebrate with them."

She huffed out a laugh. "Oh, I think they can do that without me."

"Really? Because Boomer made it clear he was divorced and wanted your company." His voice dripping with disdain, his hard gaze moved over Jane, lingering on the gaping neckline of her sweater before meeting her eyes.

Self-consciously, she moved to straighten her sweater, then fisted her hands on her hips. "What's your problem? I didn't ask them to join us, and I got rid of them as soon as I could."

Liam stalked down the stairs, stopping inches from her

and mirroring her stance. "My problem? That Neanderthal was all over you, practically drooling in your bra. And you were smiling like it was the most natural thing in the world!"

"Boomer just ended a shitty marriage. He's allowed to blow off some steam."

"He all but invited you to blow him!"

Jane pulled back as if slapped.

Liam ran a big hand through his hair, muttered something Jane couldn't hear, and stalked off to his car.

Jogging after him, Jane grabbed him by the arm and yanked him around. "Boomer is gay. He came out of the closet five years ago and married the first guy he fell in love with, who then trampled all over his heart and took him to the cleaners."

Liam blinked. "He's gay?"

"Yeah. All three of them are." She let go of his arm and stomped back to the restaurant.

In three strides, he was beside her. "I'm sorry. That was—"

"Rude, judgmental, harsh."

"Caught by surprise. I'm not used to being with women like you."

Folding her arms across her chest, Jane cocked her head. "Like *me*? What the hell does that mean?" She held her hand up. "Don't bother. I'm not interested." Jane ran up the stairs to the restaurant, leaving Liam standing in the parking lot. Blinking back tears, she blew past the hostess and strode to the restroom. She splashed water on her face and glared at herself in the mirror. Things had been going so well. She should have known better than to get her hopes up. Men were not worth the trouble. Straightening her shoulders, she blew out a sigh. With a smile pasted on her face, she exited the restroom to re-join Beth and Chuck, thinking that a cat might be her best option for companionship. She obviously sucked at dating or whatever this night was.

The next morning, Jane stumbled into the kitchen in need of coffee. With a large mug in hand, she walked over to the window and contemplated the day. The cheerful sunshine was the opposite of her mood. She felt like Eeyore, wandering around with her own personal rain cloud.

"I'm heading out." Beth stood by the counter, stuffing items into her purse. Wearing a GG polo over black slacks, she had a chef's jacket slung over her arm.

"It's Sunday. Where are you going?" Panicked, Jane searched her memory for an event she'd forgotten about.

Beth made soothing gestures with her hand. "Relax. I'm headed to the church to help out with breakfast. Wanna come?"

Shoulders slumping with relief, Jane shook her head. "Nope. Thanks anyway."

"'Kay. See you later."

The door closed behind Beth, and Jane stood in the quiet apartment. It was weird being home while Beth was out doing something non-work related. Normally, to get Beth to leave the apartment, she had to entice her with the idea of researching some pastry or other. Would Chuck be at the church breakfast? He was such a sweet guy, unlike his numb-nuts friend, who wouldn't know sweet if it was shoved in his face. She wouldn't think about how great he'd been at the paintball party, how he'd listened intently in the car, touched her, and made her feel like he was interested in starting something. It was better not to think of him at all.

Prowling around the apartment, she tried to figure out what to do with her restlessness. The place could use a good cleaning. There was always laundry, and, no doubt, the dust bunnies were now the size of actual jack rabbits, but the walls were closing in. In a compromise, Jane threw a load of towels and bedding into the washer and left for a drop-in kickboxing class.

Punching something always made her feel better. She'd

visualized Liam's face on the bag and aimed round kicks at the level she imagined his junk would be. Dripping with sweat, she toweled off, stuffed her gear into her bag, and decided to grab a coffee before walking the ten blocks back to the apartment. Newly opened, the coffee shop she chose was beginning to fill with Sunday morning Seattleites intent on enjoying the sunshine. Staring at the menu on the chalkboard, she shuffled through the line, ignoring other patrons before ordering a vanilla latte and a croissant. She moved to the side and pulled out her phone while waiting for her order. She felt a body next to her and shifted away.

"Fancy seeing you here." A carefully coiffed Delia Duncan smirked at Jane.

Perfect. Shoving her phone into her pocket, Jane forced a smile and a cheerful greeting. "Yep. Needed my fix." Her face flushed from the workout and her sweaty hair piled on top of her head, she felt like roadkill next to the tall blonde encased in designer workout clothes. She had no desire to talk to the woman, but GG did business with Delia's family, so she asked, "Did you and Kevin enjoy the party?"

Delia cocked one hip and crossed her arms. "Yes, until he ditched me. Something about going to church this morning." She shook her hair back. "Honestly, some people can be so rude. You know what I mean?"

Keeping a straight face, Jane nodded. "Absolutely." She looked past Delia for her order, hoping to escape.

"Do you know who was with my brother last night?"

"That was my sister, Beth."

"Really," Delia drawled. "Huh."

Red flags were going up everywhere, but Jane jumped right in. "What's that mean?"

"She's a bit older than the women Chuck usually dates. And not as…polished." Her attempt at politeness saved her from being popped in the nose. "Tell your sister not to expect too much. Chuck is flighty and easily swayed by big Bambi eyes."

"I'll let her know," Jane ground out through clenched teeth.

"You and Liam seemed rather cozy."

Turning to the side, Jane attempted to hide the blush creeping up her face. Discussing Liam and the way he'd made her heart go pitter-pat and then promptly crushed it was not on her to-do list today. Fortunately, Delia was far more interested in sharing her opinions than sharing secrets. "Don't *you* get your hopes up either. Liam's a cold one. I've known him for years, and he's never once shown any interest in me." She tossed her hair back and sniffed. "He's all about balance sheets and baseball."

Despite her resolve not to think about him, Jane pictured Liam at Mariners games. Did he slouch in the seats drinking beer and eating peanuts? Had he played when he was younger? She could see him leaping up to catch a ball, or running the bases, his perfect ass on display in tight pants. She shook her head to clear the image. The next time they were together, she'd ask. She blinked, doubting there would be a next time.

The barista called out Jane's name, and Jane turned to the coffee bar, stopping when Delia placed a hand on her arm.

Delia pointed to her own cheek. "That scar you have. I can refer you to a plastic surgeon who does great work. He can also help you with…" She twirled her finger in front of Jane's chest while pushing back her own shoulders. "That situation."

Jane picked up her order and fled.

The tension that had leaked out during kickboxing was back. She speed-walked back to the apartment, cursing trust fund babies and the people who spawned them.

After she'd kicked Liam to the curb the night before, she'd

gone back to the table, intending to say goodnight, leaving Chuck and Beth alone. Both insisted she stay and made every attempt to not make her feel like a third wheel or a nineteenth-century chaperone. Chuck's affection for Beth seemed genuine, so how much of what Delia said was her being catty, and how much was the truth? Should she warn Beth? Ask Chuck what his intentions were? Jane laughed out loud at the thought, drawing the attention of two women who sidled past her, eyes rounded with alarm. Reining it in, Jane went back to ruminating as she walked. She wouldn't allow herself to think about Liam. The hope and the hurt. The anniversary party for Chuck's parents was five days away; she would immerse herself in work, smile politely to Liam at the event, and never see him again.

CHAPTER 10

The week passed as each task on Jane's and Beth's prep lists was checked off. These moments of excitement and trepidation were what she'd tried to convey to Liam. She'd wake each morning, concerned she'd forgotten something, only to discover that yes, it had been taken care of.

Discussing the final tasks over coffee that Friday morning, a text came in on Beth's phone. The blissed-out look on her sister's face meant it was from Chuck. Jane got off her stool and went for the coffee pot for a refill.

"No!"

Jane whipped around to see Beth staring at her cell phone as if it had bitten her.

"What?"

Color draining from her face, Beth blinked wordlessly at her.

"Breathe. I can't help you if you don't tell me what it is."

Beth dutifully inhaled and exhaled.

"Last-minute guests?"

Beth shook her head.

"His parents know about the party?"

Beth shook her head again, but she was chomping away on the inside of her cheek.

"Okay. Something about his parents." Still holding the coffee pot, Jane paced the tiny kitchen. "He found out they're vegan?"

Beth's eye bulged out.

Jane waved the coffee pot at her. "Babe, you got to give me something."

Knuckles whitening as she gripped the counter's edge, Beth whispered, "He wants to introduce me to his parents."

Jane shrugged. "So? You've met clients before. Bring a second chef's jacket."

"No! He wants to introduce me as his girlfriend."

"Oh. Ooooh! That's good, isn't it?"

Beth stood abruptly, knocking the stool over. "Are you kidding? It's way too soon to meet his parents. Driving to the restaurant the other night is the only time we've been alone together. He hasn't kissed me. I'm *not* his girlfriend."

It took Beth three tries to right the stool. She strode around the living room, shaking out her hands and gasping for breath. Jane picked up her phone and found Chuck's text.

"It says, 'Can't wait for you to meet my parents.' I think you're reading too much into this."

Beth's head whipped from side to side, hair flying. "Did you see the emoji? It's got heart eyes. You don't send that emoji when you're introducing the event planner."

She had a point. "I thought you liked Chuck? I'm not quite seeing the problem here."

Flopping down on the couch, Beth grabbed a pillow and clutched it to her chest. "I *do* like Chuck. He's sweet and thoughtful and kind. He's pretty much perfect. But I want to go slow. After…"

Across the room in seconds, Jane sank down on the couch, drawing Beth close. Tony had been Beth's first. His betrayal had left scars that were still raw years later. Her reluctance to jump into a relationship was understandable. Wanting to introduce Beth to his parents didn't sound flighty. It sounded like he wanted to take things further. Jane was in no position to give advice. She'd dated, had a couple of boyfriends who lasted a few months, but she didn't do relationships. Having nothing to offer about Beth's love life, Jane turned to practical matters.

"The guests arrive at six. Drinks and appetizers will be served. Chuck and his parents don't get there until 6:45. Do you need to be there for that?" Jane knew the answer; they had backup plans for situations where one of them couldn't be there. They were professionals.

"No. It's our usual staff. Nothing on the menu is new."

"Right. Then you can duck out before six. I'll make an excuse."

"Thank you! You have no idea—"

Jane waved her off. "This is good. There will be times when we have two events in one night, and you and I will have to fly solo. So this is a good test run. Let's look over the list and see what needs to be changed."

$\mathscr{L}$iam timed his arrival to be part of a group, managing to avoid having to speak to Jane. Her only reaction to his presence was checking him off the guest list as he stepped onto the yacht. Armed with a glass of whiskey, he found a corner from which to observe without having to speak to anyone. The only employee from Duncan Properties, he knew few of the guests, old friends of the Duncans, and some family members. He smiled when necessary, but for the most part, people left him alone.

Jane drew his attention like a tractor beam, and he wasn't the only one who felt that way. Dressed in black slacks and a gray shirt, her hair was pulled back in a knot, and every now and then, she'd flick back the heavy bangs from her eyes. Before the arrival of the Duncan party, she'd moved among the guests, an easy smile on her face, looking relaxed and attentive at the same time. When she approached a group, they'd shift to include her, faces lighting up as if she were Oprah. She was the consummate hostess: articulate, engaging, and, from the sounds of laughter, funny as hell. She had to be watching the clock but appeared unruffled by the tardiness of the guests of honor. She was probably using the time to drum up business. He expected to see her handing out business cards, then remembered the cocktail napkins from the engagement party. He turned his over. Nothing. High quality, the cream paper napkins were neither embossed with the Grand Gestures logo nor the date of the party. Huh. He pulled out the heavy card stock invitation in the same cream color. Nowhere on it was GG mentioned. He shook his head. Jane was missing out on a great marketing opportunity. He wished Kevin were there to discuss these things with and to act as his buffer, but he, like all the other employees below the executive level, hadn't made the official guest list.

It hit him. His interactions with Kevin all week had been purely business. No casual conversation over coffee or shared lunches. There was nothing to fault about his work. He was punctual and professional, but something was off. Was he imagining it, or was Kevin giving him the cold shoulder? Mulling it over, Liam's gaze returned to Jane. Had she said something to Kevin? He doubted it. Kevin would have had his head on a platter. And Jane would not have allowed her personal life to get in the way of business. No, it was his fault. He'd been inside his head all week and had barely spoken to Kevin, which was a mistake. The younger man would have settled him about the blowup with Jane.

He regretted his words, regretted making her feel...less than. He'd been so pissed when her friends showed up, made assumptions, and made an ass of himself. No wonder she wouldn't look at him. But after tonight, he'd never have to see her again. That thought should have cheered him up, but it didn't. He shifted his stance so she was no longer in his line of sight. A laugh drew his attention.

A chorus of shushes filled the air before the guests went silent, shifting about with excited energy. A burst of applause heralded the arrival of the guests of honor. Carol Lee and Chuck Sr. looked thrilled. Liam didn't know what they'd been told, but they'd known enough for Carol Lee to have had her hair done and be dressed for the occasion. Both appeared genuinely surprised at the number of people who'd shown up for their fortieth anniversary party. That it was on the same boat they'd borrowed for their first date was the icing on the cake. GG servers moved among the guests with trays of tempting appetizers and a signature cocktail Beth had created for the event.

Carol Lee and Chuck Sr. stood near a display of photographs. Each silver frame depicted a moment from their past, and they laughingly told stories about each one. Their children stood close by, Delia looking bored while Chuck looked like a lost puppy.

Liam wandered over. "Your parents are pleased."

Chuck blinked. "Hmm? Oh yeah. They're very happy." He looked past Liam, obviously searching for something but then looked down at the drink in his hand.

"What's up?" They'd known each other since college, and Chuck was easy to read.

A blush stole up Chuck's cheeks. "Beth's not here."

"She's not in the kitchen supervising?"

He shook his head. "I asked Jane when would be a good time for Beth to meet my parents, and she told me she wasn't feeling well."

"Really?" That surprised the hell out of Liam. "Did you text her?"

"Tonight is about Mom and Dad. I need to be fully

present for them." His gaze drifted over to where Delia was taking selfies in various poses.

Liam clasped his shoulder. "I'll find out for you."

"Thanks." With a relieved smile, Chuck turned back to his parents.

Weaving through the guests, Liam spotted Jane at the bar, scrolling through her tablet. He stopped next to her. She shifted away, increasing the space between them without moving her feet. He waited for her to finish. She ignored him.

"Chuck's parents are thrilled. You've done a great job."

Jane nodded but didn't look at him.

"Everyone I've talked to is enjoying the food."

Jane nodded again.

"You'll have work coming out of your ears."

Putting the tablet on the bar, she twisted to look up at him. "I'm busy here. What do you want?"

Jane's cool stare shriveled his balls. He was the CFO of a multi-million-dollar company. Why did this one woman scare the shit out of him? "Just checking in to see how things are going from your side."

"Really?" Someone behind him caught her attention, and she flashed a smile. It disappeared the moment she focused on him.

"Yeah. I understand Beth isn't here, so wondered if you needed anything."

"This isn't my first rodeo." She flicked her bangs out of her eyes. "I've got this." She picked up her tablet and headed toward an area with bar-height tables and chairs. She pushed a chair in at one table and turned the centerpiece of another a minute amount.

He reached out and snagged her arm. "Damn it, Jane, would you give me a minute?"

She shook off his hand and huffed out an exaggerated sigh. "Fine. What do you want?"

"Is Beth okay? I'm surprised she's not here."

"Why? Did you think I needed a babysitter? Did you think a woman like me would hit on some old guy with deep pockets? Maybe take him out on the deck and show him my back tattoo?" She was moving again, picking up speed, heading toward a door from which a server emerged.

He needed to apologize, but he was running out of time, so that would have to wait. "Chuck is worried," he blurted out before she could disappear. "He can't get away from his parents to text her."

Jane stopped. Glancing over her shoulder, she said, "She has a migraine. She'll be fine."

Liam grabbed at the conversation opening like it was a life ring. "I've never had one, but I hear they're miserable. Does she get them often?"

Jane stepped to the side to let the server pass, and Liam took the opportunity to get closer.

"About once a month," she said without looking at him.

"Once a month? That's a lot. Does she—oh." His eyes widened as the light went on. "Sorry. I know nothing about women's cycles."

Jane smirked. "Why would you? Now excuse me, I have work to do."

Thinking on the fly, Liam called out to prevent her from leaving. "Acupuncture!"

"What?" She turned to face him fully, brow furrowed.

"I heard two women talking about PMS, and one said she'd had luck with acupuncture."

"I need to hear more from the person without a uterus." She made a rolling motion with one hand. "Go ahead and mansplain this to me."

He'd managed to step from one pile of shit into another. "Hear me out. I was on an overnight flight, and everyone in the cabin was asleep except me. I heard the flight attendants talking. One of them said she used to get migraines before her period and tried acupuncture. Said it worked miracles." He couldn't read her expression, but she hadn't dismissed him. "Like you said, I don't have a uterus, and I have no clue what PMS is like. But please let Beth know I hope it passes soon and she feels better. I'll leave you alone now. It really is a great party, and Grand Gestures has done a great job." He shoved his hands in his pockets before doing something stupid like brushing her hair back.

Something almost like a smile pulled at the corners of her mouth; Jane nodded before entering the kitchen.

"**S**eriously?" Beth glared at Jane, then down at her phone. "You told him I had PMS?"

Jane fortified herself with coffee before replying, "Not exactly. I told Liam you had a migraine and that you got them monthly. He made an inference. I don't know what he told Chuck. Can we get back to the good stuff now?"

"Fine. Let me tell Chuck my migraine is gone." She tapped out the text and dropped her phone on the counter.

"Chuck's mom and dad are delightful. Honestly, I don't know where Delia came from. Mrs. Duncan must have hugged me a dozen times, and when she saw their suitcases in the suite, she cried. Honest to God tears. She didn't know why Chuck insisted they keep the whole weekend free. God, I hope the weather holds for their cruise." Jane flipped her hair back and grinned at Beth. "Your ideas were brilliant, and the execution was flawless if I do say so myself."

"Thanks for that. I appreciate you covering for me."

"I get it. You aren't ready to meet his parents, and when you do, you don't want it to be when you're working. And, you know, this was a good exercise for us. Running the kitchen was easy because you've done such a good job training the staff. Your instructions were clear, and things went smoothly, other than having to run back for the lemons."

"I had complete faith in you." Beth raised her coffee mug in a salute. "If it were reversed, I don't know that I could do the front of the house."

She wasn't underselling herself. While Beth barked orders like a four-star general in the kitchen, she had no confidence with people who weren't working for her.

"We'll get back to that. Mrs. Duncan introduced me to a woman named Betty Brown. She holds monthly cocktail parties. It's part networking and part business etiquette classes."

Beth folded her arms on the counter. "I've heard of those. They're popular with companies who do business internationally."

"Right. Each month, she focuses on a different culture with guest speakers. She hasn't found a caterer who can keep up with cooking foods from different countries. And she's been putting together the information packets herself. Chuck talked us up, and she wants us to put together a presentation to do both."

"I'm listening. Is there a catch?" Beth asked, both excitement and wariness in her expression.

"I don't think so. They book the conference room of Duncan Properties the first Wednesday of each month. She has access to a kitchen on the same floor. Their next event is this coming Wednesday, and she's invited us to attend. I thought we'd ask Kevin to join us, and he can take us on a tour. You know, get the lay of the land."

Nodding slowly, Beth stared off into space. Jane poured herself another cup of coffee. A regular monthly gig would go a long way toward improving their bottom line. In addition to the cocktail parties, she'd had two other guests from the anniversary party approach her.

"Earth calling Beth." She waved a hand in front of her sister. "Where'd you go?"

"Sorry," Beth replied. "I was thinking about which of my cookbooks has the best recipes for international cuisine."

Jane looked at the shelves full of cookbooks. "I'm sure you've got something. Anyway, we're getting to the point where we need to hire someone who can cover front of the house. If we take on more than one major event per weekend, the money will roll in, but we'll be busier than a one-armed paper hanger. And I don't want to sacrifice quality."

From the start, GG was a boutique company. They priced themselves accordingly, turned down requests for parties larger than fifty people, and would *not* do weddings. Period. It was a tough decision but one they were happy with. Less moving parts, more creative control, and no dysfunctional bridal parties. They were in this for the long haul, and Jane wanted to protect Beth from burnout.

She opened the fridge and pulled out a yogurt container, holding it up in silent inquiry. Beth shook her head.

"Embossing napkins with our logo has worked well for us. So when Kevin suggested we use plain napkins for the Duncan party, I pushed back."

Beth's eyebrows rose. "I was there. I thought I was going to have to separate you two."

"He was right. The logo on my shirt and on the servers' shirts was the only advertising we did last night. And it worked like a charm. People approached me, and I was able to engage, do my elevator pitch."

"He'll be thrilled to hear that."

"Yeah. I'd love to be able to make him our third."

Beth folded her hands and propped her chin on them. "He's easy to work with and has great ideas. I know he likes it, but can we afford to do that?"

"We certainly can't afford to pay him what he's making at Duncan Properties."

Both women sighed. The dilemma of small businesses. More work than they could handle but not enough to be able to pay well.

"How about this. We meet up with him at the cocktail party and ask if he's interested in doing some contract work—specifically working front of the house, but also the creative stuff with you." Jane mirrored Beth's pose to better gauge her sister's reaction.

"It wouldn't hurt. If Kevin's not interested, we could look into an intern program with one of the culinary schools."

Jane straightened, slapping her hands on the counter. "You, my dear, are a genius. I'll tell Mrs. Brown to put us on the guest list for this Wednesday and call Kevin. What are you going to do today?"

"Now that my migraine has gone away"—she made air quotes and rolled her eyes—"I'm going to meet Chuck for lunch."

After Beth left, Jane settled on the couch with her laptop and cell phone to review her calendar, making sure she'd taken care of the items she'd written in her planner. The final payment from the Duncan anniversary party had been received, and it was nice to see a healthy balance in their bank account. Of course, it wouldn't last long with employees to pay and invoices to take care of. She dashed off an email to Betty Brown, accepting the invitation for the monthly meetup, then called Kevin to invite him to join them. Her call went to voicemail, so she left a message, hoping he'd call back soon. She wanted to tell him about the anniversary party, thank him for his suggestions, and invite him to the monthly meetup.

The last item on her to-do list was to update GG's Instagram page. Picking up her phone, she scrolled through the photos, looking for images that conveyed the excitement of an event and highlighted vendors without looking staged. Stopping on the photos from the paintball party, she found one of Liam, disheveled, splattered with paint, and laughing with Stan and Carl, a complete contrast to the man in the custom-tailored suit last night.

He'd looked so good, but after his hurtful words in the parking lot at Johnny's, she hadn't wanted to speak to him. But watching him turn twelve shades of red while discussing PMS had been worth the pain of having to talk to him. He'd seemed contrite but hadn't apologized. Had she given him an opportunity though, or had she used work and the busyness of the event to avoid him?

She looked back at the photo. It really would be good for a social media post. She already had permission from Stan and Carl to use their images but not from Liam. A tingle of anticipation coursed through her. She now had a reason to see him again.

CHAPTER 11

"**G**irl, we did a good job."

"Yeah, yeah, yeah." Jane accepted Kevin's hug instead of smacking him. Nothing was going to convince her to put on a dress or heels. She had five pairs of identical slim-fitting slacks and an assortment of button-up blouses that Beth had bought her. Thanks to Kevin, she had three knit blazers in various colors and styles. She had groused and growled at being dragged shopping but was secretly pleased. They'd found some awesome items at a consignment store. Tonight, she wore a python-printed jacket over a jade-green blouse, black slacks, and black Rothy's. "Thanks for joining us."

Kevin hugged Beth before turning back. "Not a problem. Where do you want to start?"

Fishing through her messenger bag, Jane pulled out a file folder. Opening it, she extracted two sheets of paper, giving one each to Kevin and Beth. The sisters had arrived early to tour the floor of Duncan Properties, where the conference room was located, looking for the service elevator, the amenities in the kitchen, and possible locking storage. They also wanted to take notes on Betty Brown's setup, what to emulate, and where to make improvements. From there, they would plan the presentation.

Pleased with the tour results, the three stood outside the conference room, discussing their findings. The elevator dinged, and heavy footsteps approached. Jane turned to stare at the image of masculine perfection coming her way.

"Kevin, I thought you'd gone home." Wearing a pristine white dress shirt with the sleeves rolled up, exposing muscular forearms, Liam stopped before them and nodded at Beth but focused on Jane.

"Hey, boss." Kevin spared Liam a glance before looking back down at the paper in his hand. "Heading into the Cultural Cocktail Class."

"Oh. I didn't know you went to them."

His eyes connected with Jane's, heating her from the inside out. She snapped, "Does he have to get approval from you for what he does in his free time?"

"Jane!" Beth glared at her sister.

"What?" She flicked her bangs out of her eyes, staring up at Liam's surprised face. His perfection made her feel itchy and anxious and combative. Sparring with him made her feel alive.

Liam opened his mouth, but before he could reply, the elevator doors opened again, and Betty Brown emerged. Dressed in a pearl-gray suede suit, the sixty-ish Black woman smiled at the group.

"Jane, lovely to see you. This must be Beth. How are you?" She held out her hand to Beth before turning to Kevin and Liam. "Gentlemen, are you joining us this evening as well?"

"Hi, Mrs. Brown. Nice to see you again." Kevin extended his hand. "I am. Liam just stopped by to say hi. His schedule hasn't allowed him to do so for a while." He stepped back, shooting Liam a bland smile.

"Right. It's been what? A year you've been holding these events? How's everything working out for you?"

Jane bit back a smile, watching Liam's attempt at charm.

The older woman chuckled. "I'm honored the CFO is here. Are you sure you can't join us? Perhaps say a word to the attendees?"

Liam looked like he'd rather have a root canal without anesthetic.

"Unfortunately, the boss has a Zoom meeting in fifteen minutes. Beth and I were hoping you'd explain how you choose which country you feature. Why Egypt?" Kevin smoothly stepped up and guided the woman into the conference room, looking back over his shoulder and winking at Liam. A giggling Beth followed behind.

"You owe him big time." Jane grinned up at a clearly relieved Liam.

"True. He's very good with people. I'd be lost without him." He shoved his hands into the pockets of his pants, his gaze following the backs of the others.

A twinge of guilt tickled the back of Jane's conscience; she hadn't thought about what it would mean to Liam if Kevin came to work for them. She quickly quashed the thought. "Do you have a Zoom call?" She should be heading inside but lingered anyway.

He looked down at her, full lips quirked up at the corners. "I actually do. What are you doing here? Planning on opening a franchise in Cairo?"

Jane snorted. "Absolutely. Closely followed by one in Tel Aviv. Grand Gestures will be taking over the Middle East."

Three earnest young people dressed in business casual walked toward them, and Jane shifted closer to Liam to let them enter the conference room. A blond man looked up from his phone, nodded his thanks, then slowed, his gaze running up and down Jane. As he opened his mouth to speak, Liam's hand landed on Jane's shoulder. The blond man winked. "Don't blame you," he said before joining the others.

"Really?" Twisting away from him, Jane looked up at Liam. "What was that for?"

"He was gonna—"

"What? Say hello?"

"I didn't like the way he looked at you." Liam scowled.

"How did he look at me?"

Liam's gaze roamed over her, heating her through and through. "Like he wanted to get your number, maybe buy you a drink."

"You can tell all that from a look?"

"Couldn't you?"

She tilted her head to the side, considering her answer. "Not from him."

"Good," he muttered in a low voice.

His response made her feel squishy inside. "Do you, umm, have a second?"

"Yeah. My call isn't for another half hour. What do you need?"

"Your permission to use a photo from paintball."

"Not karaoke?"

Jane shuddered. "No."

"Why not? You had everyone involved, and they were clearly enjoying themselves. Even you—after I came to your rescue."

"I did not need rescuing!" Maybe a little bit, but she wasn't going to admit it. She ignored his eyebrow raise and explained, "Chasing down parents to get permission to use their kid's image is a pain, and most of the photos were of me —and you, of course—and they don't benefit any of the vendors. For promotional purposes, they're useless." There were a couple of Liam flailing around behind the girls that she kept. One in particular where they'd collided, and they were both laughing. That one she'd tucked away.

More people approached from the elevator, and the noise level increased in anticipation of the class.

Taking her arm, Liam moved her farther away from the door to the conference room. "I see your point. Do you want to come to my office?"

The rumble of his voice shot a jolt through her. "Sure. Let me text Beth and let her know."

He waited while she dashed off the text and then escorted her through the workspace of Duncan Properties, guiding her with a hand on her elbow. A custodian emptied wastepaper baskets, but other than that, the place was empty. Light streamed through the open door of an office. Liam stepped to the side and gestured for her to enter before him. It was almost as big as her apartment—easily bigger than her living room, dining area, and kitchen alone. The sun dipped to the horizon through the big corner windows, bathing Elliott Bay with warm pink light. A sitting area with comfortable chairs surrounded a round coffee table, and two matching chairs were pulled up in front of a large desk. An open laptop and two additional monitors sat on the pristine surface, a neat pile of file folders off to one side. Behind the desk sat a credenza with more file folders, all stacked neatly, and a beat-up baseball glove with a scuffed baseball nestled inside it.

Jane turned in a circle, admiring the sleek furnishings. "Is this really your office, or are you just trying to impress me?"

"I'm pretty sure that's my name on the door." He leaned against the back of a chair, grinning down at her.

She sauntered past him to stand next to his desk chair. Unlike the rest of the furniture, it had seen better days. Silver duct tape crisscrossed the seat, and bits of chrome was missing from the armrests, revealing rusted metal underneath. "I'm suspecting there's a story behind this."

"It belonged to my dad." He waved at the high-end furniture in the room. "When Duncan Properties renovated a few years ago, they gave me this complicated ergonomic desk chair that did everything but pour you a drink. It was uncomfortable as hell, so I got rid of it and brought this from home."

Unlike most men of her acquaintance, Liam had never talked about himself in the short time they'd spent together. Looking at the old chair and the worn baseball glove on the credenza, Jane wanted to know more about him. What sentimental attachment did the two objects hold? What part of his work did he like the best? How did he manage to look so good so late in the day?

"You wanted to show me something?"

She snapped out of her daze. "Right! I have some great photos from Jessica's birthday party, but yours is the only face clearly visible, and I can't use any of the photos on social media without your permission." She came out from behind his desk and moved to stand at his side. Instead of taking the phone, he placed his hand around hers and angled the photo toward him. Long fingers cupped her own. They were warm and slightly calloused, and she was acutely aware of his firm bicep inches away from her shoulder. She wanted to press her nose against him and inhale. Since when did laundry starch make her knees weak? She forced herself to concentrate on the photograph. Framed in the center, Liam towered over the girls, who were all in the middle of high-fiving each other. Bullseye Paintball could be clearly seen in the background above Stan and Carl, whose backs were toward the camera.

He stood so close; his breath tickled her ear when he spoke. "I don't remember you taking these. Those girls sure got me good."

Jane giggled. He wasn't wrong. There was barely a spot on his coveralls that wasn't covered in pink paint. But he wore a broad smile as he stared down at the girls. The other images were similar except for the last one, which caught Liam and the two dads attempting to follow the girls' dance instructions.

"Oh, hell no. You are not using that one!"

She peeked up at him from beneath her bangs. "Really? I think this is perfect."

He narrowed his eyes and pulled the phone out of her grasp.

"Hey. Give that back."

"Not unless you promise to delete that picture."

She reached out, but his arms were too long. Grabbing his forearm, she yanked with both hands, but it didn't budge. He raised it higher until she was practically on her tiptoes.

"Looks like we're at an impasse." His dark eyes danced with amusement.

She scowled, sweeping her gaze down his chest to his flat belly and back up. "A punch to the kidneys or a well-placed knee would take care of things."

His eyes fixed on her lips, inches away from her own. "Or you could promise not to use the photo."

There was no way she could get the phone short of taking him down with violence. Grappling him to the floor would have to wait for another time. "Fine." She let go, and his other hand came up to press against her back, supporting her.

"Promise?"

"Yes."

He brought his arm down but still held the phone away from her. "How do I know you don't have any other compromising images? Perhaps I should go through all your photos."

The teasing glint in his eyes belied the threat. "That's okay. The photos I intend to use for blackmail are stored on a hard drive."

His lips quirked up as he handed over the phone. "Good to know. I'll have to—" A timer went off on his laptop. "That's my reminder for the meeting."

Disappointed that their time was cut short, she pointed at the door. "I should be going anyway. You okay with GG using the paintball photo?"

"Yeah, that's fine." He stepped back, his gaze warm as it bounced from her eyes to her mouth and back again.

"Great." She tucked her phone back into her bag and walked to the door.

"Jane."

She turned, eyebrows raised in a silent question.

In two long strides, he was next to her. "I was a jerk that night at Johnny's. You didn't deserve that, and I was totally out of line." He placed one hand on her arm. "Any chance we can try again?"

Warmth kindling in her belly, she looked down at his hand and then up into his hopeful eyes. She nodded, and he smiled fully before releasing her.

Not wanting to break the moment, she returned his smile and left his office in silence, practically skipping on the way to the conference room.

Standing at a bistro table with Beth and Kevin, Jane tried to concentrate as the last of the guests chatted with Betty Brown. The other two were taking notes, but Jane kept glancing at the window in the closed door of the conference room, wondering what Liam meant by a second chance. She was pretty sure that if the timer hadn't gone off, he would have kissed her in his office. But what exactly did he want? A casual hookup? More? Did he mean he wanted to ask her on a date? There wasn't anything stopping *her* from asking *him* out. With the anniversary party over and GG no longer doing business with Duncan Properties, there wasn't a reason for her not to see Liam socially. Not to explore this heat that flared every time he got close.

"Create a template. Plug in facts about the country, include major cultural traditions, any taboos, and some photos."

Kevin's words dragged Jane away from her thoughts.

Tucking a curl behind her ear, Beth nodded. "Whatever

food we serve, include photos of that and maybe a sample recipe?"

"I like that. Jane, what do you think?" Kevin was writing away on the checklist she'd given him earlier in the day.

"How hard is it for you to prepare and deliver that food? The kitchen here is too small to cook in, and it will all have to be finger foods."

Beth picked up a *qatayef* and studied the pancake stuffed with cheese. "Not hard at all. The distance is negligible if we continue to work out of the church kitchen, and all the events are located here. Kevin suggested renting storage here for chafing dishes, etc. I figure after we do the first one and determine the pain points, it's a two-person gig. You and I can tag-team and use one of our regular staff. Creating the menu should be easy if we have the list of countries in advance."

She was listening to Beth but watching Kevin. He'd glanced at his watch, and the animation left his face. She sent a questioning look at Beth, who nodded. She'd seen it as well.

"You got a busy day tomorrow?"

Kevin tidied up the papers before him and shook his head. "The usual. Do you need some help with anything?"

"Not really. Brainstorming session in the morning for this, and then the afternoon prepping for the weekend."

Beth snapped her fingers. "Remind me to pick up some feta cheese. There are a couple recipes I want to try out."

"You going to be at the church?" Kevin's eyebrows went up.

"No. I'm just fooling around. I'll do it at home. That way, I don't have to worry about making a mess." She grinned and winked.

Jane chuckled. "A perk of working for yourself."

"Must be nice," Kevin said with a heartfelt sigh.

Kevin picked up the empty glasses and took them to where the waiter was gathering the empty plates into a bus pan. When he returned, the sisters were leaning on the table, fingers laced together, watching him.

"What's going on?"

"We're in a bind and hoping you can help out." Jane got right to the point. "Business is picking up, which is great. We're at the point where we need someone to assist us, but we can't afford to pay them a full-time salary."

"We need someone creative and organized, who can manage clients and staff, and is willing to work part-time until we can make him full-time," Beth volleyed.

Jane picked up the ball. "Beth doesn't do front of the house. If I get sick, we're screwed. We want someone to do front of the house for weekend events, work with Beth on designing programs, menus, table setup, and be comfortable working in a kitchen."

Kevin shook his head. Beth placed a hand on his arm before he could speak. "We want you. You get us. You know what we're trying to accomplish, and you put up with our quirks. We know we can't pay you what you make here, so you could set your own hours."

He looked off to the side and cocked his head as if having a conversation with an invisible person. He shifted his glance between the two sisters. "I can't afford to leave Duncan Properties. While they're paying me, I will work only for them."

Beth sighed.

Jane's shoulders drooped.

Kevin held up a hand. "They don't pay me to work evenings and weekends. So I could do that."

"Really?"

"I won't do GG work on company time, but if you're willing to let me set my own hours, I think we can talk."

Leaping up from her chair, Jane wrapped her arms around Kevin and squealed.

More circumspect, Beth reached out a hand to clasp one of Kevin's. "Thank you. You are exactly what we need."

CHAPTER 12

*D*o you like baseball?

Before Jane could wonder who was texting, another one came in.

This is Liam.

A zing of pleasure shot through her, and she giggled. She hadn't expected to hear from him so soon.

Liam who?

It was a few seconds before his next text. **Smart ass.** And then. **Do you like baseball?**

Jane shoved her phone under a couch cushion as Beth walked into the living room, dressed for bed.

"I'm off to bed," Beth said. "You staying up for a while?"

"A bit."

Her sister stared at her. "You okay? You look…tense. Wound up." She crossed her arms and propped herself against the wall.

Her phone vibrated beside her, and Jane jerked. She stretched and let out an exaggerated groan, hoping to cover it up. "Nope. Just sore from my workout today. Goodnight now."

"Okay. You would tell me if something was up, right?"

"Of course."

Beth nodded, and Jane watched her turn and head to her room. When she heard the door close, Jane snatched her phone up.

Are you there?

Yes! Just had to do something. She hit send and continued to thumb the keys. **I do like baseball but I have a complicated relationship with it.**

Who's that? That text was quickly followed by another. **I meant how's what?**

Bubbles appeared, then disappeared. The phone vibrated with an incoming call, and she practically dropped it. "Hello?"

"Tiny screens and my fat thumbs are a bad combination. So I thought I'd call. Got time to clarify that last comment?"

"Umm, yeah. Just give me a second." She pressed the phone to her chest and tiptoed to the closet by the front door. As quietly as possible, she made space for herself among the shoes and bags on the floor and sat. She pulled the door close but not shut, not wanting to lock herself in. "Okay, I'm back."

"I didn't look at the time. If it's too late to talk, just say so."

The concern in his deep voice warmed her. "No, it's fine. I just relocated so I don't wake Beth up."

"Ah." There was a clink of something, like ice against the side of a glass. "Back to baseball. Define complicated."

Jane huffed out a laugh. "Have you ever been to a game and there's that person in the stands who knows everything? They're constantly telling the players and coaches and umps what to do at the top of their lungs?"

"Oh yeah. You just want to enjoy the game, and some jerk is ruining it for you."

"Well, that was my mom."

"Seriously."

She nodded, realized Liam couldn't see her, and said,

"Yeah. She'd been a really good player in high school and played rec league until she broke her ankle sliding into home plate. It never healed properly, and she wasn't able to play anymore. Unfortunately, she took out her frustration by going to the local games and yelling at everyone, telling them what they were doing wrong."

"That must have been embarrassing." Liam's voice rumbled in a sympathetic tone.

"Um-hmm. She got banned from the fields. For life."

"I can see the complicated feelings."

Jane remembered seeing the ball and glove in his office. "I take it you like baseball."

"I do, and umm…" He cleared his throat. "Would you like to go to the batting cages with me this weekend? If you're not busy. Or if not this weekend, sometime soon."

A thrill went through her at both the invitation and the hesitancy in his voice.

"Yesss, hang on." She thought through GG's upcoming jobs. "I'm free Saturday until two p.m. Will that work?"

"Yep. The place opens at eleven. I'll book us a cage and send you the link."

"Great. I look forward to it."

His voice lowered. "I do, too. Goodnight, Jane."

"Goodnight, Liam." She disconnected and did a happy dance in the confines of the closet.

*H*e burst through the apartment door at a dead run. The door swung wide and bounced back at him. Liam pushed it aside and raced into the kitchen to snatch up his cell phone from the charger. "You'd forget your damn head if it wasn't attached." Back out the door, he took the stairs down to the parking garage and beeped open his car. Starting up the ignition, he glanced at the clock and breathed a sigh of relief. He wasn't going to be late. He exited the parking garage with a smile on his face, the same one that had been there since he'd hung up from his phone conversation with Jane.

Hitting balls at the batting cages meant he had a chance to show off. He snorted. Nah. Jane could probably hit it out of the park without breaking a sweat. He just wished they had more time so he could take her out for lunch afterward. But he got it. Weekends were the busiest times for event planners, and he respected her dedication to her work.

He surveyed the cars in the parking lot, then realized he had no idea what kind of car she drove. His heart rate picked up as a sportscar pulled in and parked. Two guys got out. Not Jane. He decided to head to their assigned cage and warm up. She'd be there soon.

Thirty minutes later, his neck was sore from craning around whenever he heard footsteps. Where was she? Fifteen minutes after that, he gave up. Shoulders slumped and feet lagging, he left the cage and headed back to his car. His phone had been on vibrate in his pocket the whole time, and he hadn't received a call or a text. Part of him hoped it was a serious emergency preventing her from not coming or reaching out.

Back in his apartment, he squinted against the bright light streaming through his front window. It wasn't fair that the sun was shining when he felt like shit. He got a glass of water, fished his phone out of his pocket, tossed it onto the coffee table, and slumped onto the couch. Staring at the offending object, he willed it to ring. Behind him came the signal for an incoming message. "No," he said. He twisted to look over the couch at the counter that separated the kitchen from the dining area—the counter on which was a charging station for his laptop, work phone, and...personal phone. "Oh shit." He got up and went to the counter just as another message came in. While he'd been out, six text messages and three phone calls had come in. On his personal phone. He started with the text messages.

I'm fixing a flat tire. Be there as soon as I can.

The next text was an image of the damaged tire with a nail embedded in it. Then, **Just in case you doubted me.** Followed by a winking emoji.

Dammit! The spare is flat also. I am so sorry!!!

The last text said, **Tire is fixed. Ignore the voicemails.**

He opened the first voicemail. In the background, he could hear traffic. "Hey, it's me. I might not make it. I'm so sorry. I'm going to call AAA. I'll let you know."

The next one: "So it's going to be an hour before they can get here. Any chance you've got one of those inflater thingies in your car? Wanna help a damsel in distress? Let me know."

Liam growled. He did have one of those inflater thingies in his car, and he would have been happy to help her. He listened to the final voicemail: "Okay, well, umm, I'm hoping there's just too much noise around you, and that's why you aren't responding. Otherwise, well. Never mind. AAA is here."

He looked at the timestamp of the messages. The first one came in two hours ago, right about the time he was leaving the parking garage. If he'd had the right damn phone with him, he would have been able to help her. As disappointing as that was, he felt better that she hadn't blown him off. Then it hit him. Jane thought *he'd* blown her off.

His call went to voicemail, which wasn't surprising. He doubted she wanted to talk to him right now. "Hi, Jane, it's Liam. I was running late this morning and forgot my phone, and when I went back to get it, I took my work phone by mistake." He walked to the window to stare blankly at the water of Elliot Bay. "Kevin has been nagging me for ages to get a different case for it because I've made this mistake before. But not so disastrously. I will definitely do so now because I don't want this to happen again—that is, if you agree to go out with me or even speak to me, not that I'd blame you if you didn't want to, because—" The phone buzzed with an incoming call. Seeing it was Jane, Liam fumbled with the keys before speaking. "Hey."

"Is that a grovel?"

"What?"

"Were you leaving me a long, heartfelt apology for why you left me stranded on the side of the road?" Her sigh was loud and dramatic.

"Do you want to hear about how I took my work phone with me and didn't get your messages?"

"Were you stomping around thinking I wasn't going to show up?"

"Maybe?" He winced. "Okay, I was until I realized I was an idiot. I am sorry. I do have one of those inflater thingies, and I would have loved to ride to your rescue."

She laughed. "It's fine. We'll try for another time."

"Yeah?" He perked up. "Any idea when? I could meet you after your event. Maybe buy you a drink if you're not too tired."

"I can't." She cleared her throat. "We, umm, are training a new staff member today, and after the event, we'll be debriefing him."

"Oh." Liam tried to keep the disappointment out of his voice. "I get it."

"I could call you tonight. That is, if you would like to talk."

"Definitely. I'm home all night."

"Great. I need to hop into the shower before heading out. Bye, Liam."

"Bye, Jane." He pumped a fist. There was hope yet.

CHAPTER 13

The hiss of the espresso machine and the hum of conversation were audible through the open door but not loud enough to be intrusive. Glass walls surrounded the large conference table, providing a semblance of privacy. Jane had reserved the meeting space from the coffee shop owner for the afternoon. She and Beth were meeting with the organizers of a fundraising luncheon for a local nonprofit. Someone who attended the Duncan anniversary party had reached out. Initially, Jane had turned them down; the expected attendees exceeded fifty people, which was the maximum event size the sisters were comfortable with. But the woman had reached out again, explaining it would actually be three luncheons of forty people each, on different days, in different venues, around the greater Seattle area. So the meeting was arranged. Arriving early, Jane and Beth ordered drinks, set up their space, laid out their suggestions, and now waited for the others.

Jane said, "I think they're here."

Two women stood at the entry to the coffee shop, scanning the crowd, clearly looking for someone. Jane lifted her hand to draw their attention. Beth pulled it back down to the table with a jerk.

"What's wrong?"

White-faced, Beth's eyes were big, and her grip tightened on Jane's arm. "That's...that's the mother of the bride from *the wedding.*"

She didn't have to say more. Despite the many weddings Beckett Bridal Consultants had done over the years, only one stood out in their collective memory.

"Are you sure?" Jane had never met her, but she'd heard the horror stories. How the woman changed her mind three times over the menu, how she wanted the waitstaff to wear uniforms in colors that would complement the flowers, how she wanted imported sparkling water but would only pay for domestic. And that was before her daughter had sex with Beth's husband.

Beth nodded, ducking her head down and twisting away from the doorway.

Jane turned toward her, allowing her hair to fall and cover her face. "Okay. How do you want to play this?" There was no way in hell she would work with a woman who had made Beth's life miserable.

"And, oh shit, they're coming this way," Jane muttered, clutching Beth's hands. "We'll get out of this as gracefully as possible."

Beth nodded again.

"Now, bend down as if you've dropped something."

"What?"

"Pretend you've dropped your pen. Trust me, and follow my lead."

Beth dutifully bent down, her head barely visible above the table.

Jane rose and advanced toward the door, hand out and smile plastered on her face. "Elsa Wong?"

A tall, sixtyish Asian woman accepted Jane's hand and

held out her other to indicate her companion. "Jane, thank you for seeing us. Bianca Withers is organizing the luncheons with me."

"Bianca, lovely to meet you. We've never met, but you know my sister, Beth Beckett."

Beth rose from the floor at the mention of her name, looking composed except for the two spots of color riding high on her cheekbones. With a tight smile, she rounded the table to stand next to Jane. She murmured a greeting to Elsa Wong, then turned to the angular blonde next to her. "Hello, Bianca."

Bianca Withers' polite expression froze. She sucked in a breath, eyes darting back and forth between Jane and Beth.

Elsa Wong indicated the table. "Shall we sit down?"

Shaking her head, Jane addressed Elsa while continuing to look at Bianca. "I don't think so. Unfortunately, we won't be able to work with you."

"I don't understand. What's this about?"

Hands clasped tightly in front of her, Beth answered, "A few years ago, my family's business, Beckett Bridal Consultants, did the wedding for Bianca's daughter, Julie. It was a… difficult situation. I'll let Bianca fill you in on the details. I trust both of your daughters are doing well?"

Tight-lipped, Bianca nodded. "They are."

"Glad to hear it." Beth and Bianca exchanged silent stares before Beth inclined her head. "Best of luck with your event." She gathered up her things and left the room.

Jane followed suit, murmuring her goodbyes, and caught up with her sister in the parking lot. She grabbed Beth by the arm and pulled her over to their car. "Oh my God! You handled that so well."

Slumped against the car, Beth heaved out a massive sigh. "Are we done? Is that it? Is word going to get out that GG is unreliable, and all my crap will bubble up from the past?"

"Bethie, it's fine. You did good. We knew that the story

would come out someday, and you were so gracious. If it had been me, I'd have—"

"Exactly why I had to speak. We couldn't have you going off in there."

"I wouldn't have gone off!"

Beth glared at her.

"Maybe a little. You okay?"

"Yeah. I hope I haven't screwed things up for us." She rounded the car and waited for Jane to beep open the locks.

On the drive home, Jane ruminated over the interaction. The luncheons were almost a year away, and the organizers were in the preliminary planning stages. It was quite possible GG would not have gotten the contract anyway, so she didn't feel bad about saying no. It was the other part, wondering what Bianca Withers would say to Elsa Wong. Regardless of how you spun it, the bottom line was that Beth's then husband, the wedding photographer, had sex with Bianca's daughter, an underage girl, in a back room at the wedding.

Jane glanced over to see Beth staring out the window. Today had brought back the embarrassment, anger, and pain.

Making a quick decision, Jane changed lanes and turned onto a side street.

"Aren't we going home?"

"We have a stop to make first."

"Okay." Beth continued to stare out the window, not saying a word.

Twenty minutes later, they pulled up in front of an old warehouse in Lake City. Putting the car in park, Jane pulled the keys from the ignition and turned to face her sister. "Do you trust me?"

"Sometimes. Why? What is this place?"

"It's a place to take out your frustrations."

Beth shook her head, but Jane raised a hand.

"Hear me out. Deep breathing and yoga poses are great, but sometimes, you just have to hit something."

"I am not playing paintball."

"Nope. Not paintball." She opened the car door and rounded the car to open Beth's. "Come on. You'll love it."

Reluctantly, Beth climbed out of the car. "I am not doing shots and not getting a tattoo."

"They don't do that here. But those aren't bad ideas for when we're done." Inside, a petite woman stood at a counter behind which hung baseball bats, golf clubs, and sledgehammers. Above them was a sign reading, "Smash away your cares."

"Hey, Jane," the woman greeted them. "Haven't seen you in forever."

"I know! Jocelyn, this is my sister, Beth."

Jocelyn came out from behind the counter, a warm smile on her pretty Latina features. Her hair was cropped short, and tiny studs paraded up the shell of her ears. "First time here?"

Tucking a hank of hair behind her ear, Beth nodded. "Yes. What, umm, do you do here?"

Winking at Jane, Jocelyn picked up a coffee mug and threw it to the floor. Beth jumped back.

"We break things."

Jocelyn moved back around the counter and pulled out paperwork. "We provide gloves, coveralls, and safety goggles. You two have the room for half an hour, and you can break shit to your heart's content." She indicated the items behind her. "Choose your weapon. You can use any and all of these."

Jane filled out the paperwork, one eye on Beth as she roamed the storefront, looking at the glass and ceramic items on the shelves and the porcelain sinks and toilets on the floor. She bent down and looked at the items in a cardboard box. "We can break anything?"

"Pretty much," Jocelyn said. "It depends on how much you want to spend. What's caught your eye?"

Hefting up the box, Beth turned to the other women with a gleam in her eye. "Wedding cake toppers."

"All right!" Jane pumped a fist in the air.

An hour later, the two sisters sat at a table in a small café, cups of tea in front of them.

"Is there anyone you *don't* know?"

Jane shrugged and pointed her thumb over her shoulder. "That woman over there."

Beth glared.

Jane smirked.

"Seriously, how do you know Jocelyn?"

"Her wife works at Amazon. They opened up Smash Sisters a few years ago, and I was at the launch party. Did you enjoy yourself?"

"Very much. It was oddly satisfying to tee up those cake toppers and smash them into the wall."

"Who knew you were a natural at golf." Jane raised her hand for a high-five. Taking Beth to Smash Sisters was a gamble that paid off. Beth looked far more relaxed than she had earlier. "You good?"

"Better. Thank you."

"Not a problem. And we may have found a different venue idea. I'm thinking I-signed-my divorce-papers parties. People can bring their wedding china and smash the shit out of it."

Beth furrowed her brow, eyes unfocused.

"Too soon?"

"Not at all. I'm thinking about where we'd set up. There's not much space for a party."

Jane relaxed. If Beth was thinking logistics, she was going to be okay.

CHAPTER 14

Jane's text came in shortly after nine a.m. **I'm free tonight. Any chance you want to buy a girl a drink?**

Sorry, I'm washing my hair.

You funny guy. Not.

His thumbs flew over the keyboard. **Name the time and place, sugar plum.**

Sugar Plum?

I'm trying out nicknames for you.

Keep trying and I'll see you tonight.

"Yes!" Liam dropped the phone on his desk and swiveled in the creaky old chair. They were finally going to get together, and he couldn't be more excited. It had been way too long since he'd seen her smile. He turned back to his computer, hoping the hours would pass quickly.

A while later, a knock on the open door to his office alerted Liam to Kevin's presence. The slim dark man dropped a coffee in front of Liam and sat with his own in one of the chairs in front of the desk.

"Thanks." Liam sat back in his chair and stretched. "I've

been staring at the screen so long I think my eyes are crossing."

"That's appropriate, Boss Cross."

"Ha ha."

Smirking, Kevin sipped his coffee, then placed it on the desk. "Starting next week, I want to shift my hours."

"Oh, okay." Liam dragged his mind away from the leasing contract in front of him to focus on his assistant. They'd worked together for three years and had settled into a routine where Kevin showed up at 8 a.m. and left around 5 p.m. Liam usually arrived at the same time but often worked later. "What are you thinking?"

Kevin crossed one leg over the other and adjusted the crease in his trousers. "I'll come in at seven-thirty and leave at five, except for Fridays, when I leave at two-thirty. I talked to Devi in HR, and she said it's between you and me what my hours are."

"I don't see a problem with it, except for the fact that you hate getting up early."

The younger man flapped a hand. "I'll have to get used to going to bed earlier. Just stay out of my way until I've had a few cups of coffee."

Liam wrote a note in his planner for the following Monday. "What's happening Friday afternoons? You taking a class in Japanese flower arranging?"

Picking up his coffee mug, Kevin rose from the chair and moved toward the door. "More like French patisserie."

Sipping from his own coffee, Liam watched him leave. Kevin was a dabbler, forever taking classes from salsa dancing to crafting cocktails, usually in a quest to find hot, like-minded men. Baking, though, that was new. For a second, Liam wondered if Jane Beckett would be in the class. He shook his head. She'd be more likely to take a class on knife throwing.

He picked up his phone and opened up the Instagram

page for Grand Gestures. He scrolled through photos from different events before finding one from the paintball birthday party. There was the one of him he'd agreed to, but he stopped at one of Jane surrounded by the girls, head thrown back and laughing at the camera. He studied the photo. God, she was pretty, and she was going out with him tonight. Talking with her was a great way to end the day, but it wasn't the same as being able to see her. Touch her. In the middle of the night, doubts assailed him, and he wondered if it was him. Did she not find him attractive? Was he not her type? Did she have a type?

It had been forever since he'd been interested in a woman, and he was rusty at flirting, but from her reactions, he was pretty sure Jane was interested. If exchanging barbs with her was stimulating, what would it be like to spend time with her? He'd suggested the batting cages because she seemed like a restless spirit, full of energy and enthusiasm. Being with Jane would be an adventure, an adventure he wasn't sure he was up for. He liked his shirts starched and his shoes shined. She liked…he didn't know, but somehow, he thought her world would be looser and more relaxed.

Switching over to the text icon, he shot a message to Chuck.

Hey, want to go for lunch in an hour?
Sure, I'll meet you by the elevators.

That settled, Liam set an alarm for himself and dove back into his reports.

*B*etween bites of his pastrami sandwich, Chuck checked his texts.

"What's up?" Liam asked.

"Give me one second and I'll put this away." Chuck's thumbs flew across the screen, then he dutifully stuffed his phone into his jacket pocket. "Beth and Jane are looking at a storefront down near the Market. I told her not to sign anything until I've looked over the contract."

Why hadn't Jane told him that? Liam tried not to growl.

He was also getting worried that things between Chuck and the pretty blonde were getting serious. Beth was a nice girl and seemed to like Chuck, but she had way too much baggage, and her business had the potential to drain Chuck's bank account, which the dumbass would give to her with a smile. It wasn't in his job description, but Liam believed protecting Chuck from gold diggers was his responsibility. Out loud, he said, "I'm sure Jane can handle the contract."

Holding up a hand while he chewed and swallowed, Chuck replied, "That's who I was texting with. She politely told me to back off. They've been scouting around for a few months and just got approval for a business loan. Meanwhile, they've been cooking out of the kitchen at First AME church. It's got a commercial kitchen, and they've worked out a contract that benefits both GG and the church."

"First AME. Why does that sound familiar?"

"That's the church where Kevin's mother is the office manager. Duncan Properties donated to their breakfast program last year."

"That's rather cozy."

Chuck nodded, oblivious to the snide tone of Liam's comment. "Beth says that Kevin helped them find it. He and Jane are thick as thieves. She says the two of them cackle together constantly."

A stab of something that felt oddly like jealousy shot through Liam. It didn't matter that Kevin was gay; he was still spending time with Jane. Time Liam hadn't been able to. Chuck and Kevin were close, another thread drawing Chuck into the web of the Beckett sisters. Were they using Kevin to get closer to Chuck and his money? Mentally, Liam shook his head. He trusted Kevin, and from what he was learning about Jane and her sister, they were honest. Nobody had a bad thing to say about them or GG. He listened to Chuck blather on about Beth, the wonderful pastries she made, and how much his parents would like her.

"Beth is too busy. I'm hoping to introduce them next week. Beth has never been to Canlis, and you know Mom loves that place."

He went on about how much his mother and Beth had in common while Liam silently stewed, wondering if the pretty blonde was playing the long game and whether his frequent phone calls with Jane were a part of it. Was she deliberately holding him at bay? He didn't think so. She seemed genuinely frustrated that they hadn't been able to sync their calendars up until now. Neither she nor her sister was like the other women who'd taken advantage of Chuck's generous nature, or his own mother, who'd left his father gutted, then continued to hit him up for cash until the day he died. There was a good reason Liam had a hard time trusting women, but after meeting Jane, he was trying.

The bright afternoon sun glinted off the waters of Elliot Bay. Liam rose from his desk to lower the blinds and stood, staring out over the water, lost in thought. He was supposed to review a lease agreement with a new client, but his mind had drifted to Jane and the lease agreement she'd be signing. While he was a little hurt she hadn't brought it up, he understood her stubborn independence and admired her determination. A storefront near Pike Place Market was a huge step up in the world, and if she was negotiating the contract, he was sure it would come out in their favor. He wondered why they didn't go for a space with a commercial kitchen attached, like a restaurant that had gone out of business. God knows, there were plenty of those around. If she didn't bring it up, he'd ask her tonight.

"I'm heading out."

Liam turned at Chuck's words. His best friend looked harried. "What's up?"

Chuck ran a hand through his hair and sighed. "I was going to take Beth out for drinks to celebrate their signing the lease, but it fell through."

"The bank wasn't happy?" Liam turned away from the window and crossed his arms. Despite his misgivings about Beth's motives for dating Chuck, he believed that Grand Gestures was a business that deserved to succeed.

"In a way. Their parents were in an accident, and their RV was damaged. Jane and Beth will have to help them out."

"Any injuries?" Genuine concern underlaid his question. He missed his father every day.

Chuck shook his head. "No, thank God. But they'll have to stay in a hotel until the repairs are made. From what I gather, they don't have the money to pay for it. Beth won't say a word against them, but Jane's livid. I'm not sure about the details, but I'm going to see what I can do to help."

Alarmed, Liam held up a hand. "Are you sure that's a good idea? Beth may not like you throwing money around."

"I have no intention of doing that. Beth has too much pride." Chuck shoved his hands in his pants pockets, looking pleased. "But I do know a storefront near Third and Pine that's available. The property owners are very reasonable." He winked at Liam and turned on his heel.

Liam closed the door to his office and pulled out his phone to text Jane. A strip of masking tape on the back read PERSONAL.

"**H**ey, Mom. You two okay?" Jane put the phone on speaker and set it on top of the dresser. Jane made the bed as her mother chattered away about the accommodations at the Lucky Horse Saloon. While she was relieved neither Steve nor Barbara Beckett had been injured, she was pissed it was up to her to pick up the pieces. She'd arranged towing of her parents' RV, located a repair shop fifty miles from the site of the accident, and made reservations for them at a hotel. The money she and Beth had been saving to pay for the storefront would now be used to repair the RV. Once again, their dreams were put on hold. She'd hoped to surprise Liam with it. Show it off and bask in his praise.

"Jane? Did you hear me?"

"Sorry, Mom. You cut out there for a second." She didn't feel guilty about tuning out her mother.

"I asked when we could expect that money. Your father and I don't want to be a burden, but he'd feel better having a little cash for walking around money."

Jane laughed. "No one uses cash, Mom. Just put it on your credit card." She placed a pillow on the bed and gave it a good karate chop, then picked up another and gave it the same treatment. "Mom? Are you still there?"

"Yes, dear."

"Is there a reason you don't want to use your credit card?" She sat on the edge of the bed and stared at the phone. Sunshine streamed through the window, warming her back, but a chill ran up her spine. Her mother's voice sounded strained.

Her mother cleared her throat. "They're umm, very close to the limit."

"They?" She didn't want to know the answer but asked the question anyway. "How many credit cards do you have?"

When Beckett Bridal Consultants closed down, it was Jane's job to settle the books. She hadn't realized how close to the edge her parents had run the business. Instead of generating income, the final wedding cost them a small fortune. But it wasn't only those bills that needed to be paid. They lived on their line of credit and had taken out a second mortgage on the property. Selling the farm had been a painful necessity. With the proceeds from that, they'd purchased a secondhand RV. Jane then sat them down and explained that they could live the nomadic life comfortably if they were frugal.

"Three?"

Her mother's answer sounded more like a question. A movement drew Jane's attention toward the door. Beth stood silent, shifting her gaze between the phone and Jane.

"How much do you owe on them?"

Her mother mumbled a number.

Beth looked at Jane, eyebrows lifted in a silent question. Jane shook her head.

"Mom, can you repeat that? I didn't hear you."

"I said about fifteen thousand."

Jane's mouth hung open as she stared at Beth. About fifteen thousand, plus the repairs to the RV, plus the cost of putting her parents up at a hotel. They were screwed. To take care of their parents, Grand Gestures would have to say goodbye to renting a storefront. And bringing Kevin in on a full-time basis? Probably not. She stared at the phone, feeling the energy drain from her. Shoulders slumping, she stared down at the floor, unable to move. Beth's foot entered her field of vision, and she heard her sister say, "Mom? Can we call you back in a bit?"

"Sure. Beth, honey, will you be sending some cash today?"

"I don't think so, Mom. You can charge your meals to the hotel room."

"But what about—"

"Not now, Mom," Beth spoke firmly.

"Oh." Their mother cleared her throat. "Okay. We'll talk later."

"Yeah. Bye, Mom." Beth disconnected and turned to kneel in front of Jane. She grasped her sister's hands and squeezed gently.

Jane looked up, not bothering to hide the tears forming in her eyes. "About fifteen thousand? How does that happen? They're living in an RV. What the hell are they spending the money on?" Standing, she brushed past Beth and strode from the room. She needed coffee. Or tequila. Maybe a Valium. "Do you think they're gambling? There are casinos all over the place down there."

"It's possible. But that doesn't sound like them."

Restless, Jane paced the living room. "You're right." She couldn't wrap her head around the amount of money they'd blown through in less than two years. "The how and the why will have to wait. I need to figure out what to do now. I'll—"

"We."

"What?"

Beth moved to stand in front of Jane. "You said I. But it's we. *We* will figure this out. I can do more than make pastries and design invitations. This time, you're not alone. I can certainly help."

"Thank you, but—"

"No buts." Beth placed her hands on Jane's shoulders, looking directly into her eyes. "You will not shoulder the entire burden this time. I know what you were doing when I couldn't get off the couch. You took care of the farm. You took care of the lawsuit. You took care of *me*. This time, I can help. Let me." She gave Jane a little shake before letting go and stepping back. "Now. I'm going to call Mom and Dad. I'll get their credit card information and start looking into it. Then I'll call the repair shop and see what's up with the RV."

Jane wiped her nose on her sleeve. "What do you want me to do?"

"Go for a run or go to a kickboxing class. Just get out of the apartment and work off some of that frustration. We will take care of this."

"Punching something sounds like an excellent idea." She walked back into the bedroom and changed, trying not to think about her parents' mess. Beth was right; *they* would take care of this. She kicked herself mentally. Why the hell hadn't she checked in on them more often? When they first hit the road, she'd look at their bank statements. They were being frugal while still enjoying themselves. Then she and Beth started GG, which took up every waking moment, so she slacked off from worrying about her parents. Now they'd blown through their savings and maxed out three credit cards.

She pounded the pavement for an hour, trying not to think of anything but avoiding being hit by a car or bicycle. But she was anxious; she was used to making the decisions. She'd run them past Beth, but her sister would generally agree. Jane fully expected to find Beth standing in the doorway, ready to thrust the problem into her hands when she returned.

Liam's text arrived just as she was pulling out her keys. **Chuck told me about your parents. Everything okay?**

It took a few seconds for her to respond. This, this is what she appreciated. Having someone interested enough to check in with her. **Yeah. Thanks. No injuries, thank God.**

I'm assuming this means we're off for tonight?

"Damn it." With all that had happened, she'd forgotten about their date. The date she'd set up, anticipating sharing her good news. Now, there wasn't anything to share. But she could still see him and sit across a candlelit table from his handsome face. He might be the perfect cure for a shitty day. She typed back, **Let me get back to you.**

Straightening her shoulders, she opened the door to hear Beth on the phone using her kitchen commander voice. Jane had only ever heard it when they were working a job and Beth oversaw the waitstaff. She pretty much turned it off when a job was over.

Jane moved from the foyer into the living area and saw Beth seated at the counter. Her back toward her, she faced her computer, her cell phone beside her in speaker mode. Her tone was calm and patient but assertive. "Dad and Mom, I need you to listen carefully. A fax is going to come through to the hotel from each of the credit card companies. It's the authorization for me to act in your stead and for them to correspond directly with me. You both need to sign it and fax it back."

"Where do we do that? How are we going to know when to do that? The hotel has been so nice to us, I don't want to bother them."

"Mom, the hotel manager is named Carla. She has your cell phone number and will call you when the fax comes in. She will take care of this."

"Button, thanks for doing this," Stephen Beckett's voice boomed out. For some reason, he'd never learned that speaking loudly into a phone wasn't necessary. "Your mom and I really appreciate your help. Until this mess is figured out, can you send me a little walking around money? I'd like to be able to—"

"No, Dad."

Jane blinked. She'd never heard Beth speak sharply to her parents. She rounded the counter and got a glass of water. Turning to lean against the opposite counter, she watched Beth. Her sister rolled her eyes and grimaced.

"We can't send you any cash."

"You said you had lots of business. Surely, you can spare—"

"We have workers to pay and supplies to purchase. Jane and I are already paying off your bills and cannot give you spending money on top of that."

"What are we supposed to do? You won't let us use the credit cards. You won't send me cash. Do you want me to panhandle? Have your mother make up a sign for me and I'll stand on the street corner?"

Jane opened her mouth to speak, but Beth held up a hand to stop her.

"Your social security checks are automatically deposited into your account on the last day of the month. You'll have cash then."

"But that's two days away!"

"You'll live. Now I have to call the repair shop. I'll talk to you later." Beth disconnected. She scrubbed her hands over her face and growled.

"What did they do?" Jane retrieved Beth's coffee mug and refilled it.

"Thanks." She took a sip and sat back. "I can't decide if they're incredibly gullible or just terrible with money. Mom started going to church about seven months ago."

"I remember that. They'd stopped somewhere in Arizona and decided to stay there for a few weeks. Then when they were back on the road, she'd watch the services on Facebook."

"Right. The pastor messaged her a welcome, and they started chatting. While Dad was driving, Mom would put Sister Margot on speaker, and they would talk. She asked lots of questions—"

"All very friendly, I imagine."

Beth nodded. "Yep. They'd have these long conversations about life and the state of the world, and wasn't it a shame that others weren't as fortunate as they were."

"Let me guess. The pastor asked for a donation."

"Nope. She was too smart for that. Hang on." Beth typed into her laptop and turned the screen for Jane to see it. The website for Southwest Savior Church came up. Jane clicked through the site, noting that the worship area was modest yet attractive. There were many groups that people could join for fellowship and opportunities to serve the community. She found a picture of Sister Margot. A white woman who appeared to be in her sixties, with long, silver-gray hair hanging in a braid over her shoulder, warm eyes, and a warm smile, looked directly at the camera.

"She doesn't look like a nut bar." She clicked and found a video of Sister Margot surrounded by a group of Latinx children. Apparently, the church was building a school and needed funds. "Is this where Mom is sending her money?"

"Yeah. Sister Margot asked if they wanted to stop by one day and see how the build was coming along. They have work parties once a month. Mom and Dad were two states away at that time, so Mom said she'd send a donation instead." Beth reached over and brought up the donation page. "Way down at the bottom is a box you have to check if you don't want this to be a recurring payment."

"You have to opt out?"

Beth nodded, looking grim. "Yeah. Mom and Dad have been giving $750.00 every two weeks."

"Holy shit!"

"Exactly. It came right out of their bank account. They didn't realize what was happening until Dad tried to use the debit card, and it was rejected. They were too embarrassed to tell us—"

"And started living off credit cards." Jane stared back at Beth. "Are they still giving to the church?"

"Yes! Sister Margot called Mom when the money stopped coming in. I don't know what she said, but Mom apologized. Then she gave her a credit card number. But get this, Sister Margot said they could reduce the donation amount to five hundred dollars so it wouldn't be a hardship."

"How kind of her." Jane stood and stepped back to lean against the counter, trying to absorb the magnitude of the money. "Is there any way to get it back?"

Beth shook her head. "I don't know. What I'm doing right now is talking to the credit card companies. I want to freeze their accounts to stop more payments from going out. We're going to have to talk to a lawyer."

"Maybe we should bring them back here. Take whatever money we can get for the RV and put them up in an apartment."

Proving their minds worked along the same path, Beth asked, "Are we going to have to fire Kevin?"

"Maybe? I sure as hell don't want to. Let's not do that yet. But there won't be a storefront in our future for a long time."

Picking up her phone, Beth said, "That reminds me. Chuck had a couple for us to look at. I need to tell him we can't."

"Don't tell him about Mom and Dad." Chuck was way too sweet and would probably offer to bail their parents out.

"He already knows they were in an accident." Beth frowned. "He was so sweet when I told him. He's been texting me for updates."

"That's fine. Just don't tell Chuck about them giving their money away. It's just—"

"I know. It's embarrassing to admit our parents were so easily led astray."

"Yeah."

Jane hit the shower, letting the warm water beat some of the tension out of her shoulders. The face of Tony the Asswipe, Beth's ex-husband, popped into her thoughts. Their father had hired him as a photographer, and he'd wheedled his way into her mother's favor and into her sister's heart. He had great ideas about using the farm for photoshoots other than weddings. At the time, Jane was working at Amazon and wasn't paying much attention. Her parents and Beth were happy, and she was caught up in her own life in the city.

Cleaning up the mess after the last wedding, Jane discovered that Tony had taken advantage of Barbara Beckett's generosity and purchased expensive camera and computer equipment with company funds. He claimed they were in lieu of a salary, and there wasn't a paper trail to prove otherwise. When the dust settled, he made off with thirty thousand dollars' worth of equipment.

Jane shut off the water and tried to blot out the festering memory. She and Beth were working together this time. Hopefully, there wouldn't be more damage. Heading to her room, she heard Beth talking on the phone in a soft voice, probably with Chuck, and her thoughts turned to Liam. She couldn't face him tonight. She'd probably burst into tears if he said something sympathetic. She was such an unattractive crier he'd probably go running for the door. If she ever wanted a real date with the man, she couldn't afford to fall apart in front of him. Finding her phone, she texted to apologize and say she wouldn't be able to make it. Then she turned off her phone, crawled into bed, and cried into her pillow.

ith a perfunctory knock on the open door, Liam walked into Chuck's office. "Do you have time to go over the costs of upgrading that strip mall on Aurora? It looks like a total retrofit for the electrical."

"Hmm?" Chuck peered up at him distractedly. His hair was a mess, his shirt was buttoned incorrectly, and his eyes were circled with fatigue.

Liam sank into a chair on the other side of the desk. "What the hell, man? You look like shit." His eyes darted around the office, taking in the collection of empty coffee mugs and the heap of file folders stacked haphazardly on the credenza. "What's going on?"

Chuck slumped forward, pushing his face into his hands and scrubbing it; the rasp of whiskers sounded. He mumbled something.

"What was that?" Liam leaned forward.

Removing his hands from his face, Chuck pointed at the phone. "She doesn't want my help. I found four properties that would make an excellent storefront for GG, crunched the numbers to find an amount they could afford, and she said no." He shot Liam a lopsided smile. "She was very sweet and polite, saying how much she appreciated what I'd done but said, and I quote, they've 'decided to go in another direction.' I don't know what 'another direction' means. I asked, but she won't talk to me. In fact, she won't take my calls. I know her parents are stranded in Arizona while waiting for their RV to be fixed, so I don't think it's that. She texted that something came up, and I haven't heard from her for two days."

"She's not responding to your texts?"

"Oh, she responds. She'll send me a thumbs-up. Or says, 'talk later.' And she's not playing *Words with Friends*. We've been playing *Words with Friends* every day for the last few months."

Liam studied his friend, wondering what game Beth was playing. "She's not ghosting you?"

He shrugged. "Nope. She just won't…let me in."

The man looked like a whipped puppy. Liam had seen it before. Damsels in distress attracted Chuck like a magnet. There was the time a girl had, in her words, gotten behind in her rent because she was helping a sick relative, and Chuck put her up at a hotel. The credit card he'd put down for the room charges was maxed out after four days. The girl had bought a complete wardrobe at the hotel's boutique and taken off with all the linens from the hotel room. Liam had consoled his heartbroken friend, settled with the hotel, and hunted down the girl. She'd sold off everything and was living quite comfortably in West Seattle. For an extra thousand dollars, she promised never to contact Chuck again. Liam paid for that out of his own pocket, considering it money well spent. He wondered what Beth was up to. He couldn't give a shit if she was in trouble; his concern was for Chuck. But how to say that without sounding like a douche? He got up from the chair and moved toward the door.

"Come on. You need a change of scenery."

Chuck shook his head. "No. I'm fine."

"No, you're not. Besides, it smells in here. Let's go to my office."

Reaching for his phone, Chuck rose from his chair. Liam wanted to tell him to leave it but decided against saying anything. He led his friend past his assistant's desk, smiled absently when Kevin looked up, and closed his office door after Chuck entered the room. Chuck wandered over to the window and gazed out at the Sound. "How come you have a better view than I do?"

"Because I'm more important than you."

Chuck's lips tipped up at the snarky comeback, but he didn't respond. Liam walked over to stand next to him and waited for him to speak. In the distance, two ferries crossed paths, taking people to and from their busy lives.

"I think she's the one."

Liam bumped shoulders with his friend. He'd heard variations of that phrase multiple times. Not every woman Chuck fell for was after his money; he just gave his heart away too quickly. He'd purchased a ring and proposed to one who was a research scientist. She turned him down to take a job in Iceland. Chuck had been morose for months when she left. Liam did not want to see him put through the grinder again. He said, "I didn't know it had gotten that far."

"She's kind and thoughtful. Generous—did you know she cooks and serves meals for a church on Sunday mornings?" He glanced at Liam as if in wonder. "Doesn't bitch and complain. She's interested in me. She's started listening to the same podcasts I do...."

"And she's very pretty."

"That too."

Shoving his hands in his pocket, Liam turned to lean against the window frame. "Jane told me she had an awful divorce. Does Beth talk about it?"

Chuck grimaced. "The photographer? I'd like to hunt him

down and beat the shit out of him. I don't understand how he could do that to Beth. She's perfect."

"Do you think her not talking to you has anything to do with that?"

"I don't see how."

Liam picked his words carefully; trash talking Beth was not the goal. "From what I understand, she was extremely fragile. Has she done a lot of dating since then?"

He shook his head. "No. I'm the first guy she's felt comfortable with."

"Do you think you're moving too quickly?"

"No! We haven't even had sex. Mostly she works nights, and we talk on the phone more than we see each other. We've kissed at the end of a date, but she lives with her sister."

Liam held up a hand. "I get it." He hadn't even got to kiss Jane yet.

"I was planning on having her over on Sunday afternoon. I'd cook for her, and hopefully, we'd go from there. But she says she can't make it." He pulled his phone out of his pocket and checked it. Sighing, he stuffed it back in again.

"She sounds skittish."

Chuck's brows furrowed together. "Maybe."

"She might have too much going on right now to commit to a relationship. Growing a business takes a lot of energy."

"I know. But I can help with that. I could be a silent partner or loan—"

"Beth and Jane have too much pride for that. I get the feeling they want to succeed on their own." He pulled his hands out of his pockets and crossed his arms. "Maybe if you give her some space." Jane had been oddly reticent as well, begging off from their phone calls and slow to respond to his texts. He knew she had a lot going on, so he had dismissed it. Did she want space?

Chuck jerked back. "Do you think that's what she wants?"

He answered his own internal question. "No idea, man. But if she's not talking to you and she's canceling dates…."

"Should I ask her what she wants?"

Liam shrugged. "Maybe. Or maybe leave her alone until she contacts you? If she doesn't, then I guess you have your answer."

Scrubbing his hands over his face, Chuck let out a huge sigh. He nodded and turned to the door, closing it quietly behind him.

"It's for the best," Liam muttered, rubbing a hand over his chest. Was that really the case? Jane was settling things with her parents, and he understood. Truly, he did. They weren't in a relationship, and he shouldn't expect her to share everything with him, although he'd like her to. He pulled out his phone and looked at their string of texts. He had initiated each conversation for the past week. Jane's responses were either one word, emojis, or memes. Why hadn't he noticed that? Maybe he'd take his own advice.

For the next few days, he made it a point to check in with Chuck. Each time, Chuck shook his head wordlessly. Liam felt a guilty sense of satisfaction; Chuck would get over it, and he would, too. He'd survived quite nicely without Jane Beckett in his world, and he'd do so again.

An incoming text drew his attention. Seeing it was from Jane, his hand shot out, then he quickly drew it back. He wasn't going to dance to her tune. He turned his phone over and pushed it aside. It pinged again. And again. "Fine." He picked it up to read the messages.

Hey, sorry about the radio silence the last few days but I've been inundated. I'm at the healthcare pop-up today, can I buy you a coffee?

Actually, make you a coffee. I'm working the coffee cart.

Hello? All right. Well, I'm down here if you want to stop by. Or not.

He had no idea what she was talking about and wasn't sure if he wanted to answer.

His calendar app pinged with a reminder. The healthcare pop-up was due to start in one hour. He could have summoned Kevin into his office, but he needed to stretch his legs. He poked his head out the open door and asked, "Do you know anything about this healthcare pop-up?"

Kevin turned away from his monitor, smoothing the lilac tie that was a shade darker than his immaculate dress shirt. "Mrs. Duncan is using the vacant storefront downstairs to host an event. Healthcare providers are donating their time to provide services. Hang on." He turned back to his screen and clicked through until he found a website with the information. "They're doing dental and medical checkups, vision screening, mental health counseling, VA assistance, haircuts, handing out hygiene kits, and offering coffee and donuts."

"That's ambitious. Carol Lee is doing that? Which agency is hosting it?" He knew she served on several boards for nonprofits in the Seattle area, but this was the first time he'd heard of something this big.

"Not one specific agency. There are a lot represented at the event, but Duncan Properties is hosting it. Mrs. Duncan and Jane Beckett have been working on it. It's quite the organizational feat. The list of sponsors is impressive."

Liam muttered, "I'm sure the bill from Grand Gestures will be impressive as well."

"They're not charging. Look at this." He clicked on the list of sponsors. In large print, Duncan Properties was listed at the top. At the very bottom, right below Sassy Styles, was Grand Gestures. "Jane's not being paid for her work. Not everything is about profit." He flicked a glance at Liam, then went back to work.

Once again, Liam had been put in his place by his

assistant. It didn't feel any better this time. He slunk back into his office and thought about Jane's text. Maybe that's why she hadn't reached out.

Hearing Kevin leave his desk, Liam strode to the stairway. He clattered down fifteen floors to emerge in the foyer, expecting chaos. Expecting to see street people milling about, filling up the space with shopping carts and backpacks and blocking the sidewalk. The storefront had been previously occupied by a cooking supply store and was a good size, with a glass wall and entrance from the foyer and doors opening onto the street. While there were a lot of people, they were not milling about. Young people and senior citizens wearing vests saying ASK ME were moving about, chatting to the street people, jotting on clipboards, and escorting them to various spaces.

Realizing he was in the way, Liam moved across the foyer to stand against the wall and observe. A coffee cart was right on the street, a short distance from the doors. A head of dark hair moved behind it. The head turned, the hair moving in a familiar manner to reveal the face that had been haunting his dreams for weeks. He shifted to the side to see more clearly. Jane was operating the espresso machine with casual skill, laughing and chatting with the people in line. He watched while she made drinks and served them to people heading into the health clinic and those who took them and walked off. She treated volunteers and clients with the same level of respect.

He hadn't seen her in weeks, but that didn't mean he hadn't thought about her. He missed their conversations. He'd wondered how her parents were doing and how the business was going. Had they found a storefront they could afford? Were they in a position where they could even think about one? Deciding to wait for her to reach out to him had been agonizing. Now that she was here, he could stroll on over and ask her in person.

She smiled at a man in an expensive suit while making another drink. Whatever he said made her throw her head back and laugh. Liam growled. The man in the suit said something else, and Jane shot him a flirty look while handing him a coffee cup. In exchange, the suit gave Jane a business card and stuffed cash into a jar sitting on the side of the cart. Liam's blood boiled.

The suit stepped aside, making room for the next customer. But instead of placing an order, the new customer snatched up the jar of cash and darted off down the sidewalk. Not thinking, Liam dashed out the door of the building and gave chase. The thief wove between pedestrians and shoved others out of the way. He glanced back and spotted Liam, then turned and picked up the pace. Liam swore and cursed his choice of shoes. Perfect for the boardroom, they had no traction and were useless in a foot race. Rounding a corner, he almost lost his balance, but damn it, he was not going to give up. Up ahead, a delivery van emerged from an alley, and the thief skidded to a halt. Liam doubled his effort and was on him in three strides. Arm extended, he grabbed the thief by the shirt collar and jerked him back.

"What the—" The pimply-faced, young white kid glared up at Liam.

Liam shook him like a dog. He was too angry to speak. Still holding the thief by the back of his shirt, he marched him back down the sidewalk.

"I didn't do nothing to you. Let me go!"

"No. You're going to give the money back."

"That's bullshit." The kid tried to shake loose, but Liam held him tighter. "I need it more than they do."

"Yeah? Then get a job. That's what people do when they need money. They work. And that money you stole? It's being donated to a soup kitchen."

"I didn't know that," the kid whined.

Liam pointed at the jar the kid clutched like a football. "Seriously? It says so right on there."

"Oh. Well then, here. You take it back."

"Uh-uh." Liam marched him around the corner and toward his building. "You're going to apologize."

"Oh shit," they said in unison. A clearly pissed Jane Beckett bore down on them.

❄

The morning was going so well. Mrs. Duncan was a pleasure to work with, and it was a shame Beth couldn't be here; the two women would have gotten on like a house on fire.

Flirting with the cute guy in the coffee line was fun, though not nearly as fun as poking at Liam Cross. She scanned the crowd, wondering if he was around. He hadn't responded to her text. Maybe he hadn't seen it. Or maybe he was annoyed she hadn't been available the last few days. With Beth being down in Arizona, Jane had been too busy to even pee. Mrs. Duncan was a lovely woman, but organizing this event had been a bit of a nightmare.

She gnawed on her lip, knowing full well that being busy wasn't an excuse. She just didn't know what to say to Liam. *Oh, hi, my flaky parents went through all their money and we have to bail them out and now our business might go belly up?* It was pathetic, and she hated being pathetic. However, Beth was on her way home, and they had kind of sort of a plan. They'd have to tighten their belts even more than they already were, but they'd make it.

Distracted by her thoughts, she didn't notice the shifty movements of a scrawny kid in the coffee line. With his shaved head and wearing tattered jeans, broken-down sneakers, and an oversized hoodie in dire need of a wash, he looked like the kind of client the clinic was meant to attract, those who lived on the street. She flicked a smile his way, then turned back to the cute guy, who had moved away from the front of the line and around to the side of the cart.

The kid chose that moment to make his move, snatching the money jar, shoving someone aside, and racing down the sidewalk.

"Hey!" Trapped behind the coffee cart and blocked in by the cute guy, all Jane could do was stare after the thief. She muscled her way past the cute guy and made it around to the front of the cart, dismayed but not surprised the money had been stolen. She heard a noise and turned to see Liam take off like a strong safety after a wide receiver off the line of scrimmage. Wonder turned to concern, then turned to fear. She ran after the two, hoping like hell no one would get hurt.

Unwilling to cross the busy street against the light, she waited impatiently for the walk signal, cursing the thief, the cute guy, Liam, and all men everywhere. The light changed, and she darted across. Squeezing through pedestrians, she approached the corner.

Relief flooded through her at the sight greeting her. Clutching a scruffy youth, a pissed-off Liam marched toward her. Pristine white shirt wrinkled and pulled from his trousers, dark hair tumbling over his forehead, he'd never looked better. Check that. It was a close second to the bemused and helpless look he wore when the preteen girls were attempting to teach him the floss.

She stomped toward them. "What the hell were you thinking?"

Liam reared back, but she steamed ahead, not allowing him to speak.

"You could have gotten yourself killed. Running through the streets like a comic book crime fighter. That was stupid."

"Stupid?" He got into her face, eyes snapping with fury. "You were robbed. I was getting it back for you. You should be thanking me."

"Thanking you? It was money. It wasn't worth you risking your life."

"Does that mean I can keep it?" Dangling from Liam's big hand, the thief looked hopeful.

"Shut up," Jane and Liam said at the same time.

Curious onlookers stopped to watch. Jane ignored them, focused on venting her fury. "You could have run into someone or been hit by a car—"

"He chased me into a truck."

"Shut up!" Liam shook the thief.

"Is there a problem here?"

Jane turned at the sound of the new voice, ready to snap at them. Two cops leaned against their bicycles, the Black officer removing her helmet while her partner, a slim Asian man, watched the trio, his hand resting on his gun.

"This…this idiot—" Jane waved her arm at Liam.

"Chased down the thief who robbed you!" Liam glared at her. "How the hell is that a bad thing?"

"You could have…." Jane sputtered and turned away, shaking her head.

"What? What would you have had me do?"

"Sir." The female officer stepped forward. "I'll take the suspect, and my partner will get your statement. You and your wife can fight this out at home."

"Or in a therapist's office," the thief mumbled.

Jane stepped to the side, arms crossed and hands stuffed in her armpits. She was still shaking. Watching Liam run through traffic had nearly given her heart failure. She waited while he gave his statement, gave her own, and turned to find him scowling at her. She stalked past him. No match for his long legs, he caught up with her in a half dozen steps. "What the hell is wrong with you?"

Flicking her bangs, she stared straight ahead and ignored him. He kept pace with her, glancing at her now and then in confused silence.

The coffee cart was in sight. A volunteer worked behind it while a group of others huddled together, shooting worried looks their way.

Dredging up a smile, Jane called out, "It's all good. Our hero saved the day." She gestured at Liam and held the jar of money aloft. A cheer went up as she placed the money jar on top of the coffee cart. Turning, she saw a scowling Liam waiting by the door of the building. Huffing out a sigh, she joined him, stepping close to avoid the people around them. "When he grabbed the money, it shocked the shit out of me. It took me a bit to get out from behind the cart, and when I did, I saw you. You ran through oncoming traffic, and then I saw you almost go down going around that corner." She looked down.

"You were scared for me?" Liam rumbled out.

She nodded, reliving the moment he disappeared around the corner and tires screeched in alarm. She looked up to see his smirk. Eyes narrowing, she poked him in the chest. "No. Not worried for you. The write-up for the event would have been crap if you had been hurt. You becoming road pizza would have edged out any good press we got."

"You tell yourself that." His smirk turned into a grin, and he booped her on the nose. "It's good to see you. Can you get away for a minute or two?"

The volunteer at the coffee cart seemed to be doing fine. "Sure."

He took her by the hand and led her into the coffee shop proper. Acknowledging the baristas with a wave, he took her to a table in the back and pulled out a chair for her.

"Thanks," she said.

"I've missed talking to you." He propped his elbows on the table and folded his hands. "Are you okay?"

"Yeah."

"Things all right with your parents?"

"They will be."

He pressed his thumb and finger to the bridge of his nose. "Getting information out of a teenager is easier than this. You do realize that's what couples do? Tell each other stuff."

She peeked up at him from beneath her bangs. "Are we…a couple?"

"I'd like to be. At least find out if we could be. You?"

A scratch in the tabletop absorbed all her attention. She had a crappy track record at dating. Men found her abrasive and aggressive, probably for a good reason, but didn't want to see beneath that hard surface.

"When Beth and I started Grand Gestures, we decided not to do weddings. We do engagement parties and anniversary parties but not weddings. And it's not because of the shit show that was the last event she did with my parents. After they had to shut down the business, I paid the bills and cleaned up the books." She shifted in her seat, glancing at Liam, then back down at the table. "In a file cabinet, I found a record book that my mother kept. It listed the names of each bride and groom and the date they married. There was a column for the cost of the weddings and a final column listing divorce dates. A lot of those joyful celebrations ended unhappily. Way too many. It seemed disingenuous to encourage elaborate, expensive weddings when, at the back of my mind, I was estimating how long before the marriage ended.

"I know that not all relationships are doomed." She was pretty sure Chuck and Beth were going to make it. "There are couples who have been together forever. I'm sure there are days my mother would happily smother my dad with a pillow, but I know she loves him." She grinned up at Liam. "What about your parents? Are they still together?"

"My dad died ten years ago in a car accident."

She waited quietly, knowing there was more. He unfolded his hands and splayed them on the tabletop. "Dad was an accountant for a small lumber mill up in Skagit County. My parents split when I was eight. Mom took off. She'd show up on my birthday every now and then, but I never counted on it. It was just my dad and me."

She clutched her hands tightly to prevent herself from reaching out for his. "They never remarried?"

"Mom remarried many times. She's currently on husband number five. I think they live in Phoenix. Dad never remarried and never dated." A muscle ticked in his jaw. "When I cleaned out his place after he died, I went through his computer files. He kept meticulous records, and it was easy to take care of paying off bills and closing accounts. I found a file folder in his desk with my mom's name on it. In it were greeting cards and postcards from her. Breezy messages about how she was doing but could possibly use a little help. Stapled to each card was a canceled check." He shot Jane a hard look. "Right up until the month before he died, my dad was sending my mother money. She showed up at the funeral in this big black hat, sobbing all over the place. She hugged Chuck, thinking it was me."

Not thinking, Jane untangled her fingers and flattened them on the table. "She sounds like a piece of work."

"That she is." He flexed his hands, the tips of his fingers almost touching the tips of hers, before pulling back. "The first card from her arrived in the mail two months after the funeral. I read it, then shredded it. After that, when a card arrived, I just tossed them without opening them."

She inched her hands across the table and waited, watching Liam's face. His lips twitched, then he did the same. The tiny physical contact dispelled the tension surrounding them.

"It appears we both have a cynical view about marriage"— he pulled her hands toward him, engulfing them in his own — "and we may not make it as a couple. But I'd like to see more of you and try it. I want conversations with you that run a little deeper than whether the Mariners will make it to the playoffs. I want you to share what's on your mind."

He squeezed her hands. "Do you want to try that?"

Did she want to be the focus of his attention? Yes. Did she want him to hold her hands again? Yes. Did she want to see him without a shirt on? Hell yes.

She nodded and squeezed back.

"Good." His gaze heated as he looked at her lips. "Any chance you're free tonight?"

She nodded again. Beth was back, and no doubt, she and Chuck would be spending the evening together.

"Good." He tugged her out of the chair and held her hand on the way out the door. In the foyer, he leaned down and kissed her on the cheek. "Call me when you're free."

He headed to the elevator, and she returned to the pop-up, her heart going pitter-pat the entire time.

CHAPTER 16

"**A**ren't you the hero," Kevin said from the doorway to Liam's office.

Liam shot him a smug look and sat back in his chair. Jane had been worried. Chasing a punk through traffic was an asinine decision, but the look on her face had been worth it. Warmth filled his chest. If they hadn't been surrounded by people in the foyer, he would have done more than kiss her on the cheek. He could hardly wait for tonight. "Someone had to be."

"I wasn't sure if Jane was going to choke you or hug you. She was so pissed at you. She couldn't get out from behind the coffee cart fast enough."

"Probably pissed she wasn't able to do it herself."

Kevin chuckled. "Yeah. The woman is a badass. But she can sweet talk clients. Watching her is a lesson in marketing."

"You've been with her while she meets with clients?" Liam watched Kevin's eyes light up.

"Not at the interview stage. But during events." He held up a hand. "Purely on my own time, boss. I've worked a few events on weekends with them. The clients get worked up about stuff, and Jane is a master at talking them down. They, in turn, sing her praises to their friends."

"That's the best form of advertising. Are they paying you to work?"

Kevin gave him a look. "Of course! I love those women, but I am not giving up my Saturday nights without compensation." Then he sobered. "Something's up, though. Business is good for them. I see it myself. But Jane is tense. She's barely smiled all week." He shook his head and stared at his phone.

Liam watched the younger man, waiting for him to continue. Was this why she hadn't called him? And why was his personal assistant working for her? He and Kevin had a good working relationship, but in all that time, he'd never seen Kevin quite so animated, at least not about the job. He'd fallen under the spell of the Beckett sisters as well, it seemed. Should he worry about that? No. They couldn't possibly offer Kevin the salary and benefits that he had at Duncan Properties. He and Jane had so much to talk about this evening.

"Oh, good."

"Sorry?" Liam asked when Kevin's words drew his attention.

He looked up from his phone. "Beth's at the airport. She went down to Arizona to help their parents and somehow managed to break her phone. Jane has been worried sick. Hopefully, things will get back to normal." He moved away from the doorway.

Liam stared at Kevin's retreating back. Beth had been out of town. Without a phone. Unable to make calls. Oh shit. He shoved his chair back and strode toward Chuck's office. Without knocking, he walked in. A grim-faced Chuck was placing his phone on his desk.

"I took your advice. She hasn't responded to a single text in over five days. So I let her know that if she'd wanted space, she should have told me, and that I won't be calling her again."

"Just now?" All the good feelings that had been warming Liam's belly slunk away. He saw his plans for the evening slipping away as well. Swallowing hard, he sank into the chair in front of the desk.

"Yeah. I left a voice mail." Chuck rubbed the back of his neck and slumped back in his chair. "I knew she wasn't going to be at the health clinic downstairs, so I went to her apartment this morning and knocked on the door. No one answered, and as much as I wanted to tell her face-to-face, I figured that was the next best thing. I didn't want to wait any longer. I need to put her behind me." The resolute tone of his voice was not reflected in his posture.

"She's been—"

"Where the hell is he?" Jane's voice rang out.

Through the open doorway, Liam saw her stride across the floor, head twisting from side to side as she searched the inner offices. Kevin rose from his desk and approached her. But Jane wasn't to be stopped. She sidestepped him, calling out, "Where's the gutless wonder?"

"Liam?"

"No. The other one—Chuck."

Liam and Chuck rose from their chairs, Chuck looking alarmed, Liam feeling guilty. Their movement must have caught her attention because, in a flash, Jane was at the door. Liam put out his hands to stop her, but she slipped past him to get at Chuck. Chuck scrambled back behind his desk, putting his chair between himself and the angry woman.

"What did you do to my sister? I spent the morning with your mother to come home and find Beth curled into a ball and sobbing her eyes out. You left a voicemail to break up with her? What kind of asswipe does that?"

"Jane—"

"No!"

Liam tried to grab her arm, but she shook him off and rounded on him. "What's wrong with you people? Is our work too grubby? Too beneath you? We don't swan around in offices with three-hundred-dollar haircuts?" She swung back to Chuck. "She goes out of town for a week and you kick her to the curb? Is your attention span that short?"

"He didn't know." Liam placed himself in front of her, forcing her to look at him. "Chuck didn't know she was out of town."

Hair wild and eyes blazing, she glared up at him. "How the hell not?" She leaned past him to address Chuck. "You two text constantly."

He bobbed his head. "Yes, but she didn't say she was going out of town. Just that she had to take care of some things. And then she stopped texting and answering my calls." Palms up, he stretched his hands out to her. "She just stopped. No explanation."

"She broke her phone. She said that in the email."

Chuck's eyebrows furrowed together. "Email? I didn't get it."

"Uh. Yeah!" Jane's hands went to her hips. "I know she did because I was CC'd on it."

Pivoting the chair around, Chuck sat down and searched his email. "I didn't get it. And look, it's not in my junk mail, either."

Liam shifted to the side and both he and Jane leaned over Chuck's shoulders.

"There." Jane stabbed at the screen. "The one from EBbakes1955."

Chuck clicked on it. In great detail, Beth explained about being in a tiny town in Arizona and how her dad stepped on her phone and that email was the best way to reach her. Chuck slumped in the chair and stared at Jane. "I didn't recognize the email address. I was looking for one from Grand Gestures."

Jane shook her head. "We never use company email for personal stuff. Regardless. It was only a few days. You could have asked me or Kevin. Instead, you broke up with her."

Chuck turned, switching his gaze from Jane to Liam. "I thought…he said…."

It was time to man up. Liam inhaled deeply and stepped forward. "It's my fault. Chuck was worried because Beth seemed to be growing distant, and I suggested she needed some space. You said yourself that she hadn't dated since her divorce, and I thought they might have been moving too fast and she was getting cold feet."

Jane studied his face, her expression stony. "It took Beth a long time to open her heart again. You knew how vulnerable she was." She stared at Chuck, then back at Liam, eyes widening. "She was head over heels for Chuck, and you thought she was stealing your best friend."

"No. He never said that. He said you two were engrossed in growing your business and she didn't have time for a relationship. And you had some troubles and she wouldn't let me help." Chuck's words were not helping Liam out. "I could help you secure a storefront. That's what we do here. But Beth wouldn't let me. And then she went away and wasn't responding to my texts or calls. And Liam said—"

"Liam said," she sneered. "Can you not think for yourself? You could have asked me, for God's sake. What did you think? That she was playing games?" She whipped her head around and gasped, piercing Liam with her glare. "That's it. You thought Beth was playing Chuck. That she was using him to get to his money. That's what all this has been about. That's why you scrutinized everything about the anniversary party. You thought Chuck was a mark."

Her rising voice was drawing a crowd. Kevin stood at the door to Chuck's office, watching the back and forth with wide eyes. Behind him, a gaggle of staff with shocked faces listened with rapt attention.

Dismay and frustration fought with anger as Liam tried to speak over Jane. "No!" he thundered. In the sudden silence, he looked at Kevin, who shook his head, a fierce frown taking over his dark, handsome face. "I asked you what was going on, and you blew me off. If you had told me, none of this would have happened."

Jane opened her mouth to reply, but Liam was on a roll, furious at himself for leaping to conclusions and at Jane for never telling him a damn thing.

"As for Chuck, he gives his heart away too easily and has been hurt too often. I've looked after him and cleaned up after him like you did for Beth, and I was protecting him."

"I don't need protection," Chuck ground out and pushed past Jane to stand face-to-face with Liam, fierce determination on his face.

The two friends glared at each other, and Liam realized the enormity of his mistake.

"You're right. I give my heart away easily, and I have been hurt. But this is different. Beth is different. You should have seen that. If you really cared about me—me and not *Duncan Properties*—you would have told me to look for the simple solution and not jump to conclusions." He stepped around Liam and went to the coat tree in the corner, grabbing his jacket and stuffing his arms into the sleeves.

"I'm not a child, and I don't need protection. What I needed was a friend. You've been so busy brooding because you haven't got the balls to take a chance on love and risk hurting yourself. You think everyone is out to further their own agenda. Get your head out of your ass."

Chuck turned and grabbed the phone off his desk. "Jane, I am so sorry for being an idiot. Now, if you'll excuse me, I'm going to see if Beth will possibly forgive me."

Reaching into a pocket, Jane extracted a ring of keys. She pulled one off and tossed it to Chuck. "Here. Let yourself in and leave the door unlocked. I'll be home in a couple hours."

Chuck grabbed the key and jerked his chin at her. Without looking at Liam, he brushed past Kevin, through the throng of employees, and strode to the elevator.

A sinking feeling settled in the pit of Liam's stomach. He looked at Jane. She appeared to be having a silent conversation with Kevin. The younger man nodded.

Turning, Kevin said to the crowd, "Drama's over. Let's get back to work." He glanced once over his shoulder, switching his gaze between Liam and Jane, then went back to his desk.

"Jane, I—" Liam reached out a hand, but she shouldered past him, posture erect and jaw tight.

"Don't. I feel the need to hit something, and if you don't get out of my way, it's going to be you."

"Then hit me. I certainly deserve it. I know it won't make everything better but—" He folded over as the air whooshed out of him.

"There." Jane shook out her hand. "I should have aimed lower."

Liam crumpled to the carpet and watched her stomp off. When he was able to breathe again, he picked himself up. With as much dignity as he could muster, he walked to his office, concentrating on each slow step.

Arms crossed, thunderous look on his face, Kevin stood at the door. Liam staggered through it, and Kevin followed, closing the door behind them.

"What the hell is wrong with you?"

"Not now." Moving at a glacial pace, Liam reached his chair and collapsed into it.

Steam was fairly coming out of Kevin's ears. "Yes, now. Explain to me why you maligned the nicest woman in the world."

"I don't have to explain—"

"Maybe not. But you sure as hell need to apologize. To Chuck. To Beth. To Jane."

Liam held up a hand. "Yeah, yeah. I get the picture."

With both hands braced against the desk, Kevin leaned toward him. "No, I don't think you do. If you don't fix this, and fix this soon, you are going to be one lonely man because I doubt that any one of those three are going to want to be around you ever again."

Turning his back on Liam, he left the office, closing the door and leaving Liam alone.

❄

*S*he didn't need to be there; the cleanup crew had the task well in hand. A buzz of excitement filled the space where the health clinic was winding down. A few stragglers spoke with counselors, getting advice and picking up the last of the handouts. Needing to be out of the apartment to allow Chuck to state his case with Beth, Jane drifted to the back of the storefront, picking up empty coffee cups along the way and dumping them into the large trash bin, every now and then shaking out her hand. The punch had been satisfying, but only in the moment. She wanted to go back and kick him in the balls. Repeatedly. If it were physically possible, she'd kick herself in her own ass. Blame fell on her shoulders as well. If she'd confided in Liam when her parents had the accident, none of this would have happened. "Hubris, thy name is Jane," she muttered softly.

Turning on the tap, she watched water run into the sink of the tiny kitchen area. If she kept busy, she wouldn't think about Liam. He hadn't gotten close enough to break her heart, but he'd certainly bruised it. It was tender, like taking a paintball in an unprotected area. The tenderness would fade, but right then, it was a dull ache.

Picking up a sponge, she soaked it and started scouring the counters. After that, she'd clean out the fridge and empty the trash and recycle. Then she'd find a broom and do the floor. Going over her to-do list in her head, she startled when her name was called.

Leaning against the doorway, Kevin smiled apologetically. "Sorry." He glanced around the room and back at her. "Are you expecting the health department to show up? Planning to perform surgery on those countertops?"

Jane tossed the sponge into the sink. "Lost in my head."

"I get that."

"Is, umm, Liam okay?" She wanted him to suffer, but not *too* much.

He cocked his head to the side. "I think so. Why? Wait. He was moving kind of gingerly. Did you have anything to do with that?"

"Maybe. I sort of…punched him in the gut."

"You punched the CFO of Duncan Properties in the gut?" he asked incredulously, his expressive eyes wide.

She shrugged, both hands raised. "He told me to hit him, so I did."

A snort. Then a chuckle. Then Kevin bent at the waist as laughter took over. Watching him, laughter bubbled up in Jane until she too wiped tears from her eyes.

"I should have aimed lower."

Kevin held up a hand, his pink palm contrasting with his dark skin. "Stop. I can't take any more." He stepped closer and took hold of her hand, his thumb brushing over her abused knuckles. "Did you hurt yourself?"

"Nah. I'm fine."

"But it wasn't your hand that he hurt." The laughter was gone from his face as he looked into her eyes.

She tugged her hand, but he wasn't letting go. Instead, he used her captured hand to pull her in for a hug. She stiffened, then relaxed into him, leaning her head against his shoulder. He didn't say anything, just held her, stroking her back. "Why do you have to be gay? Because you're pretty much perfect," she mumbled into his shirt.

He pulled away and smiled down at her. "Right back atcha."

Leaning back against the counter, she shook the hair out of her eyes. "The worst part is I thought there might be something there. I mean, the man chased down a thief this morning. And then…he sabotages Beth and Chuck."

"It's ingrained in him to look out for Chuck. The man is a fool for love and has done some stupid things in the past."

"I get that. But this is my sister. If you had seen Beth…" She shook her head, anger and frustration once again taking root.

"Will she let Chuck explain?"

Jane nodded emphatically. "She really cares for him. So yeah, she'll take him back."

Kevin picked a piece of lint off his sleeve, then dusted off his hands. "I've been thinking. I'd like to buy into Grand Gestures." He had Jane's full attention now. "I have some money tucked aside. I like my job at Duncan Properties and, aside from being an asshole every now and then, Liam is easy to work for. But I'm not going anywhere in the company. I don't want to be an executive assistant forever. I believe in Grand Gestures. These past few weeks working with you and Beth have been the most fun I've had in a long time. I like being part of the creative process, and I want to see the business grow. I think I can be an asset. I know you're hurting for money right now, and I can help. Becoming a partner is the way I want to do it."

This was not what Jane was anticipating. She stared up at him, trying to organize her thoughts. "Wow. Umm, just wow." Kevin was the perfect combination of creative and practical. He was detail-oriented, charming, hardworking, and punctual, curious, eager, and never mansplained. He was a unicorn in the guise of a young, gay Black man. "How much are you able to invest?"

He named a figure, and she blinked. It was more than

enough to bail out her parents, repair their RV, and possibly secure a bank loan. "That would be awesome. I can't make this decision without Beth, but I'm pretty sure she'll be on board. And we would need to draw up a contract."

"Agreed. You talk to Beth, figure out what my buy-in means, I'll tell you what I want it to mean, then we can meet with someone, iron out the details, and make it legal." He held out his hand. "I'd love to say that a handshake is all I need from you, but my momma never raised no fool."

She took his hand and pulled him in for a hug. "You are an answer to a prayer. We hadn't thought of taking on a partner, but I think this will work out."

Releasing her, Kevin stepped back and sketched an arc in the air with his hand. "I think we should rename it—Kevin's Grand Gestures!"

She elbowed him out of the way and walked to the front of the store. "Nice try." Her phone dinged, and she glanced at an incoming text from Beth.

Can you be gone for a few more hours?
Yes. Things okay?

The answer was a selfie of a beaming Chuck with his arms wrapped around an equally beaming but puffy-eyed Beth.

Jane shot a thumbs-up emoji and tucked her phone back in her pocket. "They've reunited, and I need to stay away for a few hours."

Kevin grinned, waggling his eyebrows. "What are you going to do?"

She waved a hand at the storefront. "Help finish up here. Then camp out at the coffee shop, take care of emails, stuff like that."

A volunteer passed by, carrying a bag of trash. Kevin and Jane stepped aside, stopping in the corner where the windows to the street and the windows to the building's foyer met. "This space would be perfect for a storefront. Beth could prepare samples for clients in the little kitchen. That back corner could be sectioned off for office space." In her mind, she saw the perfect combination of an event space, client presentation space, and an office area/creative space for her, Beth, and now Kevin. "The monthly meetups could be down here. I don't suppose it's in our price range?"

Kevin wrapped an arm around her. "Honey, you are dreaming."

"Ah well. Maybe we can find something around SoDo. Until then"—she gestured toward her messenger bag in a corner—"I'm very good at working out of a mobile office."

He nudged her shoulder, then strolled off, calling over his shoulder, "Won't be mobile for too much longer."

She grinned and turned back to grab a broom.

An hour later, she frowned at her laptop. The write-ups about the morning's event were great. Mrs. Duncan was pleased. The response from the community was encouraging. Three hundred people had been served in the brief time period, and there was discussion of staging a similar event on a quarterly basis, perhaps rotating the venue to reach other communities. All this was good, and Jane was proud to have been a part of it. It was the photographs that were bothering her, particularly the photos of Liam. He looked like a hero in an action movie, all windblown hair and determined jaw. There were photos of him and her in heated conversation, him leaning over her, her poking him in the chest.

She closed out the browser and mentally slapped herself upside the head. Hours earlier, she'd been all tingly, twirling her hair and checking her phone, anticipating his call. But finding her sister curled up in a ball on their couch, sobbing, sobered her up. Any warm, fuzzy feelings she'd had for Liam Cross were thrown out the window. She certainly understood protectiveness, but his leading Chuck to believe that Beth was manipulating him—unacceptable. Those thoughts weren't productive, so she turned her mind to her parents' issues. Talk about being manipulated.

It was late afternoon and quiet in the coffee shop. She'd commandeered a corner seat, plugged in her laptop, and spread papers over the long table. Now, sprawled back in her chair, she contemplated the street scene over the rim of her coffee cup. If Kevin were to become a partner, they would have to reveal the full extent of their financials—including having to bail out their parents. While in Arizona, Beth had a serious "come to Jesus" conversation with them.

In addition to their mother having donated massive amounts of money, their dad was losing at poker to the tune of a hundred dollars a day, the "walking around money" he insisted he needed. It was possible there was a twelve-step program in his future.

Late one night, Beth called from the phone in the hotel's lobby, and they'd chewed over this new discovery. "Dad's never been into gambling. Why now?"

"I don't think it's the gambling itself," Beth replied. "It was the social aspect. It's a common thing to park your RV in the lot of a casino. There's like these little villages that evolve. The casinos don't mind, provided you spend money there. Dad got drawn into poker—a chance to talk to people— mostly men. He assured me he never spent more than his daily limit, and sometimes actually made money."

"When they said they wanted to take an RV down south, I thought they'd be touring the parks and staying at camp- grounds, not casinos. Does Dad know how much money he spent?"

Beth sighed. "I showed it to them. There was a lot of finger-pointing and shouting. Neither one knew what the other had gotten into."

"What did Mom think Dad was doing? What was she doing all day?"

Another sigh came through the phone. "Mom was just

glad to have a few hours to herself. Being on the road and living in an RV was pretty tight quarters."

Thinking about that conversation, Jane wondered what her parents would do now. If they moved back to Seattle, where would they stay? She made a note to research RV sites nearby—that weren't close to casinos. Kevin coming on board with an infusion of cash was awesome; GG wouldn't suffer because she and Beth were helping their parents. But their parents still had a huge credit card and the RV bill, which had depleted their savings. It was doubtful they would get the money back from the church, but she made another note to talk to a lawyer to at least try and recoup *something*.

Staring out the window, her heart picked up the pace as movement caught her eye. Liam stood on the sidewalk, looking right at her. Frowning, he pulled open the door and strode directly toward her.

He stopped across the table from her. Lines creased his forehead and bracketed his full lips.

She stared up at him, conflicted but unwilling to let go of her anger.

"May I sit down?"

She shrugged.

He pulled out a chair and sat, wincing slightly.

She hid her smirk behind the coffee cup.

He studied her face, then shifted his gaze to look at the notes in her planner. "Why do you need a lawyer?"

"None of your damn business, and stop looking at my stuff."

"Are you in trouble? Is it your parents?"

"I said, none of your damn business." She put her cup down on her notes; she wasn't going to share her family's dirty laundry with him. "I can clean up my own messes, and, like Chuck, *I* don't need your protection."

He grimaced. She wasn't sure if it was from the words or lingering pain from the punch to the gut.

"I owe you an apology."

"It's not me you need to apologize to." Jane sat up straight, gathering her things to stuff into her messenger bag. She'd stop at the gym and get in a workout. It should be safe to go home after that.

"Actually, there are many people I need to apologize to. You're here, so I figured I'd start with you."

"Fine. Go ahead."

If she kept moving, he wouldn't see her disappointment. Rising from her chair, she went to the outlet and unplugged the laptop charging cord. She wound it up, stuffed it into the bag, and then reached for the laptop.

"Would you stop and pay attention?" His hand shot out to grab the laptop.

"What?" Jane threw over her shoulder. "I'm listening." She didn't want to look at him. Instead, she focused on organizing the items in her messenger bag.

"Sit." He bit out the word, frustration evident in his deep voice.

"Fine." She flopped down into the chair and crossed her arms mutinously. "Let's get this over with." She didn't want to look at him or those hands that had held hers just a few short hours ago and those eyes that had gazed at her with warmth and understanding.

Liam ran a hand through his hair and glared at her. "I'm well aware that I overstepped." He ignored Jane's snort. "I started out in the auditing department, where I learned that not everyone is truthful and on the up and up. It taught me to—"

"Be suspicious? Pessimistic? You know, not everyone has an ulterior motive."

"I realize that." He sighed. "I've known Chuck since we were college freshmen. You know what he's like now— generous, kind, eager to try new things. Back then, he was… more so. At times, gullible. I was a scholarship student at UW and worked nights at the hospital as a custodian." His face hardened as if it hurt to speak about the past.

Jane kept quiet. Despite her bitterness, she wanted to learn as much as possible about Liam Cross.

"Late one night, right after I got off shift, a car pulled into the driveway in front of emergency. The car doors flew open, and two guys jumped out and pulled another guy out. He was totally naked and couldn't walk, so they half-carried, half-dragged him to the entrance. I was standing at the bus stop, watching, not thinking much of it. This kind of thing happened on the weekend, parties getting out of control. But the two guys dumped the other one right by the door, jumped back into the car, and took off, laughing their heads off. I expected a nurse or orderly to come out and get the guy, but nothing happened." Liam shook his head and glanced at Jane.

"Chuck?"

"Yeah. I found out it was his first frat party, and he was playing some stupid card game that, if you lost, you had to do a shot of Jägermeister."

Jane shivered. "Jägermeister is the worst. I take it Chuck lost?"

Liam nodded. "A lot. So I went back, dragged him inside, and called for help. He must have passed out, and his friends" —he emphasized the word friends—"drew all over him with markers and makeup. On his butt cheeks, they wrote his first and last name so he could be identified."

"How kind," Jane murmured.

Liam's smile was sardonic. "Yeah. The hospital staff pumped his stomach and kept him overnight. When I got to work the next day, there was a note for me to call Chuck's parents. I did. They thanked me and invited me to their house. I didn't want to go. I didn't need condescending rich people to tell me what a good person I was. But I did, and— you've met Mr. and Mrs. Duncan—they're great people, and

Chuck was this overgrown puppy of a guy. He was wide-eyed and innocent and believed the best in people, especially under the influence of alcohol or pretty girls." His gaze turned apologetic, then he continued his story. "It turned out we had a few classes together. But they were in these huge lecture halls and—"

"You were a keener sitting in the front row, and Chuck was a back row dweller." At Liam's narrow-eyed look, Jane grinned. "Was I wrong?"

"No. We became friends, and I got a summer job at the end of the year at Duncan Properties. When school started up again, I worked there part-time, and I've been there ever since."

Head cocked, she spoke in a bland tone, "So you're Chuck's self-appointed watch dog and have been fiercely loyal to the family ever since. Am I missing anything?"

"Yeah, the part where I've seen Chuck go down the relationship road too many times. Too many times where he's lost his heart and almost lost his shirt. So if I get suspicious, it's for a good reason." White-knuckled, Liam thumped the table, making the cup and saucer rattle, drawing the attention of the two baristas.

"It's fine!" Jane waved at them. When they turned away, she leaned closer, gripping the table's edge. "Do you realize that by being suspicious of Beth, you were also suspicious of me?"

His eyes filled with a mixture of guilt and remorse, he nodded slowly. "Yeah. You were right. I should have told Chuck to check in with you when he couldn't reach Beth. I just thought the past was repeating itself. I was wrong not to reach out, and I'm sorry."

She relaxed her hands and sat back, staring out the window and blinking back tears. Liam thinking she and Beth were playing Chuck had hurt. A lot.

Growing up in the chaotic world of her parents' business,

she and Beth were best friends. Two years older, her sister was the person she went to for help until she was old enough to look after herself. When Beth married, they grew apart as Beth built a world with her husband, but the two sisters talked and texted frequently. When the marriage dissolved and Beth collapsed, it frightened the hell out of Jane. So she well understood Liam's protectiveness of Chuck.

She leaned forward, folding her hands in front of her on the table, and flicked the bangs out of her eyes. "How old is Chuck?"

"Thirty-six."

"Beth is thirty-nine. It seems to me they're grown-ass adults who can figure things out for themselves. I don't know if they have a future together, but they make each other happy right now, and I think we should leave them alone to figure things out."

It was his turn to stare out the window, then his gaze returned to Jane. "You're right."

"About that, yes. But not about keeping things to myself. If I had talked to you, told you about my parents, we wouldn't have been in this mess." A lump formed in her throat, and her voice wobbled as tears leaked out. "I'm sorry for not trusting you."

He pushed back his chair and was around the table in a flash. Kneeling before her, he cradled her face in his hands, thumbing away her tears. "Oh, Jane." His deep rumble was her undoing, and the tears fell faster.

"We had a storefront all lined up, and I was going to tell you all about it, and then my parents got in that wreck, and they have no money to pay for the repairs, and they've gone through their savings and maxed out their credit cards, and we're going to have to let Kevin go." She sniffed and looked up at him with watery eyes. "And I just didn't know what to say, and I didn't know where to start." She gasped. "I never told you that Kevin was working with us."

He let go of her face and drew her head down to his shoulder. Making soothing noises, he wrapped his arms around her, rocking her side to side. She exhaled and slumped against him, exhausted and wrung out. After a moment, she sniffed again and pulled back.

"I'm sorry. I got snot all over your shirt."

He pushed her hair back and cradled her face. "I don't mind." He picked up a crumpled napkin from the table and handed it to her.

She nodded her thanks and blew her nose. Her unladylike honk didn't seem to faze Liam a bit.

"Do you need another?"

She shook her head, and he rose from the floor, grabbing a chair and pulling it close to hers.

"How about telling me what's going on with your parents?"

He listened attentively as she poured out the story, wincing at the amount of credit card debt but not saying a word. When she was finished, he pulled her toward him for another hug. "That's a lot to deal with." He pressed a kiss against the top of her head, then pulled back. "How can I help?"

She shook her head. "I don't—"

"Jane. What I said this morning still stands. I want you to share with me—the good and the bad. I know you don't need someone to solve all your problems. But maybe you need someone to talk over your problems with." He stopped and gave her a searching look.

She looked down at the soggy, twisted napkin in her hand, then back up at him. "Maybe."

"Well, then, I'm applying for that position." He slapped his hands on his knees, grinning at her.

"Aren't you going to ask about the salary? Or benefits?"

He lowered his voice and shifted closer. "I'm hoping one of the benefits is being able to kiss you properly."

"I think that can be arranged." She batted her eyelashes in what she hoped was a coquettish move.

He leaned closer and pressed his lips against hers, drawing away too soon for Jane's liking. "Are you still free this evening?"

Warmth unfurled within Jane at his heated look. "I'm free right now."

"Yeah?"

"Yeah."

He rose from his chair and extended his hand. "Then what are we waiting for?"

CHAPTER 17

The detritus of their meal lay on the dining table in Liam's apartment. Driving over to his place, they'd argued good-naturedly in his car before settling on soul food from a restaurant near the waterfront. The food arrived shortly after they did, preventing Jane from snooping through Liam's apartment, as much as she wanted to.

She craned her neck to take in the sunset. "Chuck lives on the top floor?"

"Yep." He popped the P. "Better view and more square footage."

"Seriously? This place is enormous. And I thought your office was big."

Sitting kitty-corner to her, he raised his wineglass. "Perks of working in commercial real estate. And his family owns the building."

Jane smiled and turned to take in the apartment now that she wasn't fixated on food. Having seen his office, she wasn't surprised that his home was tidy. The gray L-shaped couch was big and squashy with lots of coordinating throw pillows and a bright, ratty old afghan. The square, glass coffee table was clean except for a wooden bowl of indigenous design with some remotes sticking out of it. "I like that bowl," she said.

"Thank you. I picked it up from a native woodcarver down at the market."

"And the afghan?"

"My dad's."

She twisted around at the catch in his voice. He'd set his wineglass down and was running his fingers up and down the stem. The collar of his white dress shirt was unbuttoned, and she could see the movement of his Adam's apple. He'd been so good to her earlier, holding her while she cried, not judging, not trying to fix things, offering to listen. It was her turn to do the same.

She scooched her chair closer and pressed her knee against his, leaving it there. "Tell me about him," she invited in an encouraging voice.

"He loved two things in life: numbers and baseball." He chuckled. "After Mom took off, I'd hang out at my Aunt Diane's house in the winter until Dad got off work. When baseball season started, I'd do my homework at the ballfield, and he'd pick me up there. We'd drive into town every chance we could to watch the Mariners play. We'd both bring out mitts, and once I even caught a fly ball." He grinned and Jane grinned back, glad he had good memories of his father and happy that he'd been willing to share them.

His big hands were dusted with dark hair. One finger was bent and scarred. She touched it. "What did you do there?"

"Little League baseball. The pitcher threw a wild inside ball, and it hit my hand. Hurt like a mother." He poked at a scar on one of Jane's knuckles. "This one?"

She wiggled her fingers. "I was using a mandolin without wearing a protective glove. I'm pretty much banned from slicing vegetables. Were you a good ball player?"

He turned his palms up, revealing more scars and calluses, then placed them back on the table, his middle fingers touching hers again. "I played varsity in high school, but that's it."

"Do you play rec league now?"

He shook his head, giving her a lopsided smile. "Chuck tried to convince me, but I just…"

"The siren song of the spreadsheet kept drawing you in?"

He chuckled. "Something like that. I'm pretty boring."

She didn't think so. She thought he was fiercely loyal, highly focused, and slightly arrogant, all wrapped up in an attractive package she wanted to take her time slowly unwrapping. His gaze roamed her face before landing on her lips for a moment. Her cheeks flamed, and the corners of his mouth quirked up as if he'd read her thoughts. He twisted to the side and pulled her up from her chair to stand between his legs. His hands went to her waist. She slid her hands up his arms, appreciating the firmness of his biceps, before putting both hands in his thick, dark hair and drawing his mouth to hers.

They breathed each other in, their lips parting and sliding back and forth. In a slow glide, he claimed her mouth. Eyes closed, Jane relaxed against him. He pulled her down to sit on one thick thigh and slanted his mouth over hers. Their tongues tangled in a languorous dance.

Coming up for air, Jane met his heavy-lidded gaze. "Wow."

"Wow, indeed." He slid his nose along hers and pressed a kiss against the corner of her mouth.

She rose from his knee and stepped back. "I should be getting home." As much as she wanted to stay, it had been a long day, and she needed to talk to Beth about Kevin's offer.

"Do you have to?"

"Yes. I've got work to do, and you need to rehearse what you're going to say to Beth."

He threw his head back and let out an exaggerated groan. "Ugh. Fine. Got any suggestions?"

"Groveling is a good start."

He chuckled and stood, and they tidied up the kitchen before heading out to his car.

Jane could get used to being chauffeured around, especially by the guy next to her who made her smile like a smitten sophomore. Stopped at a red light, he said, "So you poached my personal assistant."

"Sorry. Not sorry." She looked over to catch his expression.

"Well, don't wear him out. I need him."

She wrestled with how much to tell him. But if this was going to be a relationship, she needed to share a bit more. Taking a big breath, she blurted, "Be prepared to find someone new, because he's buying into Grand Gestures."

His eyebrows winged up. "I didn't expect that."

"Neither did I, but his timing is perfect. It will ease up some of the pressure."

The light changed, and Liam pressed on the gas. "And a storefront can go back on the table?"

She waggled her hand back and forth. "Not for a while. I might be overly cautious, but I don't want to bite off more than I can chew."

"Cautious is good. When you're ready, give me a call, and I can start scouting locations for you."

"Oh. I couldn't ask you to—"

"I know. I'm offering. But you *can* ask. Chuck and I both work in commercial real estate. It's not a hardship for us to look around for likely sites. You can give us a budget and a wish list."

She made a noncommittal noise, twisting her hands in her lap. He had a point. It would be nice to talk things over with someone who had inside information. "I'll think about it."

He tugged her hand toward him to kiss the back of it, then held it loosely on the console. "That's all I'm asking for."

CHAPTER 18

*H*e stepped into the church hall and moved to the side to let others in behind him. At seven on a Sunday morning, the number of people surprised him. All volunteers, all moving around the hall with purpose. Some set tables while others were preparing the buffet line. He followed his nose to the kitchen, where the smell of bacon and coffee perfumed the air. Loud voices and laughter rose above the sounds of pots banging.

"Can I help you?" A tiny, round white woman asked, wiping her hands on the front of her apron.

"I'm Liam Cross. I signed up to volunteer." Jane had told him Beth would be working this morning.

The woman turned and called over her shoulder, "Eleanor, someone is here to volunteer." Turning back to Liam she said, "Eleanor Armstrong is the brains of the operation. She'll tell you what to do. In the meantime, the hand washing sink is over there, and find yourself a pair of gloves. Glad to have you." She nodded and went back into the kitchen.

He dutifully washed up and pulled on a pair of gloves, then stood wondering what to do next. He peeked in the kitchen, hoping for a glimpse of Beth. He turned at the sound of approaching footsteps.

"Liam Cross?" The woman looked at him over a pair of reading glasses, her face devoid of expression.

"Yes, ma'am."

"Are you the same Liam Cross for whom my son Kevin works?"

"Yes, ma'am." Somewhere in the back of his mind was the memory of Kevin talking about his mother's work as the office manager of a church. "Your son is indispensable. I enjoy working with him."

"Um-hmm. He enjoys working for you as well."

"I'm glad to hear that."

Her gaze traveled over him. Was he overdressed? It was a church, so he'd chosen a polo shirt instead of a T-shirt to wear with jeans.

"Why are you here?" She held up a hand. "I get you want to volunteer. But my son has worked for you for three years, and this is the first time I'm seeing you here. Does it have anything to do with Beth Beckett? Because on Sunday mornings, she does not have time for distractions."

Unprepared for a grilling, he blurted, "I need to apologize to her."

Eleanor pushed her glasses to the top of her head and crossed her arms. "Why?"

He blinked. "I'd rather not say. It's personal."

"Apologies normally are. Now, in about an hour, this place will be filled with people expecting to be fed, so I suggest you tell me why you're bothering Beth, or you can find the exit."

Unsure whether to be angry or entertained by the woman's intrusive nature, he bit the inside of his cheek. One thing was certain: he was not going to get anywhere without talking to her. "She's been dating my best friend, Chuck Duncan." Was there a way to explain this without sounding like a douche? Probably not. "She went out of town and wasn't answering texts and phone calls, and I led Chuck to believe she was done with him."

One elegant eyebrow arched. "Why'd you do that?"

"Because I'm an overprotective idiot. I assumed she wanted Chuck for his money."

"You don't know Beth very well, do you?"

"No, ma'am." He looked around the church hall. The place was spotless and organized, tables lined up in rows, chairs pushed in neatly, paper placemats and real cutlery set in front of each seat, and a vase of fresh flowers on each table. Beneath the cleanliness and cheerful ambiance, he could see the worn flooring and scuff marks on the wall. The church could use an influx of cash. If it would get him into Eleanor Armstrong's good graces, he'd whip out his checkbook, but the woman in front of him did not look like she'd be swayed by money. He sighed. "My friend has been used by women before, and I assumed that Beth would do the same. I jumped to conclusions, and now Chuck isn't speaking to me and I've hurt Beth deeply. I'm hoping she will forgive me."

Eleanor tapped her fingers against her arm, then walked into the kitchen, calling over her shoulder, "You can start on the dishes. When the meal is over, you can talk to Beth."

Liam followed behind and joined her in front of the sinks where dirty pots were piled to the side. Eleanor pointed to cleaning supplies. "Read the instructions before you start. Aprons are in the bottom drawer, towels are in the middle drawer. When you're done with them, take them to the washing machine." She strode off before Liam had a chance to say anything else.

He read the instructions, shifting his gaze between the three huge sinks and the soap and sanitizer dispensers on the wall above them. A big pot landed beside him.

"Sorry about this. If you soak it in hot water for a bit, it should be easier to get the oatmeal off." Beth stepped back, pushing hair out of her eyes, and turned toward him. Her cheerful smile disappeared.

"Hi." He motioned to the sinks. "I'm volunteering this morning."

Her gaze darted up at him and then away. Bright color flooded her cheeks.

He held out a hand. "Listen, I—"

"This fool needs to apologize to you. But there are people to feed, so that will happen after breakfast." Eleanor glared at Liam, then took Beth by the arm and guided her back to the stove. Beth looked back at him, lips tipped up in a small smile, and waved. He exhaled and faced the sink. Time to serve his penance.

An hour later, elbow deep in hot soapy water, a tap on the shoulder drew his attention.

"You can take a break and have something to eat."

Liam twisted around, pulling the towel off his shoulder and wiping his hands. Gratefully, he accepted the plate piled high with bacon, fluffy eggs, and crisp hash browns. It smelled heavenly, and his stomach growled in appreciation. "Thanks, Beth."

Beth stepped back and leaned against the counter behind her, sipping from a large coffee mug emblazoned with the Seattle Seahawks logo. She watched him make quick work of the food before setting the empty plate and dirty cutlery aside.

"That was really good. Thanks. Any chance I can get one of those, too?" He pointed at the mug.

She gestured for him to follow and led the way to a large coffee pot. "Cups are right there. Milk and sugar beside them."

He grabbed a mug, filled it up, and took a sip. Whoever made it knew what they were doing. He looked over to find Beth watching him, flags of color high on her cheeks.

She cleared her throat and wouldn't meet his eyes. "You

wanted to talk to me?" She didn't have Jane's confidence, but she did have Jane's habit of getting to the point.

"Yeah. I fu—screwed up and owe you an apology. I misjudged you and led Chuck to believe you were done with him." He waited for her reaction.

"Why would you think I'd do that?"

"I've seen him screwed over too many times, and I…I didn't take the time to get to know you. I was wrong not to do so."

She cleared her throat again, but this time looked up at him. "You haven't apologized."

"Yes, I did."

"No. You told me you *owe* me an apology, but you haven't actually apologized."

He cocked his head, thinking over what he'd said, then grinned. "You're right. Beth Beckett, I'm sorry I misjudged you. I was wrong. Will you forgive me for being an as—jerk?"

She nodded once, then walked away.

She stopped when he called after her. "I'm not sure if I ever told you. Your food is really good."

"I know." She grinned and continued on.

Sipping his coffee, Liam returned to the sinks. After her apology, for some reason, the mountain of dirty dishes seemed so much smaller.

An hour later, he wiped down the sinks and the drain board before tossing the wet rag into a bus pan full of towels, rags, aprons, and potholders. Hefting it, he looked around, spotted the washing machine, and headed that way. In an alcove stood two commercial-style washers and dryers. Not sure what the protocol was, he placed the bus pan on top of one machine. From a small office came the sound of adding machine keys. He poked his head in and found Eleanor staring at a ledger while entering numbers into a ten key without even looking at it. She turned as he tapped at the door.

Pushing her glasses up on her head, she turned in her chair to look at him, eyebrows raised in silent enquiry.

"I put the laundry on top of the washer. Do you have guidelines to follow, or should I just start it up?"

She rose from the chair and moved past him. "I'll take care of the laundry. How did it go with dishwashing?"

Liam followed her into the now quiet kitchen. The last of the workers were mopping the floor and smiled at Eleanor as she thanked them. Eleanor stopped beside the Hobart machine and checked the commercial dishwasher. "You emptied the drain trap, turned off the hot water, and wiped everything down. Good job." She glanced up at him. "I don't think this was your first rodeo."

Liam grinned. "I worked at a drive-in burger joint during high school. I know my way around a dish pit."

"Hey, Mrs. Armstrong. Sorry I couldn't be here this—oh." Chuck's smile disappeared when he spotted Liam. "What are you doing here?"

Liam hadn't anticipated this. Focused on what to say to Beth, he hadn't figured out what to say to Chuck.

"Let me guess. You need to apologize to him, too." Eleanor looked amused, crossing her arms and leaning back against the counter. "So much drama."

Facing his best friend, Liam took in subtle changes in Chuck's appearance. He carried himself more confidently, back straight, shoulders back, and chin lifted. Dark circles gone, his eyes were clear and bright. He looked…happy and content. Beth peeked out from behind him, then moved around him to stand at an angle between the two men. Pink-cheeked, she addressed Eleanor. "Sorry about this."

Eleanor waved away her apology. "If they're going to throw punches around, take them out back. I don't want them messing up my kitchen."

His hand going to his belly, Liam said, "Jane beat you to it."

Beth's eyes rounded.

Chuck snorted.

"I knew I liked that girl," Eleanor muttered.

"I wish I'd seen that." Chuck's lips curled up. "Washing dishes one Sunday morning isn't enough. You owe Beth an apology."

Beth uncurled the fingers of his hand and slipped her own between his. "He already did."

Chuck, his eyes wide, glanced between Beth and Liam. "Really? He actually apologized?"

She nodded. "Used the S word and everything." She leaned up to kiss Chuck on the cheek.

Liam noted the sweet look Beth gave Chuck and how Chuck relaxed under her gaze. Yeah, he'd been wrong about her. "I'm so used to looking for errors and weak points and flaws. I couldn't see what was right in front of me. She really cares for you." Chuck didn't look like he was buying it, so Liam went on. "You're so eager and optimistic, I'm always worried you're going to get hurt. So my default is to prepare for the worst. I made an assumption, one that was wrong. I hurt both you and Beth, and for that, I am deeply sorry."

Chuck glanced down at his and Beth's interlocking fingers and back up at Liam. "Opening up your heart to someone is risky. Not every woman is going to be like your mother or like some of the women I've dated before. But when you put yourself out there, you will find the perfect person." He pulled Beth's hands up to kiss her knuckles, staring into her eyes.

Hands in his pockets, Liam watched Chuck and Beth walk off, arm in arm. "I think I may have found her," he said to himself.

Driving home, he called Jane through the Bluetooth system of his car.

"Oh, thank God," she said. "I've been chewing my nails, wondering if you were still alive."

Liam laughed, pleased to know she'd been thinking about him. "Your sister was very gracious. Are you sure you two are related?"

"Ha ha. So it went okay?"

"Yeah." He gusted out a sigh. "Chuck showed up and laid into me, so I got to apologize to him as well."

"Ooh. How did that go?" His insides softened at the concern in her voice.

"We'll see. I think Beth will talk him down from being angry. They really are good for each other."

"Yes!" She squealed. "Now say the words. Admit that I was right."

He laughed again, wishing she were beside him, even if she was gloating. "You were right."

"Louder."

"Don't push it." He grinned. She was cute even when she was annoying.

"Okay. I'm glad things went well."

"Me too. I'm gonna go home and zone out in front of a ball game. Any chance you can join me?" Snuggling on the couch with her sounded like the best way to spend a Sunday afternoon.

She groaned. "I wish. I have a Zoom meeting with a prospective client in a couple hours, and I need to prep for it. Rain check?"

"Rain check." He pulled into a parking space, and put the car in park. In front of him was a cement wall, but in his mind, he could see her sparkling eyes. "Bye, Jane."

"Bye, Liam."

CHAPTER 19

"Got a minute?" Kevin stood in the doorway to Liam's office, holding two cups of coffee.

Liam pushed back from his desk and walked around it to accept a cup. "Thanks. What's up?"

Kevin handed over a folded piece of paper and took a seat in one of the chairs in front of the desk.

Frowning, Liam moved to sit next to him. He placed the cup of coffee down, glanced at Kevin, and opened the paper. His eyebrows winged up. "You're resigning?" Jane had given him a heads-up, but he hadn't expected it so soon.

"Yeah. Effective two weeks from now. I'll work with HR to find and train a replacement. I've created a file with templates for the forms and emails you prefer, listed the company corporate structure, which support person is responsible for which task, etc. It should go smoothly."

"Wow. Can I ask why? I thought you were happy here." Tossing the paper on the desk, Liam leaned forward to study his assistant. He hoped he could pull this off without giving anything away.

Kevin met his gaze directly. "It's a good company, and I like working with you. It's just...not enough. I've got the opportunity to buy into a business and do something more creative." He straightened the non-existent crease in his trousers. "It's with Grand Gestures."

"Oh. What about benefits? Do they have a 401K?"

Kevin chuckled. "Not yet. But as a partner, I'll be looking out for the employees. Jane's got big ideas, and the things Beth comes up with…" He shook his head. "That woman leaks creativity. I want in on the ground floor to help grow this company. Jane is organized and appreciates structure. They want to expand and can't do so without more hands. I'm willing to give them mine."

Duncan Properties was a family owned and run business. There weren't any rungs for Kevin to climb higher. "I get it. You've got a good future there. I'm going to miss you, though."

"I will, too. But I'm not leaving town." He sipped his coffee and met Liam's gaze over the rim. "Jane wants a storefront, preferably downtown, so we'll probably run into each other."

"May I come in? Oh—I'll come back later." Chuck stood in the doorway, eyes full of curiosity.

"Did you two make up?" Kevin waved his finger back and forth between the other men.

Liam hadn't heard from nor seen Chuck since the church kitchen. If Chuck chose to put him through the grinder, he didn't blame him. His overprotective actions had been a colossal screwup and may have cost him his best friend.

"Yeah, we're good." Chuck's easygoing smile was back in place as he sauntered into the room. "What's going on? Am I interrupting?"

Liam looked to Kevin, who nodded. "Kevin's leaving us. He's bought into Grand Gestures."

Chuck's jaw dropped. "Seriously? That's cool."

"Beth didn't tell you?" Liam asked.

Cheeks reddening, Chuck looked out the window. "No. We, uh, didn't talk business this weekend."

"What did you do?" Kevin asked with a straight face.

Chuck narrowed his eyes in return. "Actually, we were talking about our families. She's ready to meet my parents, and when hers get back up here, I'll do the same." He walked behind the desk and dropped into Liam's chair, kicking his feet up on the desk.

"Oh, do make yourself comfortable," Liam said.

Chuck grinned. "Thanks. I will. Not sure when her parents will get here. Their RV is in the shop, and they don't have the money to pay for the repairs. I'm trying to get the details from Beth, but she's embarrassed. It sounds like they were each spending money the other wasn't aware of until their bank accounts were drained."

Liam had heard as much from Jane and wondered if Kevin knew any more. "Do you know anything about this?"

He nodded but held up a hand. "Yes. That's one of the reasons they welcomed me to the company, to help out with the cash flow. They laid it all out for me, but I can't tell you anything. It's their business, and if Beth wants Chuck to know, she'll tell him."

Chuck grumbled and crossed his arms. "I wish she'd let me help."

"Won't happen. She'd feel beholden to you." Kevin rose from his chair and pushed it up against the desk.

"She's letting *you* help her," Chuck said.

"I'm buying into the business. In a few weeks, I'm going to be an active partner." He beamed and, if possible, stood straighter than his normal erect posture. "But until then, I need to get back to work. My boss is a tyrant."

Kevin walked away with Liam and Chuck grinning behind his back.

"It's not going to be the same without him around here," Chuck grumbled.

"He'll be working with Beth. You'll see him all the time."

Chuck smirked. "Did Jane really punch you?"

Reflexively, Liam rubbed his gut. It no longer hurt, but it was the memories afterward that lingered. Memories of holding Jane and kissing Jane. He wasn't prepared to share those, though. It was too new, and from the sounds of it, Jane hadn't shared with Beth. "Don't piss off your future sister-in-law."

Chuck's smirk melted into a soft smile. "I like the sound of that. But I'm not going to propose for a while. I'm not in a hurry, and neither is Beth, although I may ask her to move in with me in a few months. Do you think she'll like my apartment?"

"Who wouldn't? The way she looks at you, you could live in a shoe box and she'd be happy."

"So noted."

"Do she and Jane have a nice place?" Liam had dropped Jane off in front of the building but hadn't gone inside.

"It's an older building on Queen Anne but well-maintained. Sperry Properties owns it, and their reputation for good building management is well deserved. Jane's been there about five years and says she's never had problems with them."

Chuck *would* go into detail about the building, but what Liam wanted was a glimpse into Jane's personal life. "Is it furnished with workout equipment and exercise mats?"

"No. They run the business out of the apartment, so it's got a lot of GG stuff there. They have real furniture. Good quality, comfortable, surprisingly girly. Not sure if that's Jane or Beth." He shifted in his chair. "There were, umm, lacy bras hanging in the bathroom. They looked like they'd be too small for Beth, though."

Liam closed his eyes. "Stop right there. I don't want the image of your girlfriend's underwear in my head."

Chuck's smirk returned, and he waggled his eyebrows.

"Anyway, I think I'm going to throw a party for Kevin. I'll ask Mom or Delia to do it."

"If the company is paying for it, get your mom. We can't afford Delia."

"You're probably right." Chuck stood and walked toward the door. "I'll confer with Beth about the date so she and Jane can attend."

Hopefully, he'd be seeing Jane sooner. Liam smiled inwardly. Aloud, he said, "It's a bummer that it took so long for Beth to replace her phone. Where was she again?"

"Earp. A tiny town near Lake Havasu. Catch you later."

Liam seated himself behind his desk and reached for his laptop, murmuring the name of the town to himself.

A few days later, Jane stood in front of their open refrigerator. Beth was having dinner at Chuck's but had prepared a meal for her sister to have in her absence. Jane pulled out the plate of meatloaf and mashed potatoes with broccoli on the side. When Beth eventually moved in with Chuck, and Jane was sure it was a *when* and not an *if*, she was going to have to cook for herself—or go back to eating popcorn for dinner. The phone rang, interrupting her thoughts.

"Hi, Mom."

"Oh, Jane! You wouldn't believe the good news. Your dad and I were the 1,000th customers at the RV repair shop, and our repairs were totally paid for. Isn't that exciting? Now you and Beth don't need to worry about that. The RV will be finished late next week, and we'll be on our way home."

Jane stared at the phone, sure this was a joke. "Did I hear you correctly? There's no charge for the repairs because you were the 1,000th customer?"

Her mother squealed. "That's what I said!"

It was too good to be true. There had to be a catch and her parents were too gullible to see it. Interrupting her mother's excited babbling, Jane asked, "Did you sign anything?"

"What? No. The manager called moments before I called you. Why? Is there a problem? He didn't ask for a credit card number. Do you think it's a scam?"

Jane wanted to reassure her, but she was too much of a cynic. "I don't know, Mom. Give me the name of the manager and the phone number, and let me check it out." She put the food back in the fridge and reached for the bottle of wine. After the next phone call, she'd be either celebrating or drowning her sorrows. "You didn't do anything wrong, but I don't want you to get your hopes up. If it turns out to be false, we go back to our original plan." Her mother didn't need to know that involved maxing out a credit card to pay for the repairs.

"Okay, dear. Your dad's out for a walk, so he doesn't know yet, and I won't tell him anything until you confirm it."

"Thanks, Mom. I'll call you back as soon as I know something." Jane wrote down the name and number her mother gave her, then disconnected. Opening up a web browser, she searched for the repair shop and brought up their website. The phone number was correct. There were even photos of the employees. Identifying Manny Ortega, she enlarged the photo. Then she called the shop.

A chirpy voice answered the phone. "Havasu RV Repair, we get you back on your road to adventure!"

"May I speak with the manager please?"

"Mr. Ortega is on another line right now. Can you hold?"

"Certainly." Taking her wineglass, Jane took a seat on the couch. She put the phone on speaker and set it and the wineglass down on the coffee table next to her laptop. On it, she entered the name of the repair shop in a browser and looked for customer reviews. Yelp had good things to say, with the odd grumble about wait time or cost of parts. They were a small business in a small town, so those reviews didn't sound any alarm bells for Jane.

"Manny Ortega here. Thank you for waiting."

"Oh, hi. I know this is going to sound weird, but can we turn this into a video chat?"

"Umm…sure. I can FaceTime."

"That would be great."

After a few seconds of fumbling, the same face appeared on her phone as the one in the company photo. "Can I help you?"

"I'm Jane Beckett. You have my parents' RV in your shop, and I understand they won't be charged for the repairs." Studying his image closely while speaking, Jane thought he didn't look very confident.

"Yes!" He cleared his throat, then spoke as if reading aloud from a script. "We congratulate Steven and Barbara Beckett for being the 100th customer of Havasu RV Repair. To celebrate, we will cover the costs of repairs to their vehicle. We value their business." He avoided looking directly into the camera.

"You said 100th. I thought it was 1000th?"

"Did I say that? I meant 1000th."

His fumble making her suspicious, she pressed for more information while doing her best not to piss him off. "My parents are thrilled. Do you mind telling me how much the bill was for?"

He shuffled a few papers, then said, "$17,323.12."

"That is awfully generous of you. Have you done this kind of thing before?"

"Ahh…no ma'am. We knew that when we hit 100—I mean, 1000, we would cover their bill."

"This is so cool. I bet it will bring in a lot of publicity for you. Is there going to be some kind of reception? You know, their picture in the paper?"

He ran a hand through his receding hair. "Look, lady. I got a phone call from a guy saying he'd cover the bill and not to tell your parents. He told me to tell them about being the 1000th customer. The money got transferred and cleared my account, so I did. It's not illegal to pay someone else's bills."

"Oh, wow. I would love to be able to thank that person for their generosity. They really helped our family out of a bind. May I have their name, please?"

"I can't tell you."

"I get that. I sure would like to thank them, though." She crinkled up her nose and gave him a big-eyed smile.

"I'm sorry, ma'am. I can't give out that information. I do have the confirmation of payment I can send you. There's a phone number on it with a 206 area code."

"Thank you. I'd appreciate that."

Jane gave him her email address and disconnected. She put the phone down and picked up her wine. Staring out the window, she contemplated the generous stranger. Manny had read off an area code in Seattle. Knowing that narrowed down the field. She could count on one hand the number of people who knew about her parents and their RV accident. And the number of people who had seventeen grand to throw around? It had to be Chuck. Grabbing her phone again, she called Beth. "Hey. Is Chuck with you?"

"He's right beside me. Why?"

"Can you put me on speaker?"

"Just a sec."

There were a few mumbled words in the background, then Chuck's cheerful voice came on the line.

"Hey, Jane. What's up?"

Jane said, "Chuck, do you know anyone in Earp?"

"I don't think so? Why?"

"That's where Mom and Dad are," Beth piped in.

"Okay, but I've never met them. So no. All I know is that it's a small town in Arizona." He sounded befuddled. "Why?"

Scrambling for an answer without actually telling them, Jane said, "I'd heard Duncan Properties was buying some buildings there."

"That's news to me. We only purchase property in Washington state, although my parents have a place in Maui. Beth, can you take some time off in the fall and we can go there? It's right on the beach with lots of privacy. You'd love it. Oh, and Jane, you can come, too."

"Thanks. I'll think about it. Okay. Bye, guys."

Disconnecting, Jane flopped back on the couch. Either Chuck was an excellent liar, or he truly knew nothing. She didn't think it was the former. Kevin knew. But he was already buying into Grand Gestures. Why pay off the RV repairs and do it in such an odd way? Fleetingly, she thought of Liam, then dismissed the idea. Their relationship was far too new for him to do something that extravagant.

Checking her email, she saw Manny Ortega had made good on his word. She opened up the invoice, hoping for more detail, but all it said was Paid in Full and yesterday's date. She phoned her mother and gave her the good news, going with the lie that they were indeed the 1000th customers.

"Oh, sweetheart, see? Not everything is a scam. When the repairs are finished, we'll get the RV, check out of this place, and start driving home. We should be back in a couple of weeks."

It was Tuesday. Going through the calendar in her head, Jane said, "Take your time, Mom. There's no rush. Any idea where you're going to stay?" It wasn't like there was room to park in front of her apartment.

"There's a place in Bothell, next to the Sons of Norway lodge. You remember that. We did the Olaf wedding there when you were in high school."

"Right." There had been a wedding almost every weekend. After all the weddings and the years since them, they'd all become a blur. "Sounds good. Give us a call when you get close."

"Will do sweetheart. Bye."

Jane sipped her wine in the quiet apartment. Liam had gone up to Bellingham to visit his aunt, so she didn't want to call him, but she could certainly shoot him a text.

The phone rang. For a moment, Jane was tempted to let it go to voicemail, sure it was her parents. The name on the screen was Kevin's, so she picked it up. "Hey."

"I see we're going to have to discuss phone etiquette as a first order of business."

She grinned. "I knew it was you."

"It could have been someone using my phone."

She opened her mouth to argue but stopped. He had a point. The first time she'd spoken to Liam was on Chuck's phone. "What's up?"

"Come meet me and I'll buy you a drink."

She stared down at her sweatpants and stretched-out T-shirt. She didn't want to change, and she didn't want to move. "How about coming here?"

"Nope. This is a celebration, and it calls for overpriced cocktails in a snooty bar."

"What are we celebrating?"

"Put me on FaceTime."

Jane engaged the camera on her phone. Kevin's cocky smile was blinding against his dark skin. "I put in my notice yesterday, and I have this for you." He held up a large rectangular piece of paper.

Squinting at it, she squealed. It was a check.

He wiggled it at her. "Come and get it. I'm at McQuarry's."

The bar wasn't far from Jane's apartment but still miles away from her wardrobe. She untangled her legs and rose from the couch. "What the hell am I supposed to wear?"

"Lead me to Beth's closet. I imagine yours is full of camo and practical pantsuits."

He wasn't wrong. Opening up the closet door, she held the phone up for him to see the neatly organized row of clothing. "I refuse to wear a dress or heels, and remember, Beth has more cleavage than I do."

"Fortunately, your ass looks good in your dress slacks. Hang on, go back. Yes. Grab that salmon-colored sweater and try it on."

Jane grabbed the sweater and put down the phone, turning it away while she changed. Kevin might be gay, but she wasn't going to strip in front of him. Picking up the phone, she moved toward the mirror, angling the phone so he could see her. The boatneck neckline slid off one shoulder, and she tugged it back into place. "It's a little on the big side."

"It's perfect. Find your lip gloss and brush your hair. I'm not even going to make you put on jewelry and makeup. How long before you can get here?"

"Twenty minutes?"

"Excellent. I'll have a drink waiting for you."

He disconnected, and Jane headed to her own closet to find slacks. When she discovered Rothy's shoes, Beth convinced her to buy multiple pairs. Grinning, Jane chose the khaki camo flats just to mess with Kevin. She slicked on lip gloss and checked out her appearance in the full-length mirror attached to the bathroom door. She looked good. Not Beth good or Delia Duncan good—Jane didn't have the desire or the budget to dress like Chuck's socialite sister— but Kevin would approve. Stealing a clutch purse from Beth's closet, Jane loaded it with her wallet, phone, keys, and lip gloss and headed out.

The walk to the bar wasn't long, and Jane enjoyed the breeze coming in off the water. She pushed up the sleeves of the sweater. The neckline refused to stay put, sliding off her shoulders either one way or the other. Fortunately, she'd switched from a sports bra to a pretty black bra with lacy straps. Entering the bar, she took a moment to allow her eyes to adjust to the intimate gloom, unaware of the admiring looks pointed in her direction. Kevin was easy to spot. Seated at the corner of the bar, three men circled him, clearly thinking he was a snack and a half. Grinning, she sauntered over.

Seeing her, Kevin shooed away the men. "Sorry, gentlemen. My date is here, and she looks divine."

Jane did her best hair flip and took the stool vacated by one of the disappointed men. Smiling her thanks, she turned and murmured low, "You are a tease."

"That I am." He winked over her shoulder at a burly, bearded man. "Not to worry. I got their numbers."

Kevin waved at the bartender, who brought over two frothy cocktails and set them down on the bar. He picked his up and raised it in a toast. Jane eyed hers suspiciously. "Am I going to regret this tomorrow?"

"The drink or bringing me in as a partner?"

She nudged his shoulder and lifted her glass. "To the newest member of Grand Gestures."

Placing his glass down on the bar, Kevin reached into his shirt pocket. "I suppose you want this."

Accepting the check, Jane said, "I'll be hotfooting it down to the bank tomorrow."

"When's the first partners' meeting? I have a couple leads on events and want to build on those cocktail meetups."

"Don't you have to finish out your two weeks?"

He shrugged. "Yeah, but I've got just enough in the bank to cover my mortgage and live on for the next six months. So for GG to earn enough to pay me a salary, I need to start earning my keep."

"You own a house? I'm impressed. How old are you?"

"Thirty-two." He sipped his drink, sadness replacing his

usual smile. "My dad died in a construction accident a few years ago, and I bought a house with part of the insurance payout."

Leaning against him, Jane hurt for the young man beside her. "What was he like? Do you want to talk about it?"

He patted her hand. "It's okay. I was up in Vancouver for Pride when it happened. A crane fell and crushed him. They kept him on life support until I got home, and we…"

Jane squeezed his hand while he blinked a few times. "How did your mom do?"

"You've met my mom." He grinned and sipped his drink. "She took to her bed for a couple days. Her church lady friends were in and out of the house with food. You have never seen so many casseroles and pies. Then Mom rallied, and we had a great celebration of life. The church was packed—Dad had lots of friends, and afterward, people came to the house and told stories and laughed. Someone put together a slideshow." He looked over at Jane. "Want to see a picture?" At her nod, he pulled out his phone.

She examined the photo of a smiling man and woman, arms around each other, with a much younger Kevin standing between them. "Your dad was a handsome man. The apple doesn't fall far from the tree."

Accepting the compliment, Kevin nodded. "They were married for thirty years. He was a good husband and a great dad. And some day, I'm going to be just like him."

Jane smiled. "Including hard hat and work boots?"

"On me? I don't think so." He gave an exaggerated shudder. "Although there's something about a man working construction."

Jane raised her glass in agreement.

Kevin scrolled through photos, looking nostalgic, then put the phone back into his pocket. "Let's talk workspace. I'm not a fan of coffee shops, and I'm happy to come to your apartment, but I talked to Mom, and she said that we can use their office space, although I don't think it's optimal for client presentations. We'll have to continue going to them or meeting them at event sites."

Eyes widening, Jane grabbed Kevin's arm. "You don't know! Someone paid off the repair bill for my parents' RV. Beth and I don't have to bail them out."

"Seriously? Who did that?"

She relayed the story her mother had been given. "I grilled the manager of the repair shop, and all he'd tell me was that it was a guy calling from a Seattle area code."

"Ooh. Must be Chuck. Nicely done."

"Nope. He knew nothing about it, and I don't think he's that good of a liar."

Kevin tapped a finger against his chin. "He's not. But if not Chuck, then who?"

She flopped her hands to the side. "The thing is, it's a Seattle area code, but it doesn't mean it was someone local. It could be a fellow snowbird my parents met who's from here."

"Aren't you dying to find out?"

"Yes. But I don't want to use my phone. Then they'll have my number, and they could come after me."

"You have a vivid imagination. You can look it up online."

"I'll do that tomorrow. In the meantime, with us not having to pay out that cash, and you buying into the business, we're in a stronger position to get a storefront location."

"Hmmm." He nudged her shoulder. "It's a good thing I know a few people in commercial real estate."

"Yes, indeed."

She paid for the next round of drinks, and they ping-ponged between discussing optimal locations for the storefront and wondering who had written the check. She excused herself for a trip to the restroom and, on her return, lingered at the other end of the bar while Kevin chatted with the burly, bearded guy.

"Do you two have, like, an open relationship?" The bartender pointed his thumb between Kevin and Jane.

She snorted. "Ah, no. We're business partners and friends." She looked up. The bartender was cute, probably a few years younger than her, with thick, dark hair, dark eyes, and an olive complexion. "Do you want me to introduce you?"

He chuckled and leaned his elbows on the bar. "Thanks, but I'm more interested in meeting you. I'm Jamal." He flashed a smile and offered his hand.

"Jane," she said and extended her own. He squeezed her hand and trailed his fingers across her palm when he released it. She felt nothing.

She flicked a glance at Kevin to see him coming her way, waving goodbye to the bearded guy. She sighed in relief. Jamal was cute, but he wasn't Liam. She stepped away from the bar, said goodbye to Jamal, and walked toward Kevin, who said nothing as he held the door open for her.

Stepping out into the evening air, Jane smiled up at her friend as they walked toward his car. "Got a hot date in your future?"

"Maybe. How about you?" His phone dinged with a text, saving her from having to answer his question. On the drive home, she distracted him further by teasing him about liking lumberjacks. She and Liam were back to talking nightly, but she wasn't willing to discuss her feelings for him yet. She'd have to tell Beth soon, though. Sitting in the closet and talking in a hushed voice was getting old.

CHAPTER 20

$\mathcal{A}$ perk of owning a commercial real estate company was having access to empty spaces when you wanted them. For Kevin's party, Chuck's mom had, again, laid claim to the empty storefront on the first floor of the building. Liam was happy to see the space being used, even if it was a rent-free event.

True to his word, Kevin had found a replacement for himself. A Filipina woman in her fifties, she had multiple piercings and excellent references. She was due to start on Monday, and Liam had promised Kevin not to be an ass to her.

The alarm on Liam's laptop sounded, reminding him the party had started. Shutting down his computer, Liam grabbed his jacket and left his office. His glance fell on a file folder on Kevin's empty desk. Flipping it open, he scanned through the notes Kevin had left for the new assistant— Marjorie. Liam muttered her name a few times to commit it to memory. The pages detailed Liam's routine, contact phone numbers, passwords, and file locations. The last page was a handwritten note with Kevin's phone number.

Hi Marjorie,

Liam closed the folder. Nothing Kevin said was untrue, but he sounded like a robot with no personality or sense of humor. He thought back and realized that, indeed, that's what he was like before Jane. Now that he'd kissed her, talking with her was no longer enough. He looked forward to bringing their relationship out of the closet. He snorted, well aware that Jane sat in the closet at night to talk with him. He wanted to kiss her again, hear her sighs when she did so, and spend more than just an hour or two with her.

The remarkable woman was in the same building tonight, fifteen floors beneath him. He intended to spend as little time as possible at the party before whisking her away. Striding past empty desks on his way to find her, he thought about all that he had learned.

Like him, Jane was a caffeine addict. She routed her trips to and from the gym in order to visit her favorite espresso stands and coffee shops. Clowns didn't creep her out, but parking garages gave her the willies. After falling off a pair of high heels in front of a cute boy in ninth grade, she'd vowed never to wear heels again. She liked roller coasters and rock music, but Hallmark movies were her favorite.

Exiting the stairwell into the foyer on the first floor, laughter and music greeted him. He stood still for a minute, taking in the throng of people who'd turned out to celebrate with Kevin. The doors to the vacant store—now event space

—were flung wide and bracketed by giant balloon bouquets. More balloons, in every color of the rainbow, hung from the ceiling. In the corner farthest from the street, two bartenders worked steadily, filling orders for the thirsty crowd, while a server moved about, carrying a tray filled with champagne glasses. Two more servers were making the rounds with appetizers. He couldn't see Kevin, but he did see Chuck, a huge smile on his face. Liam suspected Beth was nearby. Entering the room, he shook his head at a server, refusing a glass of champagne, and searched through the crowd. A loud laugh caught his attention. Following the sound, he found her. Jane stood next to a bistro table, surrounded by three men, each with a predatory look in their eyes. Jane flicked her bangs out of her eyes, laughing again.

Someone moved aside, and he could see her fully. A turquoise tank top made from some silky-looking fabric clung to her frame, tucked into the high waistband of khaki-colored shorts. For the first time ever, Liam saw Jane's legs. Her long, toned, bare legs. On her feet, she wore flat gold sandals. Turning back to the server, Liam grabbed two glasses of champagne and pushed his way through the crowd, eyes locked on the smiling brunette. Liam growled as one of the men surrounding her leaned back, obviously staring at her ass. Liam changed direction, coming up from behind Jane and shouldering his way between her and the ass-gazer. Ignoring the guy's protest, Liam thrust a glass of champagne at Jane. "Here."

Jane looked down at the glass, then twisted her neck to look back and up at Liam. "Thanks?" She took the glass and brought it to her lips, a frown creasing her forehead.

Grabbing her elbow, Liam drew her away from the men. "Excuse us, we have business to discuss."

"Hey!" she said, as he dragged her toward an empty table. "What's your problem?"

What was his *problem*? Her being surrounded by ogling

men. That was his problem. He was wise enough not to say that out loud. He glared at her.

She returned his glare, coolly sipping her champagne.

His gaze drifted over her. Tank top, shorts, bare legs, pink painted toes, and back up her legs. "You're inappropriately dressed."

"Seriously?"

At her flat tone, he focused on her face. She was even wearing makeup. Not a lot, but she'd done something to emphasize her eyes, and her lips glistened. She hadn't bothered to hide the scar under her left eye, which was, in his opinion, one of her defining features.

She placed one hand on a cocked hip and waved her glass with the other. "Look around, Cross. It's a party. I'm wearing more clothes than half the women here."

He did as he was told. The men had shucked their ties and jackets and rolled up their sleeves, clearly ready to get started on the weekend. The women had either changed into party clothes or had done whatever it was women did to change their daytime outfits into after-work attire. His eyes almost popped out when he spotted one of Duncan Properties' appraisers wearing a dress that barely covered her assets. He brought his attention back to Jane and her annoyed frown.

He pulled at his tie and undid the top two buttons of his shirt, knowing he'd done it again. "That came out wrong."

"I'll say."

She looked hurt, but before he could salvage the situation, Kevin arrived.

"Look at you!" He twirled his finger. Jane turned around. "I don't think these are from Beth's closet. Did you actually go to a store?"

"Hardly." Jane flipped her hair back. "I took your advice and checked out one of those sites that curates and sends complete outfits to you."

Kevin nodded his approval. "Nicely done." He wrapped an

arm around her shoulder and kissed the top of her head. Leaning into his embrace, Jane grinned.

This wasn't the way the night was supposed to go. He was supposed to be the focus of Jane's attention. Her smiles were supposed to be just for him. Liam buried his scowl in his champagne glass. He was going to need something stronger if he stuck around.

"I didn't want to be mistaken for the help again." Jane looked at Liam while tilting her head toward the doors.

Delia Duncan was making her entrance. She'd spotted Kevin and moved toward him, stepping like a model on a catwalk. He disengaged from Jane and turned to greet her. Liam's gaze came back to Jane, watching her expression as the tall blonde approached. She didn't look annoyed, disappointed, intimidated, or flustered. Leaning back against the small table, Jane sipped her champagne, looking relaxed, like she was enjoying an amusing show. And it *was* a show. Gesturing broadly, Delia squealed over Kevin, drawing looks from the crowd. For the first time since meeting her, Liam wondered why she needed attention so much. A movement to his side brought his focus back to Jane. She waved at someone—Beth—her smile warm and indulgent. Beth approached, bright color on her cheeks, closely followed by Chuck.

Beth looked far more relaxed than Liam had ever seen her. Dressed in a sleeveless, soft pink dress, it clung to her curves yet was modest at the same time. Together, the two sisters glowed, clearly pleased that Kevin would be joining them. Envy sparked in Liam's chest. Grand Gestures was a team of people who clearly enjoyed collaborating together, bringing joy and pleasure to others. What Liam did wasn't nearly as much fun, but balancing to zero was something he was good at and something he enjoyed. Waiting for the chance to get Jane's attention, he felt a hand on his shoulder.

"Liam, so good to see you." Carol Lee smiled up at him, head tilted, ready to receive his kiss.

Warmth flooded through him as he did so. Chuck and Delia's mother always made him feel welcome.

"What do you think? Should I ask Beth and Jane if they have room for me at Grand Gestures?"

"You certainly know how to throw a party. Everyone appears to be having a good time."

Carol Lee winked. "Access to this space is helpful. I'm not sure if I'm ever going to let you rent this out."

"Hate to be a buzzkill, but your events aren't earning any income."

"Pfft." She waved away his protest. "I'm sure we can write it off somehow."

Liam grinned. He'd be alarmed if he didn't know she was kidding. Beside him, the older woman sighed.

"Isn't Beth delightful? We had dinner with them the other night, and Chuck couldn't stop smiling. I think she's the one." She tapped Liam on the arm. "I think you can stand down now."

He followed her glance. It was ingrained in him to watch Chuck's back, but looking at him with Beth, he said, "I think you're right."

"That Jane is a firecracker."

Liam coughed. "Sorry, it went down the wrong way."

Carol Lee shot him a grin. "At one time, I had hopes for you and Delia. It would be good for her, but my daughter isn't right for you. She's still figuring out who she is, but you need someone who already has that figured out. Did you know Jane has an MBA?"

"I did." He glanced at Jane over Carol Lee's head. She, Beth, and Chuck were huddled over a phone, talking and laughing. He'd learned that she'd worked on it while still at Amazon in the run-up to starting Grand Gestures.

Carol Lee chattered on. "Steve and Barbara, they're the

girls' parents, are back in town. Well, not in town, they're up near Bothell. Anyway, I'm going to have a Sunday brunch soon and invite them. Do you think Kevin is seeing someone? If not, maybe he can bring his mother. I hate it when the numbers are uneven. Beth tells me Jane isn't seeing anyone. Would you mind coming to round out the numbers? Delia is unreliable for weekend gatherings now that the weather is nice."

"Let me get back to you."

"Excellent. Now let's mingle."

Before Liam could speak, she slipped her hand through his arm and led him toward the others. Chuck hugged his mother while she exchanged air kisses with Delia, who then launched herself at Liam for a hug. Rocking back on his heels, he untangled himself and pushed her back gently. "Nice to see you too, Delia."

Kevin's mother, Eleanor, had joined them and stood with another well-dressed woman. The woman smiled up at Liam, and he froze, unable to recall her name. A presence at his side and an outstretched hand saved him.

"Mrs. Brown, it's so good to see you," Jane said with a barely detectable shoulder nudge.

Liam sighed inwardly. Right. Betty Brown, cultural cocktail nights. He nudged Jane back, glad she wasn't completely freezing him out.

"You as well, Jane. I have to tell you that your ideas are wonderful. We've already got a waiting list for the next cocktail night. And please, call me Betty. When people call me Mrs. Brown, I keep looking around for my mother-in-law." She laughed, raising her glass in an elegantly manicured hand.

Kevin made further introductions.

Betty turned her warm smile on Delia. "I follow you on Instagram. I quite like that moisturizer you recommended."

Delia beamed. "I'm glad. It's a small local company, and they'll love to hear good feedback."

Eleanor stepped closer. "If you don't mind, there's a table with chairs over there, and I would really like to sit down." She showed off a black patent pump. "These shoes are gorgeous but a killer to stand around in."

Carol Lee and Betty agreed and drifted off with Eleanor.

Pulling out her phone, Delia gestured to Kevin. "Go stand between Jane and Beth. Let's get some shots for your Insta page."

Kevin obliged, wedging himself between the sisters, draping his arms across their shoulders. Liam stood back, watching as Delia provided further instruction. Jane shook back her hair and smiled for the camera, then laughed outright at something Kevin said.

"That's great." Delia moved over to another table, concentrating on her phone. "Jane, do you want to pick the photos?"

"Sure," Jane answered, shrugging.

Sipping his drink, Liam listened with one ear to Kevin and Beth discussing the contents of the appetizers while watching Jane and Delia. Based on their interaction at the gallery, he wondered if he should be worried. The two women were intent on the phone, appearing oblivious to the party around them. Jane pointed at the screen, Delia nodded, and Jane patted her hand and broke away.

Liam caught up with her as she stood in line for the bar. "That looked like it went well."

A smile curved the corner of Jane's lips. "Did you think there was going to be a catfight?"

"Well..."

"My sister is dating her brother. I have a feeling we'll be seeing more of each other, so it behooves us to get along. Besides, Delia knows her way around a camera. Those images, and the way she applied the filters, are great. With the hashtags she's adding, she's giving us an excellent promotion." She placed her order with the bartender and turned back to Liam. "That's why I'm buying her a drink."

"It's an open bar."

"Semantics. It's the thought that counts. Haven't you heard that before?"

"In that case, can I buy you a drink?"

The bartender placed two glasses in front of Jane. She picked them up and grinned. "One step ahead of you."

Liam put a hand on her elbow and drew her to the side of the bar. "Any chance we can rewind this a bit?"

"How far back?"

"To where I tell you how great you look."

A blush stained her cheeks, and she flicked a glance up at him and then back down. "Thanks."

He stroked a finger down her forearm and watched her shiver. He wanted her all to himself. "How much longer do you need to stay?"

She crinkled her nose and lifted the glasses in her hands. "Help me get rid of these drinks and say goodbye? Shouldn't take more than ten minutes."

"Ten minutes. No longer." He narrowed his eyes at her and watched her lips quirk up. "I've been waiting all week to see you."

"You sound impatient."

He stepped closer to speak in her ear. "That's because I am."

She shivered and turned to brush her lips against his cheek. "I am, too."

They delivered the drinks, Liam hovering at her side.

"We're heading out," Jane said to her sister and smiled at Chuck. "I've got a meet-up with the *quinceañera* family at ten, then I'll join you at the church afterward. I'll find out if there are any dietary requirements." She waved and headed for the door.

Liam made to follow, but Chuck grabbed his arm. "What's this? Are you two dating?"

"We're trying to," Liam said while watching Jane walk away.

The man who'd earlier been leering at her ass detached himself from his group and trailed behind her. In the foyer, he got close and reached out to grab her arm. Jane turned, her questioning look changing to a frown as she shook her head. The guy moved in closer.

Liam shoved his way through the crowd. The guy moved his hand down to grab Jane's ass. Picking up speed, Liam batted balloons out of the way to get to Jane. He burst through the door in time to see the guy land on his ass. Jane stood over him, her foot hovering over his crotch.

"No means no, asshole. Do I need to make myself clearer?"

The guy covered up his crotch with both hands. He shook his head. "But you look—"

Her foot pressed down. "Like what?"

"Hot?" he squeaked out.

"Seriously?" Jane pivoted, dropping her foot to the floor, and pointed a finger at Liam. "Don't say a word."

He held his hands up in surrender, fighting a grin, and followed her out the street entrance. God, she was sexy when she was angry.

With long strides, she walked down the sidewalk, continuing to mutter, "Last time I listen to Kevin. I'm going back to cargo pants and sweats. I don't get groped in them. And I'm never going to a damn party again. What is it with men? Showing some skin doesn't mean a woman is looking to get laid. When I'm looking to get laid, I'll use my words, not my wardrobe." She stopped so quickly Liam had to backtrack. Standing in front of the window of a store selling beauty products, she pointed at the display. "And I spent an hour figuring out how to do smoky eyes. What a waste of time and money." She started moving again, but he grabbed her arm and spun her around to face him.

"On behalf of the entire male species, I apologize. That guy clearly overstepped, and I doubt he will ever do so again. But he was right, because you do look hot, and the time you spent learning to do smoky eyes and picking out that outfit was well worth it." He stepped closer until she had to tip her head back to meet his gaze. "You look amazing."

She blinked, her mouth opening in a silent O.

"May I buy you dinner?"

She nodded.

Entwining his fingers with hers, he guided her toward a nearby café.

A short time later, Jane buttered her dinner roll and took a healthy bite. She closed her eyes and smiled, groaning in appreciation. "I think I could live on bread alone, provided there was butter."

"I'd want some protein."

"You're probably right." She polished off the roll and licked her lips. Despite the evening getting off to a rocky start, she was having a good time. Liam was smart, funny, and devastatingly good-looking. Walking up the street, holding his hand, she'd wanted to point out to passersby that *he* was with her. She appreciated his protective streak, and once he let down his guard, he was easy to talk to. He'd ribbed her about stealing Kevin away from him, and she'd told him their plans for expanding the business. He hadn't been condescending or patronizing and not once mansplained to her. And the way he kept staring at her, she was glad she'd put effort into her appearance.

Her phone pinged, and she looked at the text. "Beth says

she's spending the night at Chuck's and I don't have to sit in the closet to talk to you."

"I wonder how long she's known."

"I'm not sure, but I'm not surprised. Not much gets past her."

Having paid the bill, they exited the restaurant and stood on the sidewalk. A group of tourists approached them, and Liam put a hand on her lower back to steer her out of the way. "Where are you parked?"

"I walked." Concentrating with his big, warm hand pressed against her was hard. "I was going to take an Uber home."

A breeze from the Sound ruffled Liam's dark hair. "How far away do you live?"

"It's about a mile."

"May I walk you home?"

Turning in the direction of her apartment, she grinned up at him. "Sure. You want to carry my books, too?"

"If you had them, yes, but I won't carry"—he waved at the small messenger bag she'd slung over her shoulder—"whatever that's called."

They fell into step and walked up the hill, discussing real estate, both commercial and residential, in Seattle, then shared their favorite restaurants. He'd stuffed his tie into his pocket, rolled up his sleeves, and unbuttoned his shirt, exposing dark hair in the open V. Smiling often, he'd take her elbow whenever they encountered pedestrians. His hand on her bare arm gave her shivers, and she unconsciously moved closer to him, brushing against him now and then.

When they reached the building, Jane fished out her keys and said, "I'm on the fourth floor." She led him to the stairs. Rounding the corner to the third floor, she glanced over her shoulder and found him staring at her ass. She whipped her head back around and stumbled. Two big hands settled on her waist.

"Are you okay?"

She looked over her shoulder at his concerned look and nodded, not trusting herself to speak. Two spots of color sat high on his cheeks. Her skin burned from the heat of his hands. Should she speed up or slow down? What would he think if she did either? She concentrated on keeping the same pace. Was he still watching her ass? She breathed a sigh when they got to her apartment door. Overcome with a sudden shyness, she fumbled her keys. Opening her door, she gestured for Liam to pass her.

Following him in, she stood by the entrance to the living room while he draped his jacket over the back of a stool and inspected the space. He took his time looking at the artwork over the couch, running his fingers over the spines of the books on the wall unit, and checking out her view from the window. While he stood there, she scooted to the bathroom, took her lingerie down from the shower rod, and tucked them into a drawer. She glanced around her bedroom. The bed was made, and the only visible clothing was neatly folded and sitting in a laundry basket. She breathed a sigh and popped back into the living room just as Liam turned around.

"Would you like coffee or some wine?"

"Wine, please. What time do you have to get up tomorrow?"

She blinked. "What?"

He walked over and leaned against the edge of the peninsula. "I don't want to overstay my welcome or keep you up too late."

"*You've* been keeping me up late for the past few weeks."

He held up a finger. "That is true. However, in my defense, *you* initiated some of those calls."

Jane grinned while getting glasses from the cupboard and the wine from the fridge.

He accepted his glass and saluted her before taking a sip. "This is good. Local?"

"Yeah. A vineyard from Walla Walla sent us a case for us to try. They hope we'll promote them to clients for upcoming events."

"Does that happen often?"

"It's starting to. We're making a name for ourselves, and businesses want to partner with us."

"Is that because of Instagram? I've been learning about the impact of influencers."

"That helps. We've reached out to wineries as well. We're happy to recommend them if the product is good and the price is right."

"Have you ever received something you didn't want to promote?" he asked.

"Yes! A horrific wine called Okanagan Porch Banger." She shuddered. "I'd recommend it only for stripping the paint off walls."

He laughed, leaning against one side of the peninsula while she leaned against the kitchen counter. There was more space between them than there had been while they'd eaten dinner, but he seemed much closer. His attention focused on her, even if they were talking shop. She gestured toward the couch. "Do you want to have a seat?"

She followed him over to the living room and hesitated. It had been so damn long since she'd done this; she didn't know the protocol. Should she sit next to him or in the chair? He looked up at her, eyebrows raised in a question. She perched on the edge of the couch, close but not too close. Scattered on the coffee table were a bunch of papers. She gathered them into a neat pile and placed them on an end table beside her.

"What was the thing on top? You were frowning?"

"It's nothing."

He nudged her foot with his own. "Now you're sighing.

Remember, I told you that I'm happy to listen if something is bugging you."

He looked so earnest; brushing him off might be insulting. She picked up the flyer she'd printed out. It was an image of the interior of a church filled with smiling faces and smaller images of children in school and elderly adults eating a meal. She handed the paper to Liam, who studied it and looked back at her. She explained about her parents' bank account being drained by unknowingly making repeated donations to the church.

His eyes widened in surprise. "That's a hell of a lot of money."

"Especially when you're on a fixed income. They were so embarrassed. I don't think they would have told us if they hadn't had the accident with the RV."

"Are you going to be able to get any of it back?"

Relaxing back into the corner of the couch, she tucked one leg underneath the other and turned to face him fully. "I don't know. I have to talk to a lawyer. My parents are probably not the first people this has happened to. How many others are out there who've been fleeced?"

"Having to opt out of a recurring payment is shady."

"Exactly." She smacked her hand down on the couch, her fingers brushing against his. "It's legal but…wrong. Know what I mean?"

He reached out for her hand and gave it a gentle squeeze. Turning it over, he stroked one long finger over each of hers, brushing the calluses and tapping a scar. "What's this from?"

"That one?" She searched her memory banks; she had so many scars from her adventures over the years. "I wiped out going around an obstacle in paintball and collided with a wall."

"Seriously?" He picked up her hand, examining it like it was an exquisite jewel. He intertwined his long fingers with her own.

"Tell me about that one?" She pointed to a faded mark on the underside of his forearm.

"Jumping a fence."

"Did you need stitches?"

"No. Bled all over the kitchen floor, though."

"Your parents must have been thrilled."

He shrugged, meeting her gaze. "Mom was gone by then. Dad patched me up, and I helped him clean the floor."

"Do you have a lot of scars?"

"A few." He leaned closer and reached out to touch the scar under her eye. "Nothing like this, though."

She held her breath, doing her best to ignore the tingling running through her. "Delia gave me the name of a plastic surgeon."

"Are you going to get it fixed?" His finger trailed along her cheekbone to trace the shell of her ear.

"Insurance won't cover it, so probably not. Does it… bother you?"

His brow furrowed. "Why should it?"

She'd never been vain, but suddenly, she wanted very much to have his approval. "Because it's not…because I'm not…perfect."

He pulled her toward him, his big hand moving to cup the back of her head. With the softest brush of his lips, he traced the scar, then pulled back. "Yeah, you are."

She shifted closer and met his lips with her own. Like the first time, they melded perfectly. Her tongue darted out to trace the seam of his lips. They opened, his tongue drawing hers in. They explored each other's mouths before breaking the kiss and pulling back to lock gazes. One hand enclosed in his, the other had made its way to his chest. It was her turn to explore. She reached up to stroke his eyebrows, run her fingers through his hair, and rub her thumb across his bottom lip. He opened his mouth and bit it, his heavy-lidded gaze zeroed in on hers. He pulled back, brought her hands together in both of his, and kissed her knuckles. "I'd like to stay, if you want me to."

"I do, if you don't mind me kicking you out early. I've got that meeting in the morning."

Pushing her deeper into the couch, he said, "I'll take whatever time I can get." He angled over her and kissed his way down her neck.

They stood on either side of the counter, drinking their first cups of coffee of the day. Jane smiled through a yawn. "I'm sorry we don't have more time this morning."

"And I'm sorry you didn't get more sleep."

"No, you're not," she said, smirking wickedly.

His grin was just as wicked. "You're right, I'm not. How about I pick you up from your event tonight? You can sleep at my place, and we can laze in bed tomorrow morning." Liam moved around the counter to put his mug in the sink and kissed her on the corner of her mouth. "I'll make waffles."

She turned to kiss him properly. "Deal." She picked up her phone, her thumbs flying over the keypad. "There, I sent you the address."

Frowning, he pulled his phone out of his pocket. "I didn't get—dammit, I did it again. I brought my work phone. I'll text you so you'll have that number as well."

He pulled her toward the door, snagging his jacket along the way. Wrapping his arms around her, he leaned down and kissed her lips, nose, and forehead before pulling back. "Have a great day, Jane Beckett." Then he was out the door, closing it softly behind him.

With her back to the door, she sighed. Weak inside, she put one hand over her heart to prevent it from leaping out of her chest. Absently touching her kiss-swollen lips, she wandered over to the counter and picked up the phone, her fingers moving to add his work number to Liam's contact profile. What was it about his number? A niggling sense of uneasiness tickled the back of her mind. She went to her emails and scrolled through them until she found it. She raced out the door and down the stairs, catching Liam as he opened the front door of the building.

"You paid for the repairs on my parents' RV," Jane accused, pointing a finger at Liam's chest. With one thing and another, she hadn't traced the phone number from the invoice.

He closed his eyes and sighed. "I was hoping you wouldn't find out."

"No shit." Her heart plummeted to her belly, tears pricked her eyes, and she blinked them back.

"Please." He released the door and faced her fully. "Hear me out. You and Beth work so damn hard. If I haven't been present, I've heard about it—one step forward, two steps back. It's not because you are bad at business. Just shit sometimes happens. And I thought it was time something good should happen to you."

She was shaking her head before he finished. "I don't need—"

"I know that. That's why I know I messed up. You don't need help. You and Beth, and now Kevin, make smart decisions. Because of those smart decisions, Grand Gestures will survive, unlike many other small businesses. I also know you're cooking at the church, working out of DP's conference room, and meeting clients all over the damn city. I know you want a permanent location, and paying for your parents' repairs set you back. So that's why I did it." He stepped closer. "I guess I wanted to be a white knight riding to the rescue. But you aren't a damsel in distress. Can you accept it as a loan?"

A headache was forming at the back of her head. She

reached behind to rub the tendons of her neck. "It will have to be a loan. I can't accept it as a gift. I'll talk to Kevin and Beth about a payment plan."

Liam looked hopeful. "Can I still pick you up tonight? Will you stay with me?"

"I don't know if I can. If I hadn't clued in, would you have told me?"

His mouth opened and closed, but nothing came out.

"That's what I thought. You'd hold this over me until the perfect opportunity to throw it in my face. Goodbye, Liam." Jane turned and walked back to the stairwell.

"Who hurt you?"

"What?"

He thrust a hand through his hair. "You heard me. Who hurt you so badly that you're unwilling to accept a gift? A gift that was made anonymously without expectations."

Her laugh rang hollow. "There are always expectations."

"What happened? I can't make it better, but I can at least try to understand. Because right now, all I see is a stubborn mule of a woman letting her pride get in the way. Tell me, Jane. If we have any kind of a future, you have to let me in."

His imploring gaze was almost her undoing. But she'd held onto the secret for so long, she didn't know how to let it out. The pounding in her temples increased to the point that shaking her head was painful.

Liam moved closer, holding out a hand. "If not me, tell somebody."

"I'll think about it," she whispered and made her way back to the apartment.

CHAPTER 21

Opening the back door to the church kitchen, Jane made a beeline for the coffeepot. After pouring the biggest mug she could find full of the life-giving elixir, she turned back to face the big eyes of Beth and Kevin.

"Did it not go well?" Beth continued to roll and drop cheese balls onto the baking sheet in front of her.

Jane waved away her concern. "The *quinceañera* will be fine. I'll give you my notes later."

"What's the problem? You look awful." Kevin's brows furrowed together.

"I found out Liam paid for the RV repairs."

"Seriously?" Beth gawked.

"You're kidding," Kevin protested.

Clutching the mug to her chest, Jane paced the kitchen. She'd been drinking coffee all morning and didn't think she could stand still if she tried.

"How did you find out?"

Groaning, Jane answered Beth's question with the details of the night before, knowing there was no point in beating around the bush.

"He spent the night with you?"

"Kevin! That is not the point."

"What *is* the point?" He stole a piece of cheese and popped it into his mouth. At Beth's glare, he said, "Quality control."

"The point is we can't accept the money." At their uncomprehending stares, she continued, "Don't you see? He thinks I'm a helpless female who can't fix her own problems. I'm perf—"

"Stop." Beth held up a glove-encased hand covered in cheese ball mix. "Maybe he wanted to make up for being a jerk to Chuck and me. Maybe he wanted to help out a small business. The point is, he made a generous, thoughtful, *anonymous* gift to help out people he'd never met before."

"We need to pay it back."

Kevin circled a finger between the three of them. "By we, do you mean Grand Gestures? 'Cause if so, I have a say in the matter, and I say no."

"No. From our personal account."

Beth shook her head. "Leave me out of this. I am going to say thank you and bake him cookies for however long he wants me to."

"But I—"

"That's right. *You*. You think this is all about you. *Your* pride is hurt because Liam did something you couldn't. Get over it. If you have to pay him back, go ahead. But use your own damn money."

"Bethie—"

"No. No, Jane, just no. I've deferred to you many times because you are smart and have great ideas. The bill has been paid. Can you just accept it? Please, let it go." Beth looked at her imploringly before stripping off her gloves and walking away.

Jane stared after her sister and then at Kevin, who shrugged. She left the kitchen and climbed into her car, unsure where she was going, unsure what she was going to do. Staring into the rearview mirror, the shadows around her eyes reflected her sleepless night. She would have to tell Beth. That was the only way she'd be able to make her understand.

Returning to the kitchen, she called out to Beth from just inside the door. "Remember when I was working for that accounting office in Ballard?"

Forehead wrinkled, Beth said, "Sort of."

Jane addressed Kevin. If he was going to be part of the company, he deserved to know all her dirty little secrets. "I'd been there about six months, got a promotion, and quit three months later."

"Yeah. That surprised me. I thought you really liked that company," Beth said.

"Not exactly." Jane picked at a chipped piece of Formica on the countertop beside her. She'd never talked about this before, but if she didn't get the words out, they would choke her. "I worked under a woman named Celia. She was tough but fair, and I sort of idolized her. She liked me and took me under her wing, and I gobbled up everything she could teach me. A fishing company based out of Ballard was one of our biggest clients, and to my surprise, the account was given to me to oversee, with a bonus and a salary increase."

While Jane spoke, Beth walked around the big island to stand next to her sister. Kevin did the same until they bracketed her. Jane smiled gratefully at first one, and then the other, but continued to tell her story, looking down at the floor.

"It was maybe four weeks later that Celia took me aside and told me that the client deserved *special* attention. Because of their size, there were regulations they didn't need to comply with and government forms that didn't need to be filled out. When I questioned her, Celia asked me if I'd liked the bonus and if anything was left of it."

Beth gasped. "You took me to Cancun and paid for everything. That's how you could afford it?"

Jane nodded.

Kevin took one of her hands in both of his. "What did you do?"

"I complied," she choked out. "I…there were massive amounts of documents I had to sign when I got the promotion and took over the account. Celia would shove a page in front of me and point to where I should sign, the whole time chattering away. I didn't bother reading anything. At the time I protested, she produced an NDA, non-disclosure agreement—with my signature on the bottom."

"How did you get out of there?" Beth rubbed big slow circles on Jane's back. As good as it felt, it didn't ease the recriminations Jane heaped upon herself so many years later.

"Celia had surgery and was going to be out for six weeks, so I tendered my resignation to the person who'd stepped into her place and left as soon as I could."

"Are they still in business?" Beth asked.

Jane shook her head. "A few years later, the fishing company got caught fishing out of season and had to pay a huge fine that eventually sank them. There was a big lawsuit, and the CEO pointed the finger at Celia, and she went down with them."

"Karma can be such a bitch," Kevin murmured. "When did this happen?"

"Fourteen years ago."

Beth stepped in front of her, forcing Jane to look at her. "I wish you would have told me about this when it happened."

"I was too scared and too embarrassed."

"You were twenty-three. Green and gullible." Beth's gaze held firm. "That was why Celia picked you. She took advantage of your inexperience and eagerness. Do you get that?"

Tears clogged the back of Jane's throat. She'd been so proud of herself for being made account manager at twenty-three, only to find out she'd been bought. She was ashamed of herself for being such an easy target and then going along with it.

Beth wrapped Jane in her arms, the scent of flour and butter and cheddar enveloping her. Jane relaxed into her embrace and felt Kevin's hug from behind her. The three rocked together for a couple moments before Beth dropped her arms and stepped back.

"This is why you can't accept Liam's gift?"

Jane nodded at her sister and wiped her nose on her sleeve.

Beth looked at Kevin. "During the three years you worked with Liam, did he ever do anything that made you feel manipulated or that he was setting you up for something?"

"No. He's very cautious and meticulous. I would say scrupulous in business dealings. The staff at DP think Liam is a bit stodgy but honest as the day is long."

Beth continued with her questions. "Has Liam ever made generous donations before?"

"That, I don't know. If he did, he didn't brag about it. Hang on..." Kevin snapped his fingers. "So this happened before I worked there. There was a woman whose son died while hiking overseas. I think it was in Croatia. It was a huge undertaking to release the body and bring it home. The government wasn't cooperating, and the woman was a mess. Liam hired a lawyer to assist her and paid for her and her husband to fly to Croatia and bring their son's body home. I don't know all the details because the woman no longer works there, and Liam has never talked about it. However, Chuck would be able to verify it."

Feeling their eyes boring into her, Jane stepped away from Kevin and Beth while digesting the information. "It was probably company money."

"No. Liam paid for everything himself. That's why people still talk about it. DP was sympathetic but didn't do anything beyond give the woman paid time off."

Beth moved over to the waiting mixture of cheese and snapped on another pair of latex gloves. Keeping her eye on Jane, she mechanically rolled and dropped cheese balls onto the baking sheet in front of her. "What Liam did is totally different from what Celia did. The only way he will benefit from his generosity is if he claims it on his taxes."

"I doubt the garage is a registered charity, so he can't even do that." Kevin held up his hands at Beth's narrow-eyed look. "What? I'm just saying."

Jane pulled out a stool from the corner and slumped down on it, continuing to brood. The gallons of coffee she'd drank roiled inside her, and she was shaky from caffeine and lack of sleep. Telling her story did ease her discomfort somewhat, but she couldn't let go of her mistrust. *Able or willing?* Through all her encounters with Liam, she'd felt his admiration for her skills and business savvy. After feeling the heat of his body and his kisses, she didn't know if she'd ever be warm again without them. Had he been laughing at her the whole time? Feeling smug about being able to write a check without worrying about the amount? If she continued to see him, when would he drop the bomb about his generosity? Because he *would* drop it. Wouldn't he?

"I think you need to accept the gift."

Jane looked up at Beth's firm tone. Kevin nodded beside her.

"I don't know if I can."

"Why not?" Beth snapped. "What can he do to you?"

"He's going to hold it over me. He's going to tell people how he bailed—"

"Now you're projecting. He's demonstrated his generosity in the past. And this *gift* is not about you. He helped our parents."

"Yeah, but—"

"No 'yeah buts.' You're just being stubborn, that's all."

Kevin had made himself scarce, leaving the Beckett sisters

alone to hash out their differences. Not able to meet her sister's eyes, Jane studied the floor. Being called stubborn by two people in less than twenty-four hours didn't sit well. No doubt there was some truth in it, although she preferred to think of it as tenacity. That's what had gotten her through the MBA and drove her to start the business with Beth.

"How would you feel if the money came from an anonymous benefactor?"

"Curious."

"Would you be able to accept it?"

"I suppose." She knew she wasn't being gracious, but she couldn't get past the feeling that Liam was patronizing her.

"I think Liam has a huge heart, and that's why he paid the bill. I also think he's opening his heart up to you, and you would be a fool to reject him. If you insist on being obstinate, pay him back out of your own money. I am going to accept his generous gift, and this is the last I'm going to talk about it with you."

Planting two gooey hands on the swinging door leading out to the church's fellowship hall, Beth made her exit, leaving Jane gaping behind her.

The numbers in front of him didn't make sense. He'd missed something—a decimal, a zero, whatever. He'd made a mistake. Liam sighed and tossed his pencil on the desk.

Boy, did he make a mistake. Well, not exactly. What was that phrase? No good deed goes unpunished. Her question haunted him. Would he have told her? Probably, if they were still together when they were eighty and there was less power in her punches. If they hadn't gone further than that first kiss, absolutely not. He would not have told anyone he'd paid that bill.

"Got a second?" Chuck's appearance stopped the thoughts from churning like a hamster on a wheel.

"Sure."

For the next half hour, they hammered out the details of renovations and retrofits.

Satisfied with the results, Chuck sat back and stretched out his arms. "Have you heard anything from her?"

"Nope." Liam hadn't told him. Beth had, then she sent a plate of cookies to the office with a thank-you note. He was glad that one Beckett sister was happy with him.

"Have you reached out?"

"Oh yeah. She replied with a text saying to stop texting and she doesn't want to talk to me."

Chuck winced. "She's not talking to Beth, either. Kevin is passing messages between the two of them. It's like fifth grade. The worst part is that they have to work together to figure out what to do about that church. Whether they can get their parents' money back."

Messing up the relationship between Beth and Jane was the last thing Liam wanted to do.

Raised voices drew their attention.

"Miss, you can't go in there."

"Of course I can. Don't you know who I am?"

Liam and Chuck exchanged grimaces and looked toward the open door. Delia strutted into Liam's office, closely followed by Marjorie, Liam's new assistant.

Looking flustered, the woman said, "I'm sorry, Mr. Cross, but she waltzed right past me. Should I call security?"

In the five days they'd been working together, Liam had developed a respect for Marjorie Barnes. Only time would tell if they'd develop the rapport he'd had with Kevin. Right now, she was pissed at Delia. He bit the inside of his cheek, trying not to laugh. "That won't be necessary."

"If you're sure." The two women glared at each other before Marjorie left the room.

Delia flopped down into the chair beside Chuck. "Who was that, and where's Kevin?"

"That is my new assistant. Kevin doesn't work here anymore."

"I know that." She crossed one long leg over the other, tapping the toe of her high-heeled sandal in the air. "Why isn't he downstairs?"

Liam looked at Chuck, who shrugged, then back at Delia. "Why would you think he'd be downstairs?"

"Isn't that what the party was for? The opening of Grand Gestures' office downstairs?"

"No. Why would you think that?" Chuck asked.

"The last two times that space has been used, one or more of the Beckham sisters was there."

"Beckett," Liam corrected her.

"Whatever." She waved a hand in the air. "Anyway, I stopped by so Kevin can go with me to the opening of that new cocktail bar in Ballard. But if he's not here, you can go with me." She smiled at Liam.

"Uh—no."

Chuck grinned. "He's dating Jane Beckett."

Liam glared at Chuck. He wished it were true. Wished he'd get a chance to hold her in his arms again. Delia didn't need to know anything about that, though.

"You don't date." She turned to her brother. "He doesn't date. Did you set this up so you could have cozy double dates? Maybe go bowling together or play canasta? Those cute little party planners must be rubbing their hands together in glee. They each hooked you good." Color rose on her cheeks with the volume of her voice. Her chest was heaving, white-knuckled hands clutching the arms of her chair. "Gold-digging bit—"

"Enough!"

Delia whipped around at the lash of Liam's voice; her pretty face twisted in anger.

"What the hell is wrong with you?" Chuck's voice was equally filled with anger.

Delia crossed her arms over her chest and continued to bounce the toe of her sandal.

"Seriously. What's it to you?" Liam had known Delia for many years. She was vapid at times but never petty.

"You two can do better," she muttered.

Chuck opened his mouth, but Liam motioned him to silence. "What don't you like about Jane and Beth? You know I looked into them when your brother got interested. I couldn't find a negative thing about them. Their clients like them, they have little staff turnover, and their creditors are happy."

"Sure. They probably feed the poor on Sundays as well," she said with a derisive snort.

Liam met Chuck's gaze. Neither one would acknowledge the truth of her statement. "What's this about?" Liam studied her, allowing the silence to grow.

Chuck reached over to rub her arm. "Are you worried about me? I'm a big boy, you know."

She jerked her arm away. "Things are changing. Kevin's gone. You're in love. Liam's almost there, and I..." She shook her head and stooped to pick up her purse. "Forget I said anything. I'm glad you're both happy." She flipped back her hair and fixed a smile on her face. "What were you talking about before I came in?"

Delia was right, Liam thought. Things were changing. He wanted Jane Beckett in his life, if she'd have him. If she could get past whatever was preventing her from accepting the money. He hoped she'd open up to him about it, because something had hurt her. He didn't know if he could make it better, but he sure wanted to try. He tucked that thought aside and answered Delia's question. "There's a church down in the Southwest that's taking advantage of people."

She flapped a hand. "What else is new? Churches do that all the time."

Liam thought of the church Kevin's mother worked at. "Not all of them. Anyway, this one targeted Jane and Beth's mother and wiped out her savings."

"That's why they're back up here," Chuck chimed in. "They're now living off their social security checks."

"Are you going to help them get their money back?" Delia glanced between the two men.

"Jane's talking to a lawyer, and Beth has closed out their credit cards," he said.

"But what are *you two* doing?"

"That's the frustrating part. Beth and Jane don't want us to get involved." Liam looked over at Chuck, who bobbed his head in agreement.

Pawing through her bag, Delia pulled out her phone. "I get that they don't want you involved with their parents' stuff, but I'm betting that other people have been impacted. You could do something for them or at least prevent others from being victimized." Seeing their confused expressions, she waved her phone at them. "There's this thing called the internet and social media. Research the church, collect stories about their practices, and release them on Twitter, TikTok, and Facebook. The mainstream media will pick up on it when enough people talk about it. The church would have to change its practices and perhaps have to give back the money."

Liam stared at Delia, leaning forward with his hands folded on the desk. "That's...that's brilliant."

Delia lifted a shoulder in acknowledgment. "What's the name of the church? I can get the ball rolling."

"Southwest Savior. What are you going to do?" Liam's voice was laced with apprehension.

"Watch me." She raised the phone in front of her and smiled at the camera. "Hi there. I've heard there's a church in

Arizona called Southwest Savior that does great work, and I want to send them some money. If you've had any experience with them—both good and bad—message me, please. Thanks!" She gave the screen a finger wave, then disconnected. "I have 200,000 followers on TikTok and about the same on Twitter and Instagram. Let's see what happens."

"Did you just post that?"

"Uh, yeah."

Dread filled his stomach. Jane was going to blow a gasket. "Can you undo it? Make it go away?"

She rolled her eyes at the two men. "Honestly. For captains of industry, you two are remarkably clueless." A ping sounded from her phone. "Here we go."

Silently, she read the messages, alternately smiling and frowning, typing all the while. The waiting was killing Liam. Would Jane see it? He had no idea if she followed Delia's posts. "What? What are they saying?"

"Well, I had to tell a few people what I'm wearing. Someone told me it was about time I started going to church. And, oh, this one is good. This person says their dad's bank account was drained." She smiled triumphantly at the men. "I'll be connecting with them."

Rising from her chair, she picked up her bag and headed to the door. "My work here is done."

Chuck turned to watch his sister. "What happens now?"

She waved a hand dismissively. "I'll chat with people and dig deeper. Weed out the misinformation. Engage with the church itself and expose them. You two aren't involved. Mr. and Mrs. Beckett won't be exposed, and good will triumph over evil." She waved again and was out the door.

"Um. Wow?" Chuck ran a hand through his hair and stared at Liam. "Is the shit going to hit the fan?"

"Probably not for you, but Jane will chop my head off and hand it to me on a platter. That is, if she ever speaks to me again."

CHAPTER 22

Swearing viciously, Jane smacked the side of the stand mixer. Not sure which level of sin it was to swear in a church, she spoke to the ceiling, "Sorry about that."

She tried the switch again. Nothing. Growling in frustration, she surveyed the giant piece of equipment that looked like a KitchenAid on steroids. Beth would know what to do. She reached for her phone, then growled again. Beth wasn't speaking to her, which was fine because Jane didn't want to speak to her anyway. It had been a rotten week, and the weekend wasn't looking any better. They had three staff members out with the flu, and Jane needed to make the dough for twenty dozen shortbread cookies in a stand mixer that wasn't working, and she couldn't ask her sister for help.

The last time she had gone this long not speaking to Beth was when she'd had laryngitis in high school. The two sisters didn't fight. Jane would be obstinate. Beth would be reasonable. They'd discuss issues, then meet in the middle. Except this time. As much as she hated to admit it, Beth was right; Jane was projecting. She had no reason to believe that Liam would screw her over. But she'd been operating for so long on the assumption that all gifts came with strings, it was hard not to doubt and be suspicious. She relied solely on herself. She didn't need help to get things done. Except for now. Because she needed to have the cookie dough made by—she looked at the time.

Crap, Beth would be here any minute to make the cookies. And she didn't have the dough made because she couldn't get the damn machine to work. She slammed her hand against the mixer again. Her sweaty hand glanced off one of the knobs, gashing a knuckle. She stared as blood welled up and dripped down into the bowl filled with high-quality, expensive butter. It would have to be thrown out, the bowl disassembled and sanitized, and—Jane slumped to the ground. Sucking on her wounded knuckle, she cried fat, silent tears.

"Janie! What happened?" Beth dropped a box on the counter and rushed to Jane's side.

Gulping down sobs, Jane pointed a shaky finger at the stand mixer. "I couldn't get it to...It wouldn't...And I didn't know how..."

"It's okay, Janie. I'm here." Rising from the floor, she pointed to a latch on the machine. "See this? It needs to be locked in place before the machine will work."

Jane wiped her nose on her shoulder. "That's it? I just had to close that latch?"

Eyes filled with sympathy, Beth nodded. She pressed a lever, swung the bowl out, and lifted it out of its cradle. She scraped the butter into the compost and took the bowl to the sink. "Do you need a Band-Aid?"

Jane rose from the floor and joined Beth by the sink. Rifling through the wall-mounted first aid kit, Beth pulled out a Band-Aid and handed it over. "Why didn't you call me?"

"'Cause I'm an idiot."

Beth rubbed her shoulder. "No, you're not. Stubborn and too independent, but not an idiot."

Smoothing the Band-Aid over her knuckle, Jane looked up at her sister. "But I was an idiot about the money."

Beth shrugged. "Maybe. I think Liam acted quickly, and if he'd known you better, knew about what happened with Celia, he would never have done it without talking to you first."

"He kinda sorta said that."

"He's a good guy."

"You say that now."

"Yes, well, he apologized right away. There are too many people who believe that an apology, an admission of fault, is a sign of weakness. And I don't believe that."

Jane watched Beth start the water running in the sink and make short work of cleaning and sanitizing the large stainless-steel bowl. Pulling a dish towel out of the drawer, Jane held out her hand to receive the bowl.

"I'm sor—"

"It's okay."

"I got all caught up in—"

"I know."

"Would you shut up and let me apologize?"

Beth mimed zipping her mouth shut.

"Thank you. I'm sorry I was so obstinate. Will you forgive me?"

At Beth's nod, Jane threw her hands up in the air. "Thank you. This has been a long miserable week."

"For me, too. And for Kevin as well. I'm surprised he didn't ask for his money back." Beth dried off her hands. "You get the butter, and I'll start with the dry ingredients."

It was good to work together, Jane thought as she headed to the fridge.

. . .

he party was hopping. Short-staffed, both Jane and Kevin worked the front while Beth supervised the kitchen. It was a retirement party for a tech guru whose wife had pulled out all the stops. Fifty people were gathered on the lawn of their Mercer Island home, eating and drinking and waiting for it to be dark enough for the fireworks. The tech guru herself would be setting them off, closely supervised by the pyrotechnic firm Jane had engaged. It had rained for the last three days, but a fire crew was also on standby.

Jane stood on the patio, watching the proceedings. At Kevin's suggestion, she, Beth, and Kevin each wore earpieces for communication. They worked like a charm. Jane blessed the day Kevin Armstrong came into her life. She figured they would be done with cleanup and get out of there in about three hours. Would it be too late to call Liam? Probably. She needed to figure out what to say to him anyway.

"Here."

Kevin stood before her with a glass held out in his hand. In it, something bubbled over ice cubes. She shook her head. He held up his hand. "It's club soda. The first rule of working events is don't touch the booze."

She accepted the drink with a rueful grin. "Or the guests." She followed his gaze to the bar, where a good-looking Asian man was smiling in their direction.

Smirking, Kevin raised his own glass. "I am well aware of that. That's why I handed him my business card. You know, in case he has any questions or wants to hire us."

Jane snort-laughed. "Well done."

Kevin shifted to stand beside her, and they silently observed the festivities before them. The sun was setting, and darkness would be upon them soon. Servers were moving about, removing plates and lighting candles. Bursts of laughter floated toward them on the warm evening air.

"Well done, you," Kevin said. "This party will be talked about for years."

"It's a team effort." She nudged his shoulder with her own. "You were the one suggesting a donation to have off-duty firefighters on hand."

He nodded his head in regal acceptance. "There will be no leftovers tonight. Those people know how to eat." He reached into his back pocket and pulled out his phone. "I know you aren't a fan of Delia Duncan's—"

"Hmm."

Ignoring the interruption, Kevin continued, "She posted something today that might pique your interest." He held up his phone for Jane to see a video on TikTok.

The sound was turned low, so Jane concentrated, then turned big eyes on Kevin. "What made her do that? Did you—?"

"Nope. She probably talked to Chuck."

Jane quietly fumed. She hated people poking into her business. The last thing she needed was Delia Duncan looking down her nose at her parents. Yes, they'd lost a ton of money. And maybe they had been foolish. But—

"Look at the comments." Kevin interrupted her thoughts. "There's a whole conversation going on about how the church has taken advantage of people. Plus, there is no evidence that the donated money has done more than line the church's coffers—or pockets—or whatever the appropriate metaphor may be."

He was right. There were many comments about the church taking advantage of people, interspersed with comments about gullibility and other comments asking Delia where she was and what she was wearing. Beth's voice came through her earpiece, and Jane held out the phone to Kevin so she could go to Beth's summons. He waved the phone off.

"I'll take care of this. Be right back." He strode off to assist the servers in bringing out the dessert offerings. Jane watched to ensure they didn't need help, then looked down at the phone. She studied the video again. Delia did look fabulous, as always. Behind her was an open door. Jane enlarged the video to its max and squinted. On the door was a plaque—Liam Cross, CFO. Crap! Was Liam behind this? First the RV repairs, and now this? After she'd told him she could handle it. Sure, the lawyer hadn't been optimistic about getting her parents' money back, but that only served to sharpen Jane's determination.

A presence interrupted her silent rant, and she turned to see Beth approaching. Considering she'd just prepared and oversaw a five-course meal for fifty people, Beth looked calm and relaxed. She raised her water bottle and smiled as she got closer. "What are you looking at?"

Jane waved the phone at her. "A TikTok video by Delia. Have you seen it?"

"The one about the church? No, but Chuck told me about it."

"And you didn't tell me about it?"

"Uh…hello?" Beth waved at the party around them. "We were a little busy."

"When did you find out?" The fact that Beth knew before her was infuriating.

"About an hour ago. I took a break and called Chuck. He told me about it."

"And you didn't come and find me?"

Beth glared at her. "I'm here now." She turned and stared out at the party.

Jane reached out and took her hand. "Sorry."

Beth squeezed it back. She shifted to lean a shoulder against the wall, glancing between Jane and the servers. "Delia stopped by, looking for Kevin, and asked the guys what they were talking about. She made the video to get people talking about Southwest Savior. I understand there's a lot of chatter."

Jane handed Beth the phone and crossed her arms mutinously. "They had no business getting Delia involved. We're handling it."

"They didn't ask her to get involved. She created and put out the video before they could blink." Scrolling through the comments, Beth flicked a glance up at her sister. "And you're looking at this the wrong way. Yes, it happened to Mom and Dad. But it happened to other people as well. Delia's question—she doesn't mention us or Mom and Dad—is drawing attention to the church. She's sparking a great deal of interest that may be able to stop the church's predatory practices. I say good for her." She smiled as Kevin drew closer and handed him back his phone.

Jane gaped at her sister. Kevin's presence prevented her from saying something scathing.

"She's right," he said. "Apparently, it's blowing up on Twitter as well. I heard a group at one of the tables talking about it."

"Talking about it doesn't mean anything."

"That depends on who's listening." Kevin winked at her and sauntered off, Beth following in his wake.

It was close to midnight when Jane turned down the street in front of her building. Miraculously, there was a parking space close by. Pulling her messenger bag out, she fisted her keys, locked the car, and trudged toward the entrance. A shadowy figure approached her. She pulled out her cell phone, ready to hit 911 if necessary.

"Hang on, it's just me."

Jane gusted out a sigh at Liam's voice.

He moved closer, hands out at his side. "You okay?"

The warmth and concern in his gaze almost overwhelmed her. For a moment, she wanted to lean against his bulk and feel his arms wrap around her. Instead, she asked,

"What are you doing here?" She brushed past him to open the door, expecting him to follow. He didn't. Turning, she saw him standing at the bottom step, hands stuffed in his pockets.

"Just checking in on you. Kevin texted and said you knew about the video. He also said that the event was spectacular."

She was exhausted, looked like roadkill, and hadn't anticipated seeing him. Standing under the streetlight, waiting for her to speak, he looked all kinds of wonderful. This patient, thoughtful man was waiting for her. Relief battled with dread inside her. Not only did she have to apologize, she needed to explain herself. If they had any chance of a future, he needed to know. She let go of the door and sank down onto the top step.

"Thank you for paying that bill. It's a huge burden off our shoulders, and I know it was supposed to be an anonymous gift. It caught me by surprise, and I wasn't gracious." Clutching her keys so tight her knuckles whitened, she looked up at him. "I'm sorry for treating you so poorly. If you have a few minutes, I'd like to explain myself."

Liam settled beside her, reached out to take her keys, and rubbed one finger over the indentations they'd left on her palms. "For you Jane, I have all the time in the world."

Letting out a huge sigh, she leaned her head against his shoulder and proceeded to tell him the story.

When she'd finished, they sat in silence. Liam wrapped an arm around her, drawing her in to kiss her on the temple. Her shoulders slumped, and the knots in her stomach untangled. For the first time in days, she relaxed and snuggled into his warmth.

"Does anyone else know?" The rumble of his deep voice soothed and settled her further.

"I told Beth and Kevin last week."

"And you've been holding this inside all this time?"

She nodded.

"Ah, Jane. I'm sorry you went through that. You've been beating yourself up for a long time, haven't you?"

Tears pricked the back of her eyes at the softness of his tone. "Yeah," she admitted. If it weren't for Liam's arm anchoring her in place, she would have floated away. That's how good it felt to tell her story. He hadn't judged or questioned; he'd simply listened, commiserated, and accepted her.

"Why were you and Beth not speaking to each other this week?"

"Because I'm stubborn."

He laughed and hugged her tighter. "I'll say." He rose from the steps and pulled her up with him. "You've had quite the week, and it's late. I should go."

She tugged on his hand. "My feet are killing me, and I want to collapse on the couch with a glass of wine. But I wouldn't mind the company."

Using her keys, he unlocked the door to the building and held it open for her. In silence, they crossed the lobby and went up the stairs to her apartment. Opening the door, she kicked off her shoes and dropped her bag and keys on the counter. A big hand massaged her shoulder.

"Go sit down. I'll get the wine."

Gratefully, she moved toward the couch. Settling back against the cushions, she propped her feet on the coffee table, tossing her phone beside them. She watched Liam move about her kitchen. He found the glasses and poured the wine.

"Did you eat? Want me to make you a snack?"

She accepted the glass he gave her and shook her head. "I ate. Beth and now Kevin is constantly forcing food on me. Apparently, I get *hangry*."

Liam huffed out a laugh and sank down beside her. "I've heard that about myself as well."

The wine was perfect. Having someone pour it and bring it to her was even better. Having that someone be Liam was comforting.

"Why were you waiting outside tonight?"

Liam placed his glass on the coffee table. "You wouldn't answer my calls and told me to stop texting you." He twisted to face her, bringing her feet with him, and settled them in his lap. One thumb pressed against the arch.

She groaned. No one had ever rubbed her feet before. "I'll tell you the passwords to all my accounts if you keep that up."

"If that's the case, I should have done this ages ago." He squeezed and pressed and continued to massage away the achiness. "You can be...prickly. I knew you'd be pissed about Delia, and I wanted to give you a chance to process it with me and, if necessary, let you hit me again."

The video. Right. She grimaced.

Liam froze. "Did I hurt you? Do you want me to stop?"

Wiggling her feet, she said, "No and no." She could stay here all night, but she knew she had to say something. Reluctantly, she said, "I was mad about the video. You've probably figured out I'm pretty private and protective. I didn't want Mom and Dad to be held up to ridicule. My much wiser sister pointed out that Delia never mentioned our family once. She's very clever. Simply asked a question and followed up comments with more questions. I was focused on our family, but Delia's video made me realize how many people have been taken advantage of. If that video can shut the church down or, at the minimum, get them to change their practices, then I'm a happy camper."

"That's good because I don't think I can be much help other than suggesting Duncan Properties buy their church."

Jane hummed a non-committal response, sipping her wine and enjoying the foot rub. She was at the point of dozing off when her eyes popped open. "Land!"

"What?"

She swung her legs off his lap and searched through the papers on the coffee table. Finding what she was looking for, she grinned at Liam. "It says in this brochure that they are taking donations for building a school. That's why my mom donated in the first place. How hard would it be to find out if that's really where the money is going?"

Liam studied the brochure. "There are hoops to jump through if you're a registered charity. And to build a school, there would be plans to submit, permits to file. So yeah, there would have to be public records."

Reaching for her phone, Jane said, "Let me call Mom to see what correspondence she has."

"Hang on." Liam plucked the phone from her hand. "It's after midnight, and your mom won't appreciate the phone call." At Jane's pout, he smiled. "Tomorrow, we can come up with a battle plan. That is, if you want me to help, no strings attached."

She didn't think about it for more than a second. If he could accept her stubbornness, she could accept his protective nature and generous spirit. "Yes. This is more than I can handle on my own. I would really appreciate your help."

He cupped an ear with his hand. "What? I don't think I heard you. Did you ask for help?"

"Ha ha." She made to stand up, but his long arm snaked out and pulled her into his lap. Eyes crinkling with mirth, he kissed her on the nose and pulled back. He was so close she could see each individual eyelash. "Would you like to meet for breakfast?"

"I can do that. Where?"

She spread her arms wide. "How about here? I'm not as good of a cook as Beth, but no one has died from eating my food."

"With that ringing endorsement, how can I refuse?"

Jane climbed off him to lean back against the arm of the sofa and plopped her feet back in his lap. Pointing at them, she said, "I think you missed a spot."

"I think you're greedy." Moving her feet to the side, he rose and moved until he was stretched out next to her, one hand propping up his head, the other trailing up her leg to rest on her belly.

She sucked in a breath, eyes fixed on his full lips. "I can be generous," she murmured.

"Show me." He leaned in and captured her lips in a searing kiss.

CHAPTER 23

Liam smiled big when Jane walked through the door of the empty space on the bottom floor of Duncan properties. Kevin, Delia, Chuck, and Beth were already there.

"Wow. Do you have a tenant moving in, or is DP finally taking over the space?" She stopped in the middle of the room and looked around. She addressed Liam but nodded at Delia. The tall blonde stood behind a small bar in front of which four stools were lined up. Behind her, an assortment of glassware and cups were arranged on shelves hanging from the mirrored wall. A high-end espresso machine occupied the counter running beneath the shelving.

"I staged it." Delia came out from behind a coffee bar and walked toward Jane. "What do you think?"

Liam watched Jane's gaze move around the room.

Delia gestured around the large area, starting with a grouping of upholstered chairs near the front window. "The concept is a gathering space as well as a functional office. This would be a conversation area to talk with clients. On the other side of the front door, I placed a few bistro tables. There are stools tucked under them. They make a great display area to showcase past work or works in progress when not in use. The room can accommodate up to forty people comfortably. That's using the conference table over here." She pointed to the right side of the bar where Chuck and Beth sat. A long rectangular table made from reclaimed wood was surrounded by chairs upholstered in a fabric that complemented the conversation area and barstools. A big screen TV was in a central place on the wall, viewable from anywhere in the room. Delia pointed to the other side of the bar where a wall had been erected. "That is the office space. Two desks, computer hookups, file cabinets, etc. The wall is movable. The office area can be closed off or opened up, depending on what the client needs at the moment."

"I'm seriously impressed and envious. This would be my dream office space." Jane smiled and sighed.

"You can drool later. We've got work to do." Kevin snagged Jane's arm and steered her toward the conference table. Chuck and Beth sat on one side, and Delia took a seat at one end while Kevin snagged the chair at the other. Saturday morning, Liam and Jane had set up a video chat with the other four, and they'd discussed and strategized Delia's findings and Jane's suspicions. Jane had created a shareable doc for their findings. Today, they would discuss their findings and figure out where they were headed.

Liam held a chair out for Jane, and she settled into it, smiling up at him. "Hi."

"Hi yourself." He leaned down and kissed her quickly. He grinned at the surprised expression on her face and sat down beside her. It felt so right, being surrounded by friends and next to Jane. Other than Saturday evening when she'd over-seen an elaborate scavenger hunt–themed party, they'd spent the weekend together. She'd made him breakfast Saturday; he'd made her breakfast Sunday. They'd talked, laughed, and walked around the city, always within touching distance of each other. There was no awkwardness. Only chemistry, comfort, affection, and, for Liam, a deep, growing love. Did she feel the same way? He wasn't sure, but the way she reached out to hold his hand gave him hope.

"Here's what we know." Delia pushed a button on a remote, and the screen above them lit up with an image of Southwest Savior Church and a bullet list beside it.

Jane murmured appreciatively, "You made a PowerPoint."

Delia flipped a dismissive hand. "The university of YouTube is a treasure trove. Anyway, as you can see, we have a few avenues to explore."

Silently, they studied the bullet points of action items she'd put together, including research building permits, track the pastor's professional background, look up legalities of donation practices. Liam was impressed with the scope of Delia's plan. He'd known her as long as he'd known Chuck, and this was the first time she'd shown herself as anything other than an overindulged, self-absorbed princess.

"Chuck and Liam, I think you two can—"

"Holy shit! Turn that thing to CNN!" Kevin gestured at the screen on the wall.

Delia glared at him. "Not now, Kevin. We have to—"

"Now! They're talking about the church."

She huffed out a sigh, pressed a few buttons on the remote, and the screen changed to the smooth, solemn face of a TV anchorwoman. In the background was an image of Southwest Savior Church beside screenshots of Twitter posts. Delia increased the volume.

"Over the past few days, social media has blown up over questions about Southwest Savior Church donation practices in Kingman, Arizona. It seems many persons, thinking they had made a single donation, unknowingly made multiple donations because they did not check a box to opt out of recurring donations. Most victims were seniors with limited tech savviness who'd visited the church while vacationing in the area. An influencer in Seattle started the ball rolling with this post." The anchorwoman turned to the side, and Delia's video was shown. Turning back, the anchorwoman continued, "That post, initially a TikTok video, was picked up on Twitter and retweeted over a million times."

"Seriously?" Chuck turned to his sister. "Well done!"

Kevin hushed him, pointing at the screen.

"This morning, the church came forward with a heartfelt apology. It seems they were unaware of a glitch in their donation software. Donors should expect a letter of apology and a check for anything above their initial contribution. And in Alaska…"

Kevin took the remote from Delia's hand and muted the broadcast. He started clapping, and all joined in. With tears in her eyes, Beth stood to hug Delia.

Jane was wiping away tears of her own as she reached out to take Delia's hand. "That was amazing. Thank you so much." She turned to Liam. "Oh my God. That is such a relief. Mom will be thrilled."

"I don't want to be a wet blanket, but it could be a while before they see any money."

Jane waved away Liam's protests. "That doesn't matter. Mom will be happy to know that she wasn't the only one and that it was a glitch." She made air quotes around the last word.

The cynic in Liam agreed with her. "That's how the church can save face, but if it doesn't happen again, that's a good thing."

Beth approached, and Jane glanced from her to Liam. "I'll make copies of the donations Mom made and send that off to the church."

Delia held up her phone. "There's a message on their website. It's the apology and instructions on how to get a refund. Oh, and a box you can check off as a request for them to keep the money." She rolled her eyes. "This is why I don't like churches."

"Hang on—" Kevin held up his hand, but Liam cut in.

"You two can argue organized religion another time. How about if we get something to eat?"

"That's my cue." Beth disappeared into the kitchen behind the coffee bar.

"And mine." Chuck headed to the coffee bar.

Liam took Jane's elbow and gestured to a chair, while Kevin and Delia exchanged conspiratorial glances and sat back down.

"What is going on?" Jane's eyes narrowed.

Liam smiled. "Just wait." He stood back to make room for Beth and Chuck. Beth placed a platter of canapes on the table and went back for plates and napkins. Chuck set fluted glasses on the table and sat down. Liam waited for Beth to take her seat before turning to address Jane. Knowing how prickly she was, this could go horribly wrong. Looking at the expectant faces, he cleared his throat.

"Grand Gestures has been working toward a storefront presence and would have one by now if they hadn't encountered so many obstacles. One of the issues is the cost and availability of space downtown. This space we're in now has been vacant for almost a year. It's a huge footprint, and few tenants want this size."

"Or can afford to pay the rent."

Liam nodded at Jane's wry comment. "That too. Delia said something in passing the other day that got me thinking. The last two times this place has been full, you've been present. She thought this was the new storefront for GG."

"I wish."

"Enough with the comments. Would you let the man finish?" Kevin glared at Jane. She, in turn, stuck her tongue out at him, then batted her eyelashes sweetly at Liam.

"While you were busy Saturday night, Duncan Properties"—he pointed at Chuck and Delia—"and the other members of Grand Gestures" —Beth and Kevin put their hands up—"met to figure out how best to make that happen. We worked out a contract that I think you'll find favorable. All it needs is your signature, and we can hand over the keys."

Everyone beamed at an open-mouthed Jane. She stared at each of them, then around the room, then up at Liam. Was it too soon?

Beth leaned across the table and took her sister's hands. "I know it seems like we did an end run around you, but this place is perfect. The office area is a permanent workspace. This table here is great for brainstorming sessions. We can meet clients here and have small gatherings here. We can move our stuff down from DP's kitchen upstairs. The cultural cocktail classes can be held here. I can work up samples in the kitchen space here. We're less than ten minutes away from the church kitchen, which we will continue to use."

"It's in DP's best interest as well," Chuck chimed in. "This is our building, and having empty space facing onto the street is bad for business. With the foot traffic Grand Gestures will bring in—both when you're interviewing clients and hosting events—and Delia's staging, we look good."

Kevin placed a folder on the table and slid it toward Jane. "This is the contract. I went over it with a fine-tooth comb. The terms are very favorable. We won't get anything better in the city."

Jane touched the contract. She looked from one face to another. "I can't believe you guys did this and kept it from me."

"Don't be angry," Beth pleaded. "You try to do everything by yourself, and we"—she indicated the group—"wanted to do something for you. It was your vision. We just put it into play."

Jane turned to Delia. "You staged the place over the week-end? Can we set up a payment plan?"

Waving a hand dismissively, Delia said, "Most of this stuff was in a storage unit, left over from my days of doing interior design. You're doing me a favor by getting it off my hands. Well, my parents' hands. They pay for the unit. If you'd rather swap stuff out, I've got some other things."

"No!" Jane placed both hands flat on the table. "I love this. You did a great job."

Delia preened. "I think so, too."

"We'll have an open house, invite all our past clients, and give Delia credit for the design," Kevin said.

"So you're happy?" Liam sat next to Jane and studied her face. She flung her arms out and engulfed him in a hug. The knots in his stomach untied, and he held her tightly.

"One last order of business." Kevin's words drew them apart. "Before the open house, we will be hosting a private event in honor of the engagement of Beth and Chuck."

Jane gasped and turned to her sister. Blushing, Beth held up a hand and wiggled her fingers. A large diamond set into a rose gold band sparkled from her finger. Chuck rose and kissed Beth on the forehead, went to the bar, and returned with a bottle of champagne. "Can I open this now?"

"Absolutely," Jane said.

When all glasses were filled, Liam raised his in the air. "To Grand Gestures." Everyone chimed in and drank.

❄

While Kevin and Delia huddled with Chuck and Beth, Jane rose and took Liam's hand, tugging him away from the table. She pulled him toward the office area and closed the door behind them.

She linked her hands behind his neck. The weight she'd been carrying for the past weeks slid from her shoulders, and she smiled up at the man in front of her.

"What are you thinking?" he asked, his gaze warm, if a

little wary.

She pressed her cheek against his chest and sighed. "There's a lot to take in. A lot has happened in the last few days."

"Are you feeling overwhelmed?"

"A little. But in a good way. Did you know about Chuck and Beth?"

He kissed the top of her head. "No, but I'm not surprised. I think they're perfect together. And it only took your fist in my gut for me to see it."

Eyes sparkling with mischief, she said, "I'm glad I didn't aim lower."

"I'm glad you didn't either."

She felt his arms tighten around her and raised her head to meet his gaze. "What you did here, arranging all of this…" She swallowed past the lump in her throat. "I think this is the nicest thing anyone has ever done for me."

"It might seem like I did it for you, Jane, but I really did it for me. You'll be here every day, in the same building as me. I'll get to see you more often. We could maybe meet up for lunch or drive in together in the morning." His open expression revealed a vulnerability that melted her insides.

"Are you saying…" Again, she couldn't find the words. The image he presented was one she wanted very badly.

He cupped her cheek. "I'm saying I love you and want to be with you. *This* is my grand gesture."

Tears prickled the back of her eyes. "For real?"

"For real," he said softly.

"I want that, too." She pressed her face into his palm. "I love you, Liam Cross." Then she was up on her toes, meeting his lips in a soft kiss that deepened until she was breathless.

He pulled back and smiled at her. "Do you think Beth would make a wedding cake for us?"

"I think we can convince her," she said before snuggling into his arms.

Fraudulent Trust

How was she supposed to know she needed to be able to support herself?

That's what trust funds are for.

Holiday Headaches

They're practically strangers but they could be roommates. What could possibly go wrong?

ABOUT THE AUTHOR

Lynne Hancock Pearson writes fun, flirty, feel-good fiction that simmers at low heat. Set in the Pacific Northwest, they are stories of people finding their way, even if it takes a while to get there. She lives near Seattle with three finicky felines, two towering offspring, and one long-suffering husband. She is a left-handed middle child who grew up in the Great White North and is a proud member of the Métis Nation of Canada.

Learn about future stories and more about Lynne at lynnehancockpearson.com and join her newsletter. You can unsubscribe at any time.

You can also follow her here:

Facebook: facebook.com/lynne.hancockpearson
Instagram: instagram.com/lynnehancockpearson